NO BIG
EASY LOVE

LORILYN WHITE

WORTHYWHITE PRESS

Published by: WORTHYWHITE PRESS

This is a work of fiction. Names, characters, places, and incidents are either used fictitiously or are the product of the author's imagination. Any resemblance to actual persons, living or dead, business establishments, events, or locales is entirely coincidental.

This novel contains mature themes. Reader discretion is advised.

ISBN Paperback: 979-8-9893691-2-6

ISBN Kindle: 979-8-9893691-3-3

Printed in the United States of America

I dedicate this book to my Masullo sisters, faithful encouragers and invaluable amateur editors, instrumental in shaping my dream into a reality.

From the Big Apple to the Big Easy.......

During the late 1960s, a New Orleans gossip columnist tried to find a way to describe New Orleans' unique lifestyle by comparing it to the "Big Apple," which references New York City. Strangely enough, New York's nickname is rumored to have come from an African-American stable hand in New Orleans during the 1920s and was later used by a New York newspaper columnist. While New Yorkers were perpetually running around in "The Big Apple," laid-back life in New Orleans reigned, hence, "The Big Easy."*

*Source: https://www.bigeasy.com/news/origins-of-new-orleans-big-easy-nickname-four-possible-theories

October 1987

Chapter 1

The fasten-seat-belt light flashed as the pilot's voice crackled over the intercom, alerting passengers to upcoming turbulence. "Ladies and gentlemen, we're hitting some rough patches ahead, so please fasten your seat belts and remain seated until further notice. We'll keep you informed. Thank you." The message was repeated in French as the plane began to bounce around in the air.

The Boeing 747 was packed with passengers. Maurice turned to Grace, curled up next to the window, asleep, with a romance book in her lap. *We were having a perfectly wonderful time until Jacque called. I'm happy we made this trip together. You are so beautiful. I love you so much.* A smile played on his lips.

Their month-long stay in Paris had been a delight, with Maurice's latest art gallery show gaining a devoted following and his paintings selling well. It was fate that Henri Penrite invited him to exhibit the same week as his thirtieth birthday. Paris was the perfect place to celebrate his big day. It was Grace's first visit to the City of Lights, and Maurice relished being her tour guide in the city he loved, showing her the best museums, restaurants, and nightlife. He also had friends there, some throwing lavish parties in his honor. The entire experience was a constant whirlwind of activity from the moment they arrived. By week four, he sensed Grace getting homesick, dropping hints that maybe it was time to go home. But Maurice was having such a blast that he'd planned to stay in France for at least one more week.

Two hours into their eight-hour flight from Paris to New York, Maurice couldn't help but shake his head in annoyance. *Jacque has become quite the party poop. What could be so serious that he would demand I end my birthday trip and come home?*

Everything changed when Jacque called. *Jacque with his ledger books and lectures on budgeting. Ever since he married Anne, he's become a complete old fart. He never wants to hang out. All he does is work and go home. Seems really boring. And now he resents that I do not want to live that way. Complaining that I'm spending too much money on partying as if he's my father. I'm making plenty of money selling my paintings.*

He recalled when the phone rang. He and Grace were about to relax in their hotel suite after an afternoon of shopping on the Champs-Élysées. Maurice's jaw tensed as Jacque's voice buzzed in his ears.

"Happy birthday, cousin. I hope you enjoyed your stay, but I need you to come home immediately. We've got a serious money issue to deal with."

After hanging up, Maurice frowned and told Grace, "We need to go home. Jacque said there's a serious situation going on with our finances. He wouldn't go into detail about it. Not that I would understand it all, anyway." Holding out his arms, he beckoned her to embrace him. Grace rubbed his head while he nuzzled her breasts. "You get your wish, mon cheri. Jacque has already booked our flight. We leave tomorrow."

Grace gently tugged his hair, forcing him to look at her face. "I don't understand what could be wrong. We had plenty of money the last time I checked our bank statement. He didn't give you any more information than that?"

"No." Maurice's eyes went back to her breasts. "Why do you still have your clothes on?" He slowly unbuttoned her silky peach blouse and removed her bra, suckling one breast. "Mm, better. C'est bon," he whispered before working on her other breast. Once he started, Grace began moaning, and they made love. Afterward, they didn't speak about it, but Maurice was concerned. They dressed comfortably in jeans and sweatshirts, packed, and went to the airport the next day.

The pilot's voice came over the loudspeaker once again. "Ladies and gentlemen, we're turning off the fasten seat belt lights as the air has settled. You are free to move about the cabin again. Thank you."

A portly, elderly gentleman squeezed his way down the plane's aisle in a rumpled gray suit, hips bumping the armrests of each seat along the way. As Maurice leaned away to make room for the man, his knees bumped against the seat in front of him. *Leave it to Jacque to book us seats in Economy. I need room for my legs. He knows I always fly first class.*

From the back of the plane, a baby's cries pierced the white noise of the jet engines. Grace continued to sleep, undisturbed. The child's wailing intensified, fraying Maurice's nerves. Shifting in his seat, grimacing, he peered over at his wife. *I don't know why you are in such a hurry to have one of those. That could be our baby making that awful racket on the plane. What would we do? I don't know anything about being a father.* Closing his eyes, he leaned back, massaging his temples.

Finally, the baby quieted down. Taking a deep breath, Maurice attempted to nap, but his mind was restless.

A bitter argument had broken out between the cousins before Maurice's departure to France. Once again, Jacque stood in his living room, scolding him as he had done repeatedly for the past few months. "Yes, your artwork may sell for a good price. But you're not making as much as you think if you spend twenty thousand dollars to sell fifty thousand dollars' worth of paintings. The parties, the expensive hotel suites, and the champagne. It's all too much!" *A gallery show is always a reason to celebrate. People want to see me and buy my paintings. I enjoy it and have a good time. He used to love to attend my art shows. Why is it a crime now?* Snippets of the Jacque lectures played like a movie reel in his head, torturing him for what seemed like hours. He must have dozed off at some point because suddenly, Grace awoke him to say the plane was about to land.

After collecting their luggage and clearing customs, they strode toward the private transport drivers holding signs with passenger names. Their designated meeting place with Jacque. Suddenly, a tall, disheveled figure standing a few feet behind the pool of drivers waved a raised arm and shouted, "Over here."

Grace and Maurice exchanged a bewildered look. "Is that Jacque?" she asked. The waving man with the scruffy beard, tussled hair, and rumpled raincoat hanging on slumped shoulders couldn't be Jacque. Jacque always stood upright, clean-shaven, with closely cropped hair, and impeccably dressed in a suit.

After taking a second look, Maurice reached down for their suitcases. "Oui. It's him."

Pushing through the drivers, they followed Jacque as he turned to walk out the exit doors. He stopped next to a yellow cab and opened the door. "This is us."

Amidst the drizzling rain, Maurice dropped the suitcases to pull Jacque into a bear hug. "Hello, cousin. I missed you too." Jacque stood stoic, barely putting his hands on Maurice. Leaning back, Maurice looked into his eyes. "Whatever it is, it cannot be this bad." Tipping his head at Grace, he signaled her over.

Grace stepped forward and cautiously hugged Jacque. "Good to see you. It's been a while."

"Yes, it has." Jacque rubbed her arm while guiding her into the cab's backseat.

Maurice chuckled as the cab driver put the suitcases into the trunk. "Boy, we really are slumming it. A yellow cab? Where's your company car?"

Jacque was unamused. "It was the best I could do on short notice. Please get in."

Attempting to ignore the building tension, Maurice gave Grace a tight-lipped smile as he slid into the seat beside her. Grace tugged at the multicolored scarf around her neck while Jacque stared out the window. They rode silently for several minutes as the taxi crept out of the airport onto the highway and sped toward Manhattan.

Maurice grabbed Grace's hand tightly as he leaned over and peered at Jacque. "How's Anne?"

Jacque never turned away from the window. "She's not feeling well, so I left her at your place. She insisted on preparing a homecoming meal for you."

"What a nice surprise," Maurice said. "Grace enjoyed her first trip to Paris. Especially the bidets, didn't you, mon cheri?"

"I did. It was amazing," Grace chuckled. "And Maurice knows everyone."

Jacque's tone stayed somber. "Yes, he's a regular there. I'm glad the show went well."

"You should have told me to take a cab," Maurice said. "You didn't have to come to the airport."

"It's all right. I wanted to come," Jacque replied.

"Merci beaucoup. So what's going on? You said something serious has happened."

Jacque finally turned to face Maurice. "Not here."

Glancing at Grace with a raised eyebrow, Maurice turned back to the window. They were silent the rest of the way. Tension swelled in the air. Maurice breathed a sigh of relief when they reached their apartment.

Jacque cradled a brown paper bag in one arm and carried a suitcase with the other. Maurice dropped his two suitcases in the entryway as he entered the door. Tossing his raincoat on the beige sectional sofa, Jacque pulled a bottle of cognac from the bag. "Would anyone else like a drink?"

Lamps glowed with a low light in the living room. Grace placed her coat and her carry-on bag on the beige sofa while Maurice followed Jacque to the kitchen. "Anne brought some white wine for Grace."

Maurice opened the wine to pour two glasses. Once Grace joined him, they turned to face Jacque at the kitchen counter. "So, cousin, what happened?"

Sighing as he gripped the counter's edge, Jacque looked down at his feet. "I know you don't read the papers or watch the news much on television, but the stock market has taken a turn for the worse. We've lost a lot of money I had invested."

Maurice gazed at Grace as he slowly sipped his wine. "How much money?"

"And he got fired." Anne sauntered toward the kitchen from the hallway bathroom in a red tank top and black sweatpants. Grace's head snapped around toward her friend. The slim Chinese girl had filled out considerably with fuller breasts and a pooch to her belly.

Grace embraced her. "Anne, so good to see you. Jacque said you weren't feeling well."

"I'm okay, just tired all the time. He knocked me up," Anne replied.

Maurice's eyes widened. "Knocked you how?"

Grace glared at Maurice. "Knocked up. She's pregnant." Going back to the counter, she lifted her wine glass. "Congratulations. That's wonderful news. Congratulations, Jacque."

"It was until he told me we've got no money to raise this kid," Anne smirked, staring at Jacque. Jacque drained his glass of cognac and poured himself another.

"Why did they fire you?" Maurice asked. "It's not your fault the stock market went down, is it?"

"No, of course not. But when things go bad on Wall Street, there are always casualties. My foreign exchange currency division did poorly, so I took a hit." Jacque glared at Anne. "And I wasn't the only one. Plenty of people were let go this week."

"I'm sorry you lost your job, but Goldman Sachs is not the only game in town. You'll find a new job." Maurice sipped his wine. "It's not the end of the world. C'est la vie."

Grace asked, "How much money did we lose, Jacque?"

"A few hundred thousand. I'll lay all the numbers out for you later, Grace."

Grace and Maurice's backs stiffened as they looked at one another, unsure what to say.

"You guys must be hungry after that long flight," Anne said. "I brought fried chicken and potato salad."

Grace joined Anne behind the kitchen counter. "Thanks, let me help you."

Jacque grabbed Maurice's arm to pull him away from the women to the furthest corner of the living room. Maurice frowned at his cousin in his wrinkled shirt, smelling of alcohol.

Leaning in, Jacque whispered, "You are in quite a messy situation now. This is exactly the type of thing I've been warning you about. A situation I wanted you to avoid. I told you months ago that you cannot continue extravagant spending beyond what you earn. Now you have a real problem. Grace isn't working at all, and your income is not predictable or steady. Now you can't rely so heavily upon the nest egg you invested in to supplement your income. How will you pay your bills? Take care of your wife? I cannot be responsible for you." Jacque stopped talking when the microwave beeped and headed down the hallway to the bathroom.

Maurice flushed, glaring at his back. *My mother left me half a million dollars. A few hundred thousand? How could you lose so much money?*

A minute later, Grace and Anne marched into the living room carrying plates piled high with chicken and potato salad. Maurice sat alone on the sofa, holding his head in his hands.

"Where's Jacque?" Grace asked.

Maurice pointed toward the bathroom before grabbing a plate.

Plastering on a smile, he focused on Anne. "Congratulations, Mama. When is the little bundle of joy going to arrive?"

"March 15th is my due date. But it could be before or after."

"Wow, Papa Bear didn't waste any time now, did he?" Maurice laughed. "You just got married in June."

Anne laughed. "I know, right? We both wanted to start a family. Though, I must say, if I'd known the stock market would crash and Jacque would lose his job, I would have waited."

"Anytime is the right time to have a baby. Babies are a blessing." Grace put her arm around Anne and squeezed her shoulder. "I'm so happy for you. How does it feel? Are you excited about being a mother?"

"I am. And I'm also scared to death. I mean, what if I'm no good at it? How am I going to work and take care of a baby?"

"Women do it all the time. Don't worry. You'll figure it out. You'll be a great mom, and Jacque will be a great father. He'll find another job soon."

With a chuckle, Maurice promised, "You will be well taken care of. I'm sure Jacque has saved plenty of money for you and your baby. He's certainly not spending any on having fun. Does he ever take you out anymore?"

"Maurice is jealous because he can't get Grace pregnant." Jacque walked back into the room and went for another cognac.

Anne looked at Grace. "I didn't know you guys were trying."

Maurice's eyes narrowed, glaring at Jacque, and he snorted. "We're not."

"But I'd like to." Grace gazed at Maurice, taking his hand. "I've told you that."

"We have time. Can't we enjoy married life a little longer before

I have to share you with someone else?"

"You're not getting any younger, cousin," Jacque said as he sipped his cognac.

"Jacque," Anne said, "Please eat something. Here's a plate."

Jacque sipped his drink. "I'm not hungry."

"From the look of you," Maurice said, "You need to eat. You look frail."

"I'll still kick your ass, cousin." Jacque drained his glass and slammed it on the kitchen counter. "You want to test me?"

Maurice pretended he couldn't reply because his mouth was full, making quick work of his plate. An uncomfortable silence filled the room for minutes, but it seemed like an hour. Maurice looked at Grace, glad to see that she was almost done with her food. "Why don't we all meet at La Brasserie tomorrow for dinner? We can finish going over the details of the money afterward." Maurice looked to his wife for support. "Right, mon cheri?"

Grace yawned and stretched. "Yeah, I'm tired. Now that my belly is full, I feel like I could sleep for a week."

"It's jet lag, mon cheri," Maurice said. "You'll feel better tomorrow."

Anne stood up as Grace collected the empty plates and headed to the kitchen. "Do you want me to help you clean up before we go?"

"No, we'll do it in the morning," Grace replied. "Thank you for the dinner and for seeing us home."

Maurice jumped from the sofa to escort Jacque and Anne to the door. He leaned over to say something in French to Jacque as they put on their coats before kissing Anne on the cheek as they walked out the door. He wanted to slam it behind Jacque.

"That was ugly," Grace said once they were alone. "What is going on between you and Jacque?"

Maurice's jaw tightened. "I don't know if we can trust Jacque with our money anymore." Maurice pulled Grace closer. "We will go over the numbers with Jacque tomorrow. Thank God you have a head for these things. Once we find out where we stand financially, we can decide what's best to do." Despite the uncertainty, he remained hopeful as he kissed Grace softly. "Everything will be all right. C'est la vie."

Chapter 2

The aroma of coffee and gentle humming stirred Grace out of deep sleep. As her eyes slid open, Maurice stood there, holding a mug out to her. "Good morning, my love. I made you some coffee."

The sight of him still made her heart leap like it did the first day she saw him. Bare-chested, wearing only gray sweatpants, his full lips and sexy green eyes were irresistible. She fought the urge to pull him onto her and instead took the warm cup from his hand as he sat beside her on the bed. She gazed into his eyes before taking a sip. "You're in a good mood. Did you sleep well?"

"I did. There's nothing like sleeping in your own bed. I'm glad to be home," he replied, surprising Grace since he had seemed reluctant to come back.

"Me too." Putting the coffee cup on the nightstand, she slid her arm around Maurice's neck, pulling him down for a deep, long kiss. "Good morning."

Gently swatting her hand as she reached to rub the crotch of his pants, he wiggled his eyebrows. "Not now, naughty. I went to the market while you were asleep, and I'm making omelets for breakfast. I'm hungry." Upon standing, he handed her the coffee cup from the nightstand. "After I eat, I'll do anything you want me to do. Oui?" He winked at her and headed back to the kitchen before she could answer.

Grace got out of bed, took her mug, and followed him to the kitchen. Perched on a bar stool at the counter in her pink cotton nightgown, she let her Adonis work his magic. Giddiness bubbled inside her as she admired his wavy black hair and smooth olive skin covering his sculpted torso. *How have I fallen in love and married this beautiful man? Maurice could have had anyone, but he chose me.* At first, she had been unsure whether they would get along as they were so different in many ways. Maurice's favorite phrase, "C'est la vie," expressed his carefree attitude, while she came from a more conservative middle-class background.

Since their wedding, Maurice had shown her there was an entirely different way to live and be happy. They never worried about money. He painted masterpieces while she attended graduate school, and they had a vibrant social life. There were Broadway shows, museum visits, shopping, nightclubs, and regular parties with friends. Living in the city with him was like a beautiful, never-ending dream. But now, she was ready to trade in that life to have a family. A twinge of jealousy ran through her, thinking of Anne and Jacque.

Maurice smiled at her as he scrambled eggs in a bowl before he turned to pour the mixture over the sauteed vegetables in the frying pan. Humming away, he readied the stoneware plates and silverware before returning to the pan. Not long ago, Maurice didn't know how to boil water. Grace was proud of how he quickly mastered simple cooking skills once they started living together.

"Voila. Let's eat." Setting the plates on the counter, he sat beside her.

"Looks delicious." Grace picked up her fork to taste the eggs, accompanied by buttered whole wheat toast.

"We're meeting Jacque and Anne for dinner tonight, and we'll discuss money afterward." Leaning in, wiggling his eyebrows, he continued, "And I want you to know I heard you about the baby. Our second anniversary is coming up soon. After that, we can start trying."

Grace swallowed. "After our first anniversary, you said we'd start trying soon. But you weren't ready every time I would bring it up." Taking his hand, she gazed into his eyes. "Have you changed your mind about having a family? You used to say you wanted a big family because you never had one."

Maurice looked away. "I said that before I found out the truth about my heritage. You know, I only recently found out who my real father is. Honestly, I'm a bit afraid now."

Gently, she tugged his hand. "Afraid of what?"

"I may pass on the criminal gene. I told you my father is a murderous, drug-dealing piece of scum." Maurice pulled his hand away from her grasp.

"You don't have a criminal gene. You are nothing like Philippe, and our children won't be either."

Maurice finally turned to face her. "How can you be so certain? Maybe the gene skips a generation, like twins or red hair."

Grace sighed. "Did you talk to Jacque about this? Is that why he remarked you're jealous you cannot get me pregnant?"

"Oui. Jacque told me Anne was pregnant before we left for Paris, and he asked me why we had not had a baby yet. So I told him about my fear. I thought he would keep it to himself."

"And he said…"

"The same as you. There's no such thing as a criminal gene."

"If the criminal gene you've conjured up is the only reason stopping you, please stop believing it. I want to have a family, and deep down, you do too."

Maurice took her hand and kissed it. "I promise, after our second anniversary, we will start trying to have a baby. Is that agreeable to you?"

Grace smiled. "Oui. As long as you keep your word."

Maurice snorted. "I've kept my word about everything thus far. Why would you doubt me?"

Grace gave him a skeptical look. "You've kept your word since we've been married, but we've got history, Monsieur."

"Forget about everything that happened before we wed. It has no bearing on our future."

Grace shook her head and put a forkful of eggs into her mouth. It was true. Since they got married, Maurice seemed to have become a changed man. He had kept his promise to stop leaving her alone for his painting adventures which included philandering with other women. Their apartment now had a studio for him to paint, and there were regular art shows in Manhattan. The recent gallery opening in Paris was the first time he had left town in two years, but she was by his side this time. He had been possessive of her in Paris, always holding her hand and proudly introducing her as his wife. All the fawning he did over her was unexpected, but enjoyable. She had prepared herself to be left in a corner like a wallflower while he mingled with his friends and fans. Instead, he'd been loving and attentive throughout the trip. Despite this, a nagging thought remained. *Will he tire of me and leave again?*

"For our anniversary," Grace said, "is there anything special you want to do?"

"I have some ideas, but don't want to plan anything until we have the money conversation. I mean, hundreds of thousands is a lot of money to lose. I don't understand how Jacque let this happen." Maurice's face tensed up.

"It's not Jacque's fault. I bet a lot of people lost money in this stock market crash. Please don't blame him."

Maurice sighed. "Oui, I know. At least we're not destitute. I suppose it could be worse."

"What did you say to him before we left?"

Maurice eyed her as he picked up the empty plates. "Basically, he needs to get his shit together." He put all of the dishes in the sink. "You wash, I dry?"

Grace joined him at the sink, putting her hands into the warm, soapy water filled with dishes. She playfully bumped him with her hip as they worked side by side to lighten the mood, and he chuckled in response. Once they finished washing, drying, and stacking the dishes, Maurice swept her into his arms and kissed her softly. "Where do you want it? Here? Or in the bedroom?"

"Let's go to bed. I'm sure I'm going to need a nap afterward."

He carried her back to the bedroom, laid her gently on the bed, and then stripped naked before joining her.

When Grace awoke, the apartment was dim. Maurice was sleeping peacefully beside her. It swelled her heart with love for him. But she couldn't forget the past easily. Two years ago, she had almost died in a fire. It was a whole tragedy of her own making because she didn't believe Maurice would ever settle down and marry her. Instead of keeping the faith and waiting, she married another man who turned out to be unscrupulous and deceitful. Still, for all the wrong Trevor had done, he didn't deserve to die in a fire. *I shouldn't have given up on Maurice and our love. I'm so thankful we got a second chance. No matter what is going on with the money, we'll figure it out together. I don't want anything to come between us ever again.*

It was almost six. Grace leaned over, kissing Maurice on his shoulder as she whispered his name. His eyes fluttered open. "I think we need to get up if we are going to make dinner with Jacque and Anne. I'll shower first. I had no idea jet lag would make me so tired, but after this nap, I'm feeling better."

Maurice moaned as Grace dragged herself from the bed to the bathroom. As the water cascaded over her curly brown hair and smooth caramel-colored skin, she prayed Maurice and Jacque would be more amicable this evening. *Naturally, Maurice is upset about losing the money. I am, too. Something else is going on between him and Jacque. They have always been so close. This isn't just about money.* Before she could think about it further, Maurice slipped into the shower behind her.

"No need to waste all of this hot water on one body. Would you like me to soap your back?"

She handed him her washcloth. "No monkey business, or else we'll be late."

"I'll behave." He intently scrubbed her back briefly, then threw the washcloth aside and pushed himself against her backside. "Okay, I lied."

"I knew you couldn't do it," Grace giggled. Stepping away, she went directly under the rain shower head to rinse. "You stay. I'm done." She crept around him to exit.

The chilly weather warranted warm woolen black slacks for both of them, with Grace donning a red cable sweater and Maurice a black turtleneck. Luckily, it didn't take too long to hail a taxi, and they made it to the restaurant a little after seven.

La Brasserie on West 65th Street was their usual meeting place. The décor was simple yet elegant, with polished dark wood. Dots of maroon and pink accents graced the walls and tablecloths. Their menu offered a variety of American cuisine, served with excellence. Jacque and Anne had already taken their seats at a table. He appeared a bit more put together in his navy sweater and slacks, while Anne glowed in a white velour jogger.

"Bonjour." Jacque sipped his cognac. "Glad you could make it."

"Bonjour. Are you feeling better, Anne?" Maurice asked.

"I am, thanks. And I'm starving. I hope you don't mind, but we ordered some appetizers." Anne leaned to Grace for a hug and an air kiss as she settled beside her. "You like stuffed mushrooms, don't you?"

"Both Maurice and I love stuffed mushrooms. Good choice." Grace smiled, picking up her menu to peruse the entrees. Jacque slid a large manila envelope in her direction, and she asked, "What's this?"

"Your investment portfolio from beginning to end. I couldn't sleep last night, so I compiled a schedule of all the financial moves I made on your behalf. You'll notice that I rebalanced the asset allocation last week when I realized where the market was headed," Jacque replied, taking a sip of his cognac. "The good news is we've had a couple of good days since Black Monday."

Maurice scrunched up his nose. "Black Monday?"

"Yeah," Anne said, "that's what they're calling the stock market crash in the newspapers. They are saying it's the worst crash since the Great Depression. The biggest drop ever in the Dow Jones Industrial Average. Totally unexpected. A lot of people got screwed."

The waiter arrived with the stuffed mushrooms, and Anne immediately started eating. "Mm. These are yummy. So tell me, how was Paris?"

Grace happily shared the details of their trip, peppered with Maurice's flowery comments. The conversation flowed smoothly throughout dinner, and things seemed back to normal again.

Jacque paid the check, and they prepared to leave. "We can go to our place and review the budget I've set up for you."

"Budget?" Maurice said it as if it was a dirty word.

"Yes, cousin. We will all have to make a few sacrifices in our spending, but I think we'll be able to recoup most of our losses in time."

"How much time?" Maurice asked.

Jacque exhaled. "I have no idea. Nothing in the world like this has ever happened before. It could take a year, maybe two?"

Maurice scowled, taking Grace's hand. "Perhaps we could have the budget talk another day. Allow Grace some time to review the papers you've given her."

Jacque looked at Grace and asked, "Do you want to wait?"

Grace leaned into Maurice. "I think we should go. We'll both sleep better once we have the full picture."

Maurice snorted. "As you wish."

The restaurant was only eight blocks from Jacque and Anne's apartment on West 57th Street. They walked ahead as Grace and Maurice lagged behind. There was tension on Maurice's face. She wanted to say something comforting, but knowing they were about to have a very uncomfortable conversation, she couldn't find the right words.

Anne announced she was off to bed when they arrived at the apartment. "You guys don't need me for this. Goodnight, all." Standing on her tiptoes, she gave Jacque a peck on the lips and slipped off to the bedroom.

At the bar, Jacque poured himself a cognac. "Anyone else?"

Maurice stood by the bar as Grace sat on the black leather sofa. "I'll have what you're having. Grace will have wine."

Drinks in hand, Jacque suggested they gather at the dining room table. After disappearing in his office, he returned with a small stack of manila folders, plunking them down on the table. "These are all for you." He picked up the folder on top of the pile. "This is the most important one right now. Your apartment lease is up for renewal in December."

Grace's eyebrows furrowed as she looked at Maurice. "I thought we owned the apartment." Maurice broke eye contact with her and looked down, shaking his head.

"The landlord is offering you a good deal as he did before. Four percent discount if you pay one full year at signing. Ten percent if you pay for two years. I recommend you take the two-year deal," Jacque explained, handing the folder to Grace. Her eyes widened, shocked by the total price. "This is more than my annual salary was at Ernst and Young." She looked at Jacque. "Can we afford to pay this?"

"Yes." Jacque sipped his drink while Maurice stared at him with contempt. "Here's the long and short of it. The majority of your money was invested, and the income generated from the invested nest egg was enough to pay your monthly bills. The nest egg has been cracked, and little more than half remains. Therefore, your income has been halved as well. The money Maurice earned from his Paris show will get you through the rest of the year."

Grace nodded, understanding the situation, while Maurice's eyes narrowed, staring at Jacque as he spoke. "You have a few assets at your disposal that you could sell and increase your monthly cash flow. If Maurice would sell his mother's house and stop paying Pierre, you'd have more than enough money to live on for a couple of years. And in a couple of years, your assets will grow if you keep what remains of the nest egg invested. It could go back to their level before the crash and probably more."

"I cannot stop paying Pierre." Maurice threw up his hands. "You know he has been with my family since before I was born. Where is he going to live? He's seventy years old."

Grace wrinkled her nose. "Who's Pierre?"

"Pierre is the caretaker of the house in New Orleans. He worked for my mother and our grandfather." Maurice looked at Jacque. "Any other suggestions?"

"I could ask my father to find a place for him," Jacque replied. "I don't know why you keep holding on to that house. You're never going to live in it."

Maurice drained his glass and stood up. "I need another drink." Jacque handed him his empty glass as well. "What else do we need to know?"

As Maurice went to refill the glasses with cognac, Grace sipped her wine. Her head was swirling with the revelations she'd heard. When Maurice came back and sat down, Jacque lifted the second folder on the stack and handed it to Grace. "This is the budget. The first column has the actual spending from this year, and the second column is what I recommend for the new year's budget. I could only reduce the discretionary items, like expenditures for dining out. Still, it works based on the lower income you'll have." Grace opened the folder and scanned the spreadsheet inside. Jacque pushed the rest of the folders toward

Maurice. "These are all your bill statements, taxes, etc. If Grace can't handle it, you should hire an accountant."

Maurice snorted. "Grace can handle it. Anything else, cousin?"

Jacque stood up and lifted his glass as if toasting Maurice. "Il est temps de mettre ton pantatlon de grand garcon, hein?" Grace didn't understand what he'd said, but from Maurice's reddening face, she knew it wasn't a compliment.

Maurice started gathering the folders up as he glanced at Grace. "Come on, let's go."

Once seated in a cab, Grace asked, "What is going on with you two? You've been going at it since we returned from Paris. What did he just say to you?"

"He has been coming for me." Maurice waved her off, still scowling. "Jacque has been giving me a lot of unsolicited advice lately. I don't like it."

Grace waited, expecting to hear more, but Maurice fell silent. *I knew he inherited money and a house when his mother died. But I had no idea Maurice was paying a caretaker. And when he told me the apartment was ours, I thought we owned it. I had no idea we were spending so much money every month.* The cab stopped in front of their building on East 96th Street, and they walked up to their second-floor apartment. Once inside, he pulled her to join him on the sofa. "Jacque told me, 'Time to put my big boy pants on.' He and I fought before we left for Paris." Sighing, he hunched over, hands twisting between his knees. "First, he told me his baby news. Then he said he would no longer be able to act as my father. That it was time for me to grow up. Stop spending so much money on partying and running about town." Maurice sat up and gazed at Grace. "He pissed me off so much I punched him in the mouth."

Grace's eyes widened. "You did what?"

"Busted his lip wide open. He tackled me and gave me a few good licks of his own. I had to concede." Frustrated, he continued, hands waving wildly in the air. "He acted as if his life was completely together and mine was not. What a farce. You see how he is crumbling at the first sign of trouble. So he lost his job. He'll get another one."

Grace bristled, recalling his body's bruises before the Paris flight. *He told me he got roughed up during a basketball game.* "I had no idea Jacque was handling all of our finances on his own." Taking the envelope Jacque gave her at dinner, she went to the kitchen counter, pulled the stack of papers out, and flipped through a few pages. "I look at our bank statements when they come in the mail and do a reconciliation, but that's all." She faced Maurice. "You should have told me you needed my help managing our money. I'm not an expert in investing large sums of money, but I can handle our bills and taxes."

Maurice stood beside her. "I know. You're studying to be a CPA. But Jacque has been managing my finances for years. He is supposed to be an expert money manager, and he never complained before. I don't want you to worry. It's my job to take care of you."

Grace took his hand. "From now on, we will manage our finances together. I will review the budget Jacque's already prepared, and then we'll take it from there. Okay?"

"Oui, mon cheri," Maurice replied, kissing her passionately.

Chapter 3

Maurice carefully untangled himself from Grace's arms to slip out of bed. He hadn't slept well. The conversation with Jacque was still heavy on his mind. Putting on his sweatpants, he headed to his studio, where the sunlight poured through the large, undressed windows. Leaning against one wall were easels and blank canvases of various sizes, while his drawing table held a few of his sketch pads. Maurice picked up one of the pads with his penciled outline of a man rollerblading in Central Park. Before they left for Paris, he had planned to paint an entire series of people in the park performing various activities. Now, he wasn't sure he even wanted to finish this picture.

I cannot sell my mother's house. It is the only thing I have left of her. He still missed her terribly and thought of her every day. Envisioning Nettie's face brought a small smile to his lips. He put the pad down and went to the windows, staring at the street below. *I love New York City, but New Orleans is my home.* Fond memories of his time with his mother on Napoleon Avenue floated through his mind.

Gingerly stepping back into the bedroom, he viewed his beautiful sleeping angel becoming overwhelmed. *You are the only person I love as much as Nettie. Maybe even more. How will I take care of you? And provide for a family? Am I behaving immaturely?* Too many questions to answer now, but he needed to come up with a solution.

Creeping from the doorway, he entered the kitchen, flicking on Mr. Coffee. While waiting for the brew, he opened the budget folders left on the kitchen counter and studied the numbers until his wife shuffled in.

"Good morning, mon cheri. Coffee will be ready in a moment. Did you sleep well?"

"Not really. You?" Grace yawned.

"No, but I've been thinking. What if we moved to New Orleans?"

Her head jerked back. "New Orleans? I never thought about it before. I didn't know you had any interest in living there."

"My hometown is wonderful." Maurice's face lit up with a big smile. "A good place to raise children. You don't want to raise children here in the city, right?"

"Well, no. I assumed we'd move closer to my parents when we were ready to have a family."

"We're going to start soon, aren't we? I don't think we should sign another two-year lease for this place." He stopped to get two mugs from the cabinet and poured coffee into each one, adding milk and sugar to Grace's. "If we'll have to move anyway, why not move there? We can live off the money we'll save on renting this place for at least a year. The house in New Orleans is fully paid for and has five bedrooms. Plenty of room for kids and a big backyard for them to play in." Grace's initial apprehension began to dissipate as she sipped her coffee. "And bonus," he said, wiggling his eyebrows. "No snow. You hate snow as much as I do."

"But it's so far from my parents. And I don't know about living in the South." She eyed him warily. "I've never lived anywhere else but here."

"Living in the South isn't any worse than anywhere else. Southern crackers are the same as the ones around here. Racism exists everywhere, including in New York. At least in the South, it's more out in the open, so you'll know where you're not wanted." He sipped his coffee, giving her time to think before he continued. "There are several universities where you can finish your studies, and all the big accounting firms have offices there. It will be easy to find work if you want to work."

"And what about your work? Are there a lot of galleries for shows?"

"Yes, but I think it would also be a great place for us to open our own. The Chenault Gallery. It's got a nice ring to it, doesn't it?"

Grace didn't answer as she rose from her stool. She grabbed some yogurt from the fridge, offering Maurice one as well. "Let me think about it some more."

"Oui." He took the yogurt from her hand and quickly ate it. "I'm going to the Y for a swim. Do you want to join me?"

"No, you go ahead. The suitcases need to be unpacked, and I need to review these papers from Jacque." Grace patted the stack of folders with her hand.

Maurice kissed her softly. "See you in a couple of hours, then." His vision of their new life in New Orleans grew brighter as he walked to the YMCA and swam laps in the pool. *It will be a fresh start. Settle down. Stop partying. Have a family. I don't need Jacque running my life. Grace and I will be fine doing things on our own.*

Stepping out of the pool, a nagging thought he'd kept pressing down came bubbling to the surface. *Philippe.* Maurice's body tensed. *He'd better stay out of my way.*

His friend, Bill, greeted him excitedly as he dressed in the locker room. "Hey man, we're getting a game together. You want in?"

Maurice glanced at the wall clock. "When are you starting?"

"Bout thirty minutes. I came a little early to warm up." Bill opened a locker and began to change. "We could use you, Moe. You ain't been around lately. Where you been?"

"I had an art show in France. Just got back a couple of days ago."

"Hey, that's great. Everything good?"

"Oui, all good. I guess I could stay and play for a while. I'll warm up with you."

They went to the gymnasium and practiced dribbling with the basketball and some shots at the rim. Other men slowly joined them, and the game began. His mind cleared of Philippe as he played, and he was breathing hard and sweating profusely when the game was over. As they returned to the locker room, Bill gave Maurice a high five. "Good game, man." They dressed, and as they were leaving, Bill pulled him aside. "You should stop by my place later. I got that good good, man. I know you gonna want some."

"Cool," Maurice replied. "I'll call you when I'm on my way. Later." He walked home feeling buoyant. Only happy thoughts of New Orleans were in his mind. When he arrived home, a delicious scent floated through the air as he put his bag down by the door, drawing him to the kitchen. He admired Grace's backside in a tight pair of jeans as she stirred a pot on the stove. "Bonjour mon amour. What's smells so good?"

She smiled. "Baked chicken. It's in the oven. I am making rice to go with it for dinner later." She went back to stirring before putting a lid on the pot and surveying the freezer's contents. "You want green beans or peas?"

"Green beans. I brought us a sandwich for lunch, but first, I need to shower."

When he returned refreshed in jeans and an NYU sweatshirt, Grace was busy reading papers from the folders. Her head sprang up, her voice incredulous. "You have a Mercedes? You don't even know how to drive."

"Pierre drove me whenever I was in town. But I've decided I will learn to drive if we move to New Orleans. Have you given my idea any more thought?" Maurice unwrapped the hero sandwich and offered her half.

"I have, and I'm warming up to the idea. But I have to ask. What about Philippe?"

"What about him?"

"Maurice."

He waved her off. "New Orleans is a big city. We don't have to see him."

"Is that likely?"

"I spoke with Philippe after my mother's funeral. He knows I don't want anything to do with him or his business." Maurice went for a glass of water to go with his meal. He didn't want to talk about his father. "What have you been up to? Are we unpacked?"

"Mostly. I sent the clothes to the cleaners and the laundry mat. I called my parents, and Mom wants us to come for Sunday service and dinner."

"Tres bien. How are Bev and Abe? Is everything good with them?"

"Yes. They can't wait to hear all about Paris."

Maurice focused on eating while Grace studied the paperwork. "I ran into Bill at the Y. He invited us over this afternoon. Do you want to go?"

"No, I want to finish this. You go ahead." Grace took a bite of her sandwich and returned to reading.

Later, Maurice called Bill to say he was on his way. Walking to 103rd Street, he was optimistic as Grace was giving his proposal to move serious consideration. As Bill opened the apartment door, Maurice's nose filled with the scent of marijuana. "Smells good in here. Where's that good good you were telling me about?" Reggae music was blasting as he followed Bill into the living room. A basketball game was on a large television with the sound turned down. He recognized the dark-skinned man with long dreadlocks in jeans, sitting on the worn floral sofa smoking a blunt. "What's up, Paul."

They gave each other a fist bump, and Paul handed Maurice the blunt. He toked on it as Bill went to the kitchen and returned with a large black garbage bag filled with weed. "Here it is, Moe. How much you want?"

Reaching into the bag, Maurice pulled out a large bud to examine and sniff. "Oh this is tres magnifique. Give me an ounce." He sat in a dilapidated, overstuffed armchair and passed the blunt back to Paul. Bill began weighing out marijuana on a scale in the kitchen.

Maurice asked Paul, "Why weren't you at the Y today?"

Paul groaned. "Me back is botherin' me again." He held up the blunt before putting it between his lips. "Dis is my pain medicine."

Maurice laughed. "Best medicine in the world."

"I hear you was in France." Paul passed the blunt back to Maurice. "You had a good time?"

"The best. It was my wife's first time, and I enjoyed showing her around. What did I miss around here?"

"Ah, nuthin, Moe. Same ole stuff goin' on here."

Bill returned from the kitchen and handed Maurice his bag of good good. "We're having a party next week at the Crystal Lounge. You and wifey should come through." Bill handed him a postcard flyer with all the party details on it. Jacque's voice piped up in his head as he read the postcard. *You need to stop partying. Grow up.* The postcard went in his pocket along with the weed, and he took out some money to pay Bill. They sat around talking, getting high, and drinking beer for a few hours before Maurice said he needed to get home.

****************** *************

Once Maurice left her alone in the apartment, Grace drew a deep breath. *Wow, that was a lot. I thought I knew everything there was to know about him. Now, I feel as if I know very little. And he wants to move across the country?*

The shock of last night's revelations had not worn off. Opening the budget folder, her eyes bugged, seeing the vast amounts of money her husband spent every month. Much of it stemmed from the cost of dining out, event tickets, and other expenses for their nights out on the town. *Things I don't need to be happy. Having a family is more important now.*

Delving deeper revealed that someone completely mismanaged his art business. Maurice's paintings were selling, but his spending for parties surrounding the gallery showings was outrageous. There were a million ways she could have cut expenses for what would still be an elegant affair. *Jacque is not managing Maurice's finances if he's letting him waste money like this. Maurice definitely needs my help. I don't know why he never asked for it. We can do much better with our expenses and increase our profits.*

Closing the folder, she recalled the last time Maurice asked her to go to New Orleans with him. His mother was dying, and he didn't want to face her death alone. But at that time, she couldn't give up her job and just pick up and move. And Maurice hadn't proposed marriage then. Trevor had.

Things were different now. Closing her eyes, she tried to imagine their life in New Orleans but couldn't. *We could manage here in New York, with a smaller apartment and staying home more often. But having a baby would mean we would need more space, not less.*

Reopening the budget folder, she reviewed Jacque's schedule again. *This budget will go even further in New Orleans. And if Maurice has another art show within the year, we won't need to touch our investments. I'm glad he didn't use lack of money as an excuse for not having a baby. I'm so ready to start our family. I think New Orleans might be the right choice, but I hope he's not keeping anything else from me.*

When Maurice arrived, Grace was busy in the bedroom, putting toiletries from their suitcases back into their place. She kissed him. "How's Bill? Did you have fun?"

"I did, and I got this." Holding up the ounce of weed from his pocket, he waved it around. He went to the nightstand for a pack of rolling paper and sat on the bed to roll a joint. "Did you finish reviewing all of Jacque's paperwork?"

"Yes, and after looking at the numbers both ways, moving to New Orleans may not be a bad idea. It will be cheaper than living in New York. While I have enjoyed our life here, I think I'm ready for a change. It could be a good place for us to take charge of our finances. After all, we're going to start a family, right?"

Maurice jumped off the bed and swept her up into his arms. "You mean it? You'll move with me?"

Planting a deep, sensual kiss on his lips, Grace said, "Yes."

Chapter 4

Grace was nervous yet excited about the move to New Orleans and eager to share their big news. The day began as a regular Sunday service and dinner. Maurice and Grace rode the Metro-North train from Grand Central Station to Greenburgh in semi-formal attire. Choppy waves churned up the Hudson River outside the window, flowing alongside the railroad tracks. Grace anticipated her parents' reaction would be much the same. *I need them to recognize that I'm a grown woman now. Maurice is my husband and we will take care of one another, no matter where we are.* They greeted them, all smiles, at the train station in time to attend the eleven o'clock service at the AME Zion Church. Afterward, they would have dinner at her parent's home.

Being in the cozy red brick raised ranch house where Grace grew up put her at ease. The men removed their suit jackets, adjourning to the living room to discuss Abe's favorite subject, politics. The ladies worked in the kitchen preparing the meal.

"Honey, pass me the spatula, please." Beverly pointed at the canister holding her utensils behind Grace on the counter, her white apron covering her blue paisley dress. "I can't wait to hear all about your trip to Paris. You said you had a good time, but I want details."

Grace laughed, handing her the spatula. "We brought pictures, too. It's a beautiful city. The gallery opening was amazing. You didn't see all the paintings Maurice completed for the show. He sold most of them." Sweaty palms smoothed the skirt of her maroon suit.

"Good for Maurice." Beverly used the spatula to scoop steak fries from a baking sheet into a serving dish. Her head tipped to the side as she faced Grace. "Is everything all right with you two? You seem a little squeamish."

"Everything is fine," Grace chuckled. "We have some other news to share with you over dinner."

Beverly's hands went to her face as her eyes widened. "You're pregnant?"

Looking away, Grace replied, "No, that's not it." *I wish we were delivering baby news.* She picked up the platter of roasted chicken. "Let's get this food on the table, and we'll tell you together."

Once seated around the dining room table, Abe blessed the food, and everyone dug in. Grace and Maurice recounted their Paris trip as they ate. As the conversation dwindled, Beverly piped up. "So what's this other news you have today, honey?"

Grace cleared her throat. "We're moving to New Orleans."

"My hometown," Maurice added. "Grace and I want to start a family, and I have a house there that will be the perfect place to raise our children." Putting his arm around Grace's shoulder, he squeezed her.

"New Orleans?" Beverly's face flushed as her hand touched her throat. "That's more than halfway across the country. How am I going to see you? Our grandchildren?"

"We'll visit you, Mom. And it will give you and Dad an excuse to take a trip once in a while." Smiling, Grace batted her eyes at each of them. "When's the last time you two did that?"

"You're going to need help when you start having babies. I want to be there." Beverly glared at Maurice, shaking her head. "You talked her into this, didn't you? Why would you want to move my baby all the way down there?"

Remaining calm, Maurice raised his hand. "Bev, Grace, and I made this decision together."

"He's right, Mom," Grace said, defending her husband. "We are going to New Orleans for a fresh start. We're going to have a family and open an art gallery."

Abe grunted. "You got money for that? You got family down there?"

Maurice turned to Abe with sincerity. "I do. And many friends. Grace and I will get plenty of support there. I will take excellent care of her. She is precious to me. I love her."

"Well," Abe said, "no one is questioning your love. We're concerned, is all. Grace has never lived outside of New York." He peered at Grace. "You realize this is going to be a big change for you. Are you ready for that?"

"I am." Grace and Maurice shared an intimate, glowing gaze. "It's a change we both need right now. Right, babe?"

Maurice kissed her lightly on the nose. "Oui, mon cheri."

Stiffening her back, Grace addressed her parents. "We brought pictures of the house for you to see. It's beautiful, and it's in a nice, safe neighborhood. With excellent schools."

Standing, Beverly picked up an empty serving dish from the table, glowering at Maurice. "Well, you always have a home here, honey, if things don't work out." Shaking her head, she went into the kitchen.

Maurice whined on the train ride home. "I don't understand why your mother doesn't like me. I like her and your father. I try to be charming whenever I am around her."

"Mom likes you." Cupping his cheek, Grace attempted to soothe him. "I'm the baby of the family and her only girl. She's just being overprotective."

Leaning back, he glared at her. "Your mother sicced the police on me. After the fire, she accused me of setting it."

"Stop being dramatic." Grace giggled. "She didn't know you then. Now that she knows you, she likes you. Loves you like a son."

Maurice snorted, waving her off.

Over time, her mother seemed to be adjusting to the fact they were moving. When they last spoke on the phone, Beverly sounded a little excited about the prospect of making a trip to New Orleans for a visit.

Maurice insisted they wait to tell Jacque and Anne. As usual, they gathered at La Brasserie for dinner the following Wednesday. Grace and Maurice stopped mid-stride when Jacque stood at their table clean-shaven with a fresh haircut, donning a dark gray three-piece suit.

Anne's smile beamed with delight. "Hey, you two. How are you?" Her red cowl neck sweater accented her rosy cheeks.

"Bonjour. We're good. How are you, mama?" Maurice and Grace sat at the table across from them.

"I'm great." Tapping her hand on the table for each word, Anne continued. "Guess who got a new job?".

Grace's eyes widened. "Jacque? Already? Wow, that was fast. Congratulations."

"Congratulations, cousin." Maurice hugged Jacque. "See, I told you another job would come along."

A broad smile filled Jacque's face. "Merci. I got a call from Lehman Brothers on Monday. I met with an Executive Director yesterday, and they made me a generous offer on the spot." As they took their seats, a waiter came with an ice bucket containing a bottle of Dom Perignon champagne. Jacque instructed the waiter to pour for everyone but Anne. "Please, bring her a sparkling cider."

While they waited for Anne's cider to arrive, Maurice said, "We also have good news. We're moving to New Orleans."

A dark scowl covered Jacque's face as he leaned across the table. "What? Are you crazy? Why would you want to do a stupid thing like that?"

Maurice's eyebrow went up as he leaned back. "It's not crazy nor stupid. Grace and I need a fresh start, and we decided New Orleans is the place to do it."

Grace was proud of her husband for staying calm. But Jacque was irritated and wasn't about to let it go. "I have one perfect reason why you should not do this. Philippe."

"I'm not afraid of Philippe."

"I know, but you should be. He is going to be a thorn in your side. The man is trouble. Big trouble." Jacque shook his head as the waiter brought Anne's glass of cider.

Maurice picked up his glass and lifted it into the air. Glancing at Grace, he encouraged her to do the same. "To Jacque and his new job. Bonne chance." Anne and Jacque raised their glasses, and they all clinked. After a sip, Maurice put his glass up again. "To Grace and me on our move." Jacque wouldn't put his glass up, and Anne slowly lowered hers.

"This means you won't be here when the baby is born," Anne said. "Grace, I'm going to need you."

"No, you won't," Grace replied. "You'll have your mother and Jacque by your side. Everything will be beautiful. It's not as if we'll never come back for visits. Don't forget, I must come and see my parents on occasion too. We'll see each other and probably talk on the phone every week like we do now."

Maurice glared at Jacque. "This is about me doing what you've been telling me. Take charge of my life. Settle down. Grace is with me. That's all that matters." He sipped his champagne and softened his tone. "Please try to be happy for us."

"Fine," Jacque snapped. "Just don't call me when you need to be bailed out of jail." Jacque stood and raised his glass, and everyone followed suit. "To Maurice and Grace on their move to New Orleans. Bonne chance." They clicked their glasses, and Jacque smirked. "You will need all the good luck you can get."

On the way home from dinner, Grace silently prayed Maurice wasn't being too cavalier about Philippe. Jacque made it clear he believed Philippe would be a problem. A shiver ran through her as she recalled the day Maurice told her, "My father is a monster responsible for most of the crime in New Orleans. He kills people who get in his way." It was unbelievable. *I hope Maurice is right about us not seeing Philippe.*

Weeks later, Grace stood amongst the boxes she and Maurice had packed in the living room. The apartment was almost empty. *We had so many good times here.*

Maurice came through the apartment door, interrupting Grace's reminiscing. "Bonjour, mon amour. I brought a few more boxes." He dropped the flattened cardboard pieces on the floor, grabbed Grace, lifted her, and spun her around. "I can't believe we're doing this. I'm so excited. Are you?" Grace nodded as he pulled her into a heated kiss. "Have I told you how much I love you?" he whispered.

"Not today." As Maurice placed her feet back on the floor, she rubbed his stiffening crotch. "Why don't you show me how much you love me? Right here. Right now."

Maurice started removing his clothes. "As you wish."

They made love on the living room floor until they were both exhausted. Grace rolled over onto her stomach. "Why don't you roll us a joint while I get us some wine? We still have a few hours before we meet Jacque and Anne." Watching Maurice as he strolled naked down the hall to the bedroom, goosebumps popped on her forearms. *I love you. I will follow you anywhere.*

Grace got an opened bottle of Chardonnay out of the refrigerator. Glancing around the apartment, a chill went down her spine. Tonight would be their last night here. They arranged with the landlord to allow the movers to collect their remaining furniture and boxes. Tomorrow, they would go to a hotel in Greenburgh to celebrate their anniversary and Christmas with her parents. From there, they would board a plane to New Orleans and start their new life. Grace closed her eyes, repeating once again her silent prayer. *Lord, please bless us and protect us on this journey.*

Maurice came back with a lit joint in his mouth. Grace handed him a glass of wine as he sat on a bar stool, and she joined him. He passed the joint to her while blowing a cloud of smoke into the air. "You'd better enjoy this now because come the New Year, no more drinking or smoking for you."

"Why?"

"Once we start trying for a baby, you have to stay clean. You don't want to be drinking when you find out you're pregnant, do you?"

"I'll stop once I know I'm pregnant. A little wine in the early weeks won't hurt the baby."

Maurice gave her a skeptical look. "You read that somewhere?"

Grace playfully punched him in the arm. "Don't worry about it. I just know." She passed the joint back to him and sipped her wine.

"Please don't freak out when you first see the house. It's been sitting empty for two years, so there's bound to be cobwebs and dust to be cleaned up."

"Isn't Pierre acting as a caretaker?"

"He is, but he doesn't use the whole house. He has an apartment over the garage."

"I see." As Maurice passed the joint, she asked, "Is there anything else I should know?"

A thoughtful expression clouded Maurice's face. "Philippe told me I have two sisters in New Orleans, but I have never met them, and I have no desire to do so."

Grace's eyebrows went up. "What? You have sisters? You have always said you were an only child."

"Philippe married another woman after my mother married Michel, my supposed father. He has two daughters with his wife. Since I have no relationship with him, why would I want to be in a relationship with his children?"

"Wow, that's a lot." Grace shook her head. "I'm afraid to ask, but is there anything else?"

He took the joint from her. "If I think of anything, I'll tell you."

"I hope so because lately, you've been holding back on sharing information."

"What are you talking about?"

"You knew about Anne's baby before we went to Paris, and you didn't tell me. Or about the fight you had with Jacque. I didn't know you had a car or a caretaker. Now, you have two half-sisters. I thought I knew everything about you. Boy, was I wrong."

"I didn't tell you about the fight with Jacque because it embarrassed me he beat me up. And as far as the baby news goes, it was not mine to tell. Jacque wanted Anne to tell you." Taking her hand, he kissed her wedding ring. "Whatever is going on with me, I tell you. I never imagined we'd be moving to my house in New Orleans. Pierre and the car were irrelevant. Sisters I do not know and don't want to know are irrelevant. I have not intentionally kept anything from you. We promised not to lie to one another, and I have kept my word." He pulled her closer to give her a soft kiss on the lips. "Is there anything you want to tell me?"

"No. But I'm having difficulty considering your father and sisters as irrelevant."

Putting his hands on her face, he whispered, "Don't worry about them." They kissed again, this time slowly and deeply. Their passion ignited, and Maurice stood up, took her hand, and led her to the bedroom. "Once on the floor is enough."

Grace made sure they were not late for dinner. They arrived at La Brasserie before Jacque and Anne for a change. They were sipping white wine and being silly with one another when the couple strolled into the restaurant. Jacque set a glittery gold gift bag on the table before them. "Happy Anniversary."

Anne came from behind and kissed each of them on the cheek before taking her seat. "Happy Anniversary and bon voyage. We love you guys and are really going to miss you."

"We're going to miss you too." Grace peeked inside the bag. "Should I open it now?"

Jacque chuckled. "Of course."

Grace drew out a box wrapped in gold paper and tore it off. From that box, she pulled out a white china music box with gold inlay around the sides. The top of the music box had a golden heart with M&G engraved on it. "It's beautiful." Grace carefully handed it to Maurice for him to examine. When he opened the lid, the melody of their wedding song, "For The Love of You," started playing in soft, bell tones. "Amazing," Grace said. "It doesn't need to be wound up for the music to play. Thank you so much."

"China is the traditional gift for a second wedding anniversary," Jacque said. "I had it custom-made for you. I'm glad you like it. It's exquisite. Much better than a set of dishes."

Anne whined, "Let's order. I'm hungry."

They traded stories and laughed about the old days when Grace and Anne were still in college and all of them were dating. Eventually, it was time to say their goodbyes. They hugged each other long and strong.

Jacque kissed Maurice on each cheek. "I didn't mean what I said before. Please call me if you get into any trouble with Philippe."

Maurice returned the kisses. "I will."

Grace was relieved to see Maurice and Jacque hugging and kissing one another, not wanting them to part with bad blood. Once home, she prepared for bed. "We've got to get up early tomorrow morning to see Mom and Dad." Their gift went into her packed suitcase.

Tossing and turning, sleep escaped her, all the news of Maurice's two sisters and Philippe swirling around her mind. *Am I moving to a strange place with a stranger? What else don't I know?* A shadow partially covered one side of Maurice's peaceful, sleeping face. Gently stroking his hair, her heart melted. *I do know you. I love you, and you love me. I trust you.* The journey ahead was uncertain, but she was determined to face it alongside the man she loved.

Chapter 5

The plane landing in New Orleans was extremely bumpy, and
Maurice held Grace's hand through the entire ordeal. At JFK Airport in
New York, swarms of people were going in a million directions, and they
had to push through the crowds to reach their terminal. Now, as they
waited for their luggage to come onto the carousel, the airport named
Louis Armstrong seemed calm in comparison as a few people milled
about. Immediately, Grace was at peace, and the worst part of the
journey was over. After pulling them off the carousel, Maurice found a
skycap to help with their four large suitcases. The gentleman dressed in a
red uniform followed behind them, pushing the luggage cart as they
headed toward the exit.

Near the exit doors stood a thin, dark-skinned man with gray hair
waving at them. Maurice raced over and embraced him in a bear hug.
"Pierre. It's so good to see you. I missed you."

Once Maurice let him breathe, Pierre looked him up and down.
"Good to see you, too. The infamous painter. Your mother would be so
proud of you." He peered around Maurice as Grace stepped forward to
shake his hand. "You must be Grace. It's lovely to finally meet you.
Maurice has told me so much about you."

Grace wished she could say the same. "Nice to meet you, too."

"The car is right out here." They followed Pierre out to the
passenger pickup lanes. Maurice's eyes widened when they stopped
beside a brand-new silver Mercedes Benz 560 SEL.

"Whose car is this?"

"It's yours. The other car was getting old and started giving
trouble." Pierre opened the trunk, and he and Maurice put the bags

inside. "The mechanic said getting a new car rather than repairing the old one would be better."

Maurice asked, "Jacque sent you money to buy this?"

Pierre got into the driver's seat. Maurice opened the passenger door for Grace to sit up front, and he sat in the back seat. "Pierre, you didn't answer my question."

As Pierre pulled the car from the curb to exit the airport, he looked at Maurice through the rearview mirror. "It was a gift from your father." Grace turned around and watched Maurice's face redden, but he said nothing. Pierre continued, "I tried to tell him you didn't want him buying you anything, but he insisted. He's been stopping by the house a lot lately since he heard you were moving back."

"You told him?"

"No, but word has gotten around."

"And what is he stopping by for?"

"You'll see."

Pierre acted as a tour guide for Grace, pointing out places of interest as they drove to the Garden District. The weather was warm compared to the freezing temperatures they left behind in New York. Grace removed her overcoat as she chatted with Pierre in the front seat and Maurice sat silently in the back seat.

When they pulled into the driveway beyond the tall green hedges and stopped beside the big, yellow two-story house on Napoleon Avenue, Maurice started loudly cursing, stepping out of the car. Pierre kept saying, "Calm down, calm down," but Maurice ignored him until his eyes met Grace's. He shut his mouth and opened the passenger door for her.

"I don't understand why you're so upset. The house is beautiful and looks brand new. I love it." She reached for his hand, but he stomped toward the car's trunk.

Pierre smiled and winked at her. "Wait till you see the inside." Opening the trunk, he helped Maurice remove the suitcases. He reached into his pocket and handed Maurice a set of keys. "New locks on the doors."

Maurice snatched the keys from Pierre's hand. "And I can bet he has one of his own." They each grabbed a suitcase and went to the front door. Maurice struggled to open one of the locks but finally opened the door. Amazement filled Grace when they walked into the large foyer with marble flooring. The scent of fresh paint was in the air. Maurice put the suitcase down and went back to the car for the other two.

Pierre eyed Grace as she walked further into the house. A few of their boxes, which were shipped before they left the apartment, had arrived and were sitting in the middle of a large, empty room. "Do you like it?" he asked.

Grace gave him a big smile. "Yes, yes, I do."

"This is the formal living room. If you follow me, I'll show you the great room and the old conservatory, which was converted into a studio for Maurice. There's also a guest suite down here." Grace was wide-eyed as she walked through the house, listening to Pierre describe each room's purpose. Visions of how to furnish and decorate each one danced through her head. They walked back to the formal living room and up the grand staircase to view the bedrooms.

"This is the master bedroom." Pierre opened the door with a sweeping gesture. The only piece of furniture was a king-size bed with pillows still covered in plastic. "I know you probably have your furniture coming along soon, but Philippe wanted to make sure you had a comfortable place to sleep tonight."

Grace entered the room and opened the large closets on the wall across from the bed. Another door led to a large master bath, freshly renovated with beige ceramic tile on the floors and walls, mahogany cabinetry, white countertops, and large oval mirrors. White towels were hanging on a steel rack on the wall. From there, she walked back into the main bedroom, opened the mini blinds on the long windows, and gazed out at the green lawn below. She turned to face Pierre. "It's beautiful. I don't think our furniture will do this room justice."

Pierre chuckled. "I know your husband won't want to hear this, but I'm certain Philippe will purchase any furniture you want for this room. The entire house, even." As Grace walked back towards the door where he stood, he whispered, "He's doing this because he wants a chance to be a father to his son. It's true, he can be dangerous, but he would never hurt you or Maurice." He turned and walked into the hallway. "Come on. There's still more to see up here."

After viewing all the rooms upstairs, they went down a smaller stairwell at the end of the hall and wound up in the large gourmet kitchen. It gleamed with new mahogany cabinets, light gray granite countertops, and brand-new black appliances. A large wrought iron pot rack hung from the ceiling with various copper bottom pots and pans. Grace's mouth dropped open at the sight. She'd never seen such a vast, gorgeous cooking space.

Maurice sat at the large farmhouse kitchen table, sipping a glass of white wine. "Do you like it?"

"Yes, the whole house is amazing. From the pictures you showed me of the outside, I never imagined an interior like this."

Maurice gave her a weak smile. "I'm glad you're happy. Would you like some wine? The refrigerator is fully stocked. So is the pantry." Grace went to the refrigerator and opened it. Inside were eggs, butter, milk, and juices, along with a variety of fresh fruit and vegetables. Stunned, she turned to Maurice as he took a wine glass from one of the cabinets. He shook his head as he joined her at the refrigerator door and took the opened wine bottle out before closing it. She followed him to the kitchen table, and he filled her glass.

"I'm going to head home now," Pierre said as he stood by the back door. "Babeth expects you for dinner tonight. Please call her."

"I will," Maurice replied. He hugged Pierre. "Merci beaucoup."

Rejoining Grace at the kitchen table, they sat quietly, sipping wine for a moment. Maurice put his elbows on the table and his hands in his hair. It surprised Grace as tears formed in his eyes. "I am so stupid." His sob ripped through Grace's soul as she drew him into her arms, cradling his head near her breasts. "Jacque was right. It was stupid of me to think Philippe would leave us alone."

"It's all right," Grace whispered. "He didn't do anything to hurt us. He wanted to help us." She waited a moment for his sobs to subside. "You're not stupid. Everything is going to be fine. You'll see."

Maurice looked up at her with red eyes. "You think so? You're not sorry we came?"

Grace put her hand under his chin to gaze into his eyes. "Not at all. Pierre said all of this is Philippe holding out an olive branch. He wants to be a father to you. Maybe instead of resisting it, you should lean into it. Get to know him better. There must be some good in the man for your mother to have loved him." She released her grip on him long enough to get some paper towels from the roll hanging beneath one cabinet and handed them to him. As he wiped his face, she continued. "We're both tired. It's been quite a day. Let's set up the bed and rest a little while."

"First, I need to call Babeth."

"Okay. I'll go find the box with our bedding while you do that, and then you can join me upstairs." She kissed him softly and took a knife from the wooden block on the counter before heading to the formal living room. Finding the box marked bedding, she cut it open, pulling out a large green cotton blanket. After rummaging through the box further, she grabbed some pillowcases and sheets. Taking it all upstairs to the master bedroom, she removed the plastic from the mattress and pillows. Not having king-size fitted sheets, she took the flat queen-size sheet, draped it over the large bed, and put the pillows in their cases. As she laid the blanket on top, Maurice came and stood in the doorway. She stretched her hand toward him. "Come lie down."

They lay down together, fully clothed, atop the green blanket. Maurice gathered Grace up in his arms and softly stroked her hair. "Have I told you how much I love you?"

"Not today." She held him tightly to feel his heartbeat as his chest rose and fell with each breath.

"I love you so much. I don't know what I would do if anything happened to you."

"Nothing is going to happen to me or you. Did you get your aunt on the phone?"

"Yes. Dinner is in an hour. It will only take fifteen minutes to walk to their house."

"Good. Rest now." After a few minutes, his breathing slowed, and when she glanced up, he was asleep.

Thoughts of her father-in-law raced through Grace's mind as she lay there. *I always pictured Philippe as some horrible ogre with a bloody ax in his hands. Now, I can't wait to meet him, look him in the eye, and judge what kind of person he is. He must have some redeeming qualities, or Maurice's mother would not have stuck by him for so long. I don't know their whole story, but I know they had been deeply in love. And Philippe obviously loves his son. A mean old ogre wouldn't buy you a new car and renovate your house, would he? I don't understand why Maurice was so disturbed by all of it.* Once again, she sent up her silent prayer. After all, neither one of them really knew Philippe since Maurice was raised by his mother alone. Pierre had assured her Philippe would not harm them, and she believed him.

Maurice stirred and rubbed his eyes. "What time is it?"

Grace checked her watch. "We should probably get ready for dinner."

He got up and went into the bathroom to splash water on his face and came back. "Do I look all right?"

"You look great. I hope your aunt is a good cook because I'm hungry."

"Babeth has an excellent cook. You won't be disappointed." He reached out his hand, and they walked down the grand staircase and out the front door. It felt like spring outside rather than December as they strolled on the tree-lined sidewalk to Prytania Street. Within minutes, they were standing at the front door of a two-story white plantation-style house.

Before Maurice could ring the bell, Babeth swung the door open. "Oh, Maurice, Grace, I'm so happy to see you. Come in, come in." She stepped aside so they could enter, and Maurice bent over to kiss her cheek. The small honey-colored woman wearing a bright yellow dress hugged Grace. "Welcome to our home." They followed her down a short hall into a large living room. A thin, pale man with round wire-rim glasses perched on his nose arose from a brown leather recliner. He matched Maurice in height as he shook his hand.

"Yves, you remember Maurice's wife, Grace," Babeth said. "We met her at Jacque's wedding."

Yves bowed slightly before taking Grace's hand. "A pleasure to see you again. Let's go into the dining room. Dinner is ready."

Babeth looped her arm through Grace's and led her to the dining room. "How do you like your new home? Is there anything you need?"

Grace admired Babeth's light brown eyes and warm smile and noted her resemblance to Jacque. "The house is beautiful. But it's going to take time to get everything in order. If I need anything, I'll let you know. Thank you."

Maurice smiled at Grace as he pulled a chair out and sat beside her. A large chocolate-colored woman wearing a long navy-blue dress and matching turban came in carrying a platter with prime rib and set it on the table. "Bonjour Monsieur Maurice. Long time no see. How are you?"

"I'm good, Marva." He introduced her to Grace.

"She reminds me of Miss Nettie. Lord, do I miss her."

Maurice agreed. "Me too."

Yves cleared his throat. "Marva, what about the rest of the food?"

"Yes, sir." Marva quickly headed for the kitchen door she had come through. She swiftly returned with mashed potatoes and a colorful vegetable medley. She placed them on the table and looked at Yves. "Shall I pour the wine?"

Yves waved her off. "No, go on. I'll do it. Merci."

As he poured the Bordeaux, Babeth asked, "How is my son?"

"Jacque is fine," Maurice replied. "Excited about becoming a father. How do you feel about becoming a grand mere?"

"Thrilled beyond words. I hope Anne is taking good care of herself."

"She is. We had dinner with them before we left."

"Yves and I are taking a trip to New York soon. I want to be there when the baby is born."

"We will go after the baby is born," Yves said. "Please, everyone, help themselves."

They continued to talk about the baby due to arrive as they ate. Then, Yves changed the subject. "Maurice, what do you plan to do in New Orleans? For work, I mean."

"I'll continue to paint. Eventually, Grace and I want to open our own art gallery."

"Hm, ambitious," Yves said. He turned to Grace. "And what do you do?

Grace replied, "I worked as an accountant, and now I'm studying for my CPA."

"C'est bon. Ever done any banking? I am the chief manager at First National Bank. We're always looking for good people. Come see me if you want a job."

"Thank you. I may do that." Something about Yves was off-putting, and Grace wasn't sure she would want to work with him. She shifted her focus back to Babeth. "Mrs. Benet, this food is delicious. Thank you for inviting us this evening."

"Please, dear, call me Babeth. You are family now. No need to be formal. I'll pass on your compliments regarding the food to Marva."

The evening ended on an amicable note, and Maurice and Grace walked back home. "Babeth is very nice. I like her," Grace said. "But Yves, I don't know."

Maurice chuckled. "Yves is an ass. Always has been, always will be."

After lugging the suitcases upstairs, hanging a few clothes in the closets, and finding their toiletries, they went into the shower together and had a quickie. Wrapped in a towel, Grace fell flat onto the bed. Maurice got into bed nude. He pulled on the towel. "Why would you wear this wet thing to bed? You know I'm going to take it off you."

She leaned up and kissed him. "Please do."

He removed the towel and massaged her breasts while lightly biting her neck. Grace giggled. "We just did it in the shower."

Maurice whispered, "That was just the warm-up." He nibbled on her earlobe.

"I hope this means you are feeling better about our move."

"I do, and it's all because of you." He covered her mouth with his own. "Je t'aime. I love you."

Chapter 6

Eyes still closed, Maurice's arms wandered around the bed sheet, searching for the familiar touch of warm, silky skin. When he continued to feel nothing but cool, wrinkled cotton, his eyes opened. "Grace?" The door to the bathroom was slightly ajar. Sitting up, he called a bit louder. "Grace? Cheri, are you in there?" He swung his legs over the side of the bed and looked around the room that had once been his mother's bedroom. *Philippe, with his renovations, has removed every hint of Nettie.* It seemed much larger without her white French provincial bedroom furniture inside the room. He closed his eyes for a moment, letting memories of his time with his mother wash over him. Lying in bed with her as a little boy, she would tell him stories or nurse him back to health if he were sick.

Going to the closet, he pulled out a blue terry cloth robe with an M stitched in white on the lapel. An anniversary gift from Grace's parents. He chuckled, remembering opening the present on Christmas Eve.

Beverly had placed a large box with a bow in his lap and a matching box in Grace's. Grace opened her gift and pulled out a pink terry cloth robe with a G stitched on the lapel. "Cotton is the traditional gift for a second wedding anniversary," Bev said. She smiled at Maurice. "Go ahead, open yours."

Opening his box, he remarked, "My cousin said China is the traditional gift."

Beverly burst into laughter. "Well, your cousin is wrong. It's cotton. You men. Always talking about things you know nothing about." Maurice was surprised. Jacque was rarely wrong about anything. Later, he checked for himself and discovered either cotton or china was acceptable. *C'est la vie.*

Putting on the robe, he went downstairs to find his wife.

Grace stood at the counter in the kitchen, wearing her pink robe, stirring batter in a bowl. "Good morning, sleepy head." She turned to give him a peck on the lips as he stood behind her.

"Good morning. What are you cooking?"

"Pancakes. You know it's a tradition at my mom's to have pancakes and sausage on Saturday mornings."

Maurice snorted. "It's Tuesday."

"I know, but it feels like Saturday to me." Grace stopped stirring to focus on him. "I wanted to make coffee, but there's no Mr. Coffee machine."

Maurice entered the walk-in pantry and came out carrying a French press with a bag of ground coffee. "You make coffee in this."

Grace eyed him warily. "You know how to use it?"

"I watched Claire do it a thousand times. I think I can manage."

"Who's Claire?"

"No need to get jealous. Claire was my mother's cook and housekeeper."

Grace laughed. "I'm not jealous. I know I fell in love with a ladies' man."

"Ex-ladies' man," Maurice playfully corrected, pulling her into his embrace. Their kiss was slow and deep. "Now I am a one-woman man. You are my woman."

"Good because you're stuck with me. You think Pierre would like to join us for breakfast?"

"I'll ask him." He pressed the intercom button on the kitchen wall phone. Pierre's voice crackled through the speaker, "Hello."

"Bonjour. Would you like to come for breakfast? Grace is making pancakes."

"I'll be right there."

Maurice wiggled his eyebrows at her as he filled a copper kettle with water. He placed it on the stove and lit a fire under it. Carefully measured out coffee grounds went into the French press. While he waited for the water to boil, Grace cut thick slices from a sausage roll and placed them in a frying pan. The kitchen filled with a delightful aroma as Pierre came in through the back door, clad in jeans and a red plaid shirt.

"Morning. Everyone sleep all right last night?" Maurice and Grace both answered yes as Pierre settled at the table. He eyed Maurice pouring hot water from the kettle into the French press. "You don't have enough coffee in there. Add some more," he advised.

Maurice raised his eyebrow, glancing at him. "You sure?"

"Yeah. With those few grounds, it's going to taste like dishwater."

Maurice scooped another heaping of ground coffee into the press along with a little more hot water. He checked with Pierre. "This good?"

Pierre nodded. "Now you have to wait and let it sit a few before pressing it down."

Grace placed a plate filled with sausage patties on the table. "Pierre, you get the first pancake. Maurice, would you please find the maple syrup? And some butter."

She returned to the stove, pouring circles of batter into the frying pan. Maurice put a bottle of syrup and butter on the table and then pressed the plunger to finish making the coffee. Once done, he poured a cup for Pierre to sample.

"It's a little weak, but it'll do," Pierre said.

He poured a cup for himself and tasted it. "Hm, you're right." He poured another cup for Grace, and she came and placed a stack of three pancakes on a plate in front of Pierre.

Pierre added butter and syrup before putting a forkful of the fluffy cake in his mouth. "Mm, this is good." He added a few sausage patties to his plate and tried a small piece. He looked at Maurice. "You did real good choosing her for a wife. Beautiful, and she can cook."

"She's very wise, too," Maurice said, his eyes fixed on Grace at the stove. "Always offering good advice and encouraging me."

"That," Pierre said between bites, "Is how marriage is supposed to be."

Grace brought a stack of pancakes for Maurice and then sat down at the table with her plate. "There are more pancakes if you want more, Pierre."

"I'm good. So what are you two planning to do today?"

"There's some shopping we need to do, and I would like you to take us to Le Beau Riviere," Maurice said. "I want Grace to see my mother's portrait."

Pierre glanced up from his plate. "I can't. It's not there anymore."

Maurice felt a flush of anger but kept his composure. "What do you mean?"

Pierre sighed. "Months after your mother passed away, business went down, and it closed. Last year, it was remodeled and reopened as a sports bar. It's called Sophie's."

Maurice could not believe what he was hearing. *That damned demon has ruined my mother's legacy.* "I want to see it. We'll have lunch at Sophie's."

"There is a good possibility," Pierre said, "you're going to run into you know who there. He hangs out there quite frequently."

Maurice waved his fork in the air. "It's fine. I'm going to see him eventually. Might as well be today."

Pierre exchanged a glance with Grace before returning to his pancakes.

"I personally," Grace said, "cannot wait to meet Philippe."

Maurice glared at her, shaking his head. He didn't want to introduce her to Philippe but knew he had no choice.

Grace turned to Pierre. "You don't have to drive us today. I can drive."

Maurice snorted. "It's better if Pierre drives. He knows the way and where all the stores are." He turned to Pierre. "Where can we buy a Mr. Coffee machine?"

They discussed the local stores and Grace's shopping list. When breakfast was over, Pierre prepared to leave. "Call me when you're ready to go."

Maurice carried the dishes to the sink. Grace smiled from her seat, coffee in hand. "We've got a dishwasher now. I only need to wash out the frying pans. Why don't you see what else is in those boxes and start unpacking? I can finish up in here."

The knife Grace had used the day before rested on one of the unopened boxes. Maurice cut the tape on all the remaining boxes and began pulling out items. Moments later, Grace joined him, and they put things away together. Time passed quickly, and a few hours later, Maurice suggested they get dressed for shopping and lunch.

A chill in the air caused Maurice to add his army jacket over his t-shirt and jeans, while Grace sported jeans with a matching jacket. As they rode from the Garden District toward the bustling French Quarter, Pierre again acted as a tour guide, pointing out landmarks to Grace. Maurice sat in the back seat contemplating what to say when he came face to face with Philippe. *Maybe I should take Grace's advice. Get to know Philippe.* He'd been shocked when his mother delivered the news that Philippe was his father on her deathbed. They had one brief conversation after her funeral. The "I want nothing to do with you" talk. He left New Orleans and returned to New York shortly after that.

Pierre parked at a mall, and they went inside to purchase the Mr. Coffee machine, king-size sheets, and other items on Grace's list of must-haves. After loading the bags into the car, they headed for Sophie's.

Outside the restaurant were a dozen empty wrought iron tables with neatly folded red umbrellas. Inside, Maurice was shocked by the transformation. The once elegant mahogany furnishings and chandeliers that defined Le Beau Riviere were replaced by plain oak tables with seating for four. Sports memorabilia adorned the walls, showcasing NBA, NFL, and MLB teams and the local teams of Louisiana universities and colleges. Oak cabinets hosted large televisions behind the long bar, with additional screens lining the dining area. Nothing was familiar here. Not a single remnant of Nettie was left. He didn't like it.

A bubbly young lady with long dark hair in a red shirtdress greeted them at the door. "Table for three?"

Pierre said, "No, just two." He turned to Maurice. "I'm going to go visit a friend while you have lunch. I'll come back in about an hour." He quickly exited and went back to the car.

Grace looked around. "Seems like a nice place."

Maurice snorted.

The place was only half full of patrons, and they were quickly seated. Maurice asked the young lady, "Is the manager here?"

"Sorry, the manager has the day off today," she replied. "But the owner is here. Would you like to speak to her? Is there a problem?"

"No problem," Maurice said, "but I would like to speak with her."

After the young lady walked away, Grace asked, "What's wrong?"

"I want to know what happened to all my artwork when they remodeled this place. Especially my mother's portrait."

While they waited for the owner, another young blond lady wearing a red shirtdress came to their table. "Hi. My name is Stella. I'll be your server today." She handed each of them a menu. "Would you like to start with something to drink?"

"Go on, Stella, I'll take care of these two." A tall, thick woman with long, black, wavy hair strolled toward the table. Her red floral dress flowed around her calves as she waved her hand at the girl. She stood at the table, and her green eyes settled on Maurice. "Well, well. If it isn't my big brother."

Maurice looked up at her, perplexed. "Have we met?"

"No," she laughed, "but I know you." She extended her hand. "I'm Sophie La Coeur. Your sister."

Maurice was stunned, slowly rising to shake her hand and introducing her to Grace, trying not to fixate on the freckles peppering her beak-like nose.

Sophie continued as they sat at the table, "Papa said you were returning to New Orleans. You are all he has talked about for weeks. Would you like a drink?"

Grace quickly piped up. "Chardonnay, please."

Sophie yelled to the bartender. "Nick, bring us a bottle of the good Chardonnay." She turned to Grace, still holding her menu. "I recommend the chicken piccata. It is the best dish our chef makes."

"Sounds good to me." Grace, glancing at Maurice, closed her menu. "Good for you?"

He nodded. "Oui."

Sophie yelled at another young man to bring two orders of the chicken special. Besides her green eyes and dark hair, there was little familial resemblance. Her skin was very fair, and he assumed Sophie was completely Caucasian. Her loud and brassy voice began grating on Maurice's nerves, intensifying with each word. As she smiled at him with a big toothy grin, he tried to focus on what she was saying, still recovering from the shock of their meeting. Nick came with the wine to pour out three glasses. Sophie smacked Nick hard on the ass as he headed back to the bar.

"How do you like my place? This used to be your mother's, but I wanted to create a new vibe. Appeal to the younger college kids, mostly."

His mouth opened, but he couldn't speak and was relieved when Grace picked up the conversation, saying how nice the place was. While they talked, Maurice pulled himself together. Remembering his mission, he asked, "Do you know what happened to the artwork from my mother's place?"

"It's probably in Papa's warehouse along with the rest of your mother's things. He would not dispose of anything that belonged to her." Sophie turned her attention back to Grace. "Do you like the kitchen I designed for you? I helped with the renovations of your house."

"You did a fine job. It's lovely," Grace replied.

"It was my idea to convert that old conservatory into an art studio. Removing the glass ceiling was a bitch. Created quite a mess. And I made sure there's a separate entrance to it, so you won't have clients traipsing through your house."

"That was very thoughtful of you." Grace sipped her wine.

Stella brought the plates of chicken piccata. Sophie eyed Grace and Maurice as they sampled the food. Grace gave her a nod of approval. "It's tasty."

Sophie leaned over to Grace. "Is he always this quiet?"

Grace giggled. "No. I think he's a bit worn out. I had him out shopping all morning. We needed some things for the house. Our furniture and the rest of our belongings will arrive tomorrow."

"We're having a big New Year's bash here on Thursday. I'll add you to the guest list if you want to come. Do you have plans?"

Maurice spoke up before Grace could accept Sophie's invitation. "We do but thank you for the invitation." He gulped some wine to wash down the dry, tasteless chicken. "It's a shame you didn't keep some of my artwork for your decor. I think college students can appreciate a little touch of class. This bar feels so basic." Maurice waved his hand around in the air.

Sophie leaned in, her eyes narrowing. "Papa offered you the restaurant first. You refused." Suddenly, her expression softened into a smile. "My customers must be pleased with my upgrades. They keep coming back, big brother. "

"Please, call me Maurice." He shook his head. "I hardly feel worthy to be called your brother." He sighed. "I need to speak with Philippe. Do you know where he is now?"

"He should be here any minute."

As soon as she said it, Philippe walked in the door. Dressed in a black suit, unbuttoned jacket, and a white shirt without a tie, he exuded confidence. His short, gelled-back black hair and clean-shaven face radiated warmth. Maurice fought the nauseous feeling rising within and stood.

Philippe walked to embrace Maurice, who willed his arms to embrace his father. Stepping back, Philippe gently cupped his son's face to gaze into his eyes. "That's progress. That's good." His blue eyes shifted to Grace as he stepped in her direction. "And this lovely buttercup must be your wife."

Grace stuck out her hand, and Philippe took it to pull her closer, bending over to kiss her cheek. Reclaiming his seat, Maurice draped his arm around Grace's shoulder. "She is my buttercup."

Philippe laughed as he claimed the last available chair. "I know." He leaned over, planting a kiss on Sophie's cheek. His gaze returned to Grace, a playful glint in his eyes. "You'd better keep your eye on her. She's quite a beauty. Whatever possessed you to marry a rogue like him?"

Grace blushed under Philippe's gaze. "He's settled down since we got married."

Maurice did not like the way his father was staring at his wife. "Philippe, may I speak to you in private?"

"Use my office," Sophie said. "And while you're in there, take a look at the special New Year's menu I put together. It's on the desk. Let me know what you think."

Maurice followed Philippe to the office. The red furniture his mother once had was replaced with a grand maple desk and matching wing chairs. Philippe sat behind the desk as Maurice took a chair. "How do you like the house?"

"Grace loves it. That's all that matters to me. What happened to Nettie's furniture? And the artwork from Le Beau Riviere?"

"Everything is stored in my warehouse. I can take you there, and you can pick out anything you like. You point it out, and I will arrange for it to be delivered to you."

"Thank you. Now, about the car. How much do I owe you?"

"Stop." Philippe chuckled as he put up his hand. "Please accept it as a belated wedding gift." His gaze intensified. "I hope you will allow me to be a part of your life. We are family. Blood."

Maurice looked down at his hands. "And if I'm not willing?"

"That would be a pity. Not at all what your mother wanted."

Maurice lost his composure, glaring at Philippe. "How do you know what she wanted? She never even told me you were my father until the very end. I'm sure she had a good reason for that."

"Your mother did not want you to bear the stigma of being acknowledged as a bastard. She didn't want to insult my wife and children. I told her I really didn't give a damn what anyone thought. I wanted to be in your life. But she only allowed me to do it from afar. Once you were older, I begged her to tell you the truth." He paused before saying, "At least she didn't cut me out of her life. She had a good reason for that, too."

"Which was?"

"I loved her. I understood her. She loved me and needed me to take care of her. Around me, she could be herself without excuses."

"And it had nothing to do with your illegal activities?"

"I always kept your mother shielded from my business. And I will do the same for you."

"The only thing I want you to do is to leave me and Grace alone. We came here to get a fresh start and have a family. I don't want your money or your interference. I am taking charge of my life."

Philippe snorted. "I thought, if I give you time and space, you will open yourself to me. But you're a stubborn one. You need to realize that you wouldn't have a penny to your name if it wasn't for me."

"That may have been true once, but I earn a good living now. I sold most of my paintings at my last show in Paris for a good price. And I plan to open an art gallery of my own here."

Philippe raised his voice, his hands waving wildly in the air. "And you want to pay me for the car and all the renovations to your house? You won't have a dime left to open a gallery. I bought that house for your mother and put the deed in her name. Without me, you wouldn't have a home or an inheritance."

Silence hung between them. Maurice's blood was boiling as he clenched and unclenched his fist. *I want to strangle him. I must calm down. Breathe.*

Philippe's tone softened. "Listen, you came here with your wife for a fresh start. I want us to have a fresh start, too. Instead of listening to the gossips in this town, give me a chance. Get to know me. I promise no harm will come to you or your wife."

Grace had said the same thing. Maybe I should try. Even Nettie said I should go to him.

Philippe reached into his pocket, took out a business card, and held it to Maurice. "My office is in the same location, but I have a new phone number. I can be quite helpful. I know all the influential people in this city. The people with deep pockets who can afford to pay for fine art and have their portraits painted."

Maurice exhaled, plucking the card from his hand. "Okay. I will try. Next week, I will call you to set a date to visit the warehouse." He stood up, extending his hand to Philippe.

Philippe came around from the desk and hugged him. "Thank you, son." Gradually, he released him. "You'd better go out there and rescue Grace. I'm certain Sophie is talking her to death."

Pierre was talking with Grace and Sophie when Maurice returned to the table. Leaning down, he kissed his sister's cheek. "Nice meeting you." Pierre and Grace also said their goodbyes before departing for home.

Grace waited until they were alone in the house before asking what happened in the office. Maurice relayed the conversation with Philippe to her. "I decided to take your advice and give him a chance."

"I'm so proud of you. I thought Philippe was nice, nothing like I had expected. And Sophie, what a hoot. I can't wait to meet your other sister."

Maurice snorted. "Me neither."

Grace grabbed another bottle of Chardonnay from the fridge and passed it to Maurice. "Can you open this while I grab glasses?" she asked, moving to the cabinet. "You said we have plans for New Year's Eve. What are we doing?"

"We're going to a dance hall in the Quarter. I'm going to teach you zydeco dancing."

"Zydeco dancing?"

"A Louisiana specialty. It's a bit like the hustle. The place we are going has an excellent zydeco band."

"Sounds exciting."

"Then," he wiggled his eyebrows, "I'm going to bring you home and put a baby in you."

Grace laughed. "Ooh. That sounds very exciting."

He sipped his wine. "Tonight, I'm taking you to dinner at The Commander's Palace. It's right here in the neighborhood. We can walk there. The chicken piccata we had for lunch was awful, but the food at this restaurant is superb. I'll call now to make a reservation."

After their wine break, they went back to unpacking the boxes and finally emptied them all. "Tomorrow, we'll let the movers do most of the work," Grace said. "Our bedroom furniture might be perfect for the guest suite down here." She went for the bags from their shopping trip to retrieve the new king-size sheets. "Let's go put these on our bed upstairs."

After Maurice helped her make the bed, they laid down on it. Grace asked, "Can I go with you to the warehouse? I'd like to see the furniture your mother had in here."

"Oui, mon cheri." He rolled over on his side to face her. "I hope we're not making a mistake by trusting Philippe."

Grace faced him, placing her hand on his cheek. "If he doesn't do right by us, we will cut all ties with him. I don't see the harm in giving him a chance." She kissed him softly on his lips, nose, and forehead.

Maurice pulled her closer. "We have some time before dinner."

Grace giggled. "Oh no. We are not getting undressed and then have to shower and redress again before dinner. You will have to wait for your dessert tonight."

He playfully tickled her, nuzzling her neck. "Are you sure?"

Grace burst into laughter. "Yes, yes, I'm sure."

Later, they enjoyed a delightful dinner at the Commander's Palace. Maurice almost spit his drink out when Grace asked, "Why do they put chicken wings on a fried seafood platter?"

"It's not chicken, mon cheri. They are frog legs."

"Oh, my god. I ate a frog?"

He howled with laughter. It warmed his heart. She made him so happy.

The following day, the truck arrived with their furniture and more boxes. They toiled the entire day getting their house in order, and by nighttime, they collapsed into bed exhausted.

Chapter 7

Maurice was dressed by the time Grace stirred. She rubbed her eyes, squinting at him. "What time is it?"

"It's almost eleven. You rest, and I'll bring you coffee, mon cheri." Maurice went to the kitchen to set up the new Mr. Coffee and start a pot brewing. He telephoned his friend, Claude, arranging a meeting before hitting the intercom.

"Pierre, did you eat?"

"Yes, I did, thanks. You going out tonight? Do you need me?" Pierre's voice crackled.

"Grace and I will take the streetcar into the Quarter tonight. It's the safest way to travel on New Year's with all the drunks on the road. Most likely, we'll sleep all day tomorrow. You take a couple of days off. Happy New Year."

"Happy New Year."

He poured two mugs of coffee and carried them to the bedroom. Grace propped herself up, taking a cup from his hand. "Thanks. I'm sore all over."

"I know, mon cheri. You rest today. I'll whip up some breakfast. After that, I need to run an errand."

Grace raised her eyebrow as she sipped her coffee.

"I'm going to get some weed for tonight."

"Okay."

Once breakfast was done, Maurice stood up. "I should be back in a few hours." Grace nodded and laid back down.

The air was brisk outside, and Maurice wore his army jacket over his black shirt and jeans. The taxi he'd called for arrived fifteen minutes later and dropped him a block from Claude's apartment. Claude was also an artist and ran a gallery on a quiet street near the Quarter. His apartment was above it.

Claude answered the door in a red jogging suit that clung to his wiry chocolate frame. A lightning bolt parted his fade haircut. Maurice talked about his latest showing in Paris and previewed some of Claude's latest work. They handled their weed business before Maurice called for another cab and walked to the street to wait.

With only a handful of people milling about on the streets, most heading into the Quarter for the New Year's celebration, a police cruiser rolled up on him, lights flashing. A white cop with a buzz cut yelled out his car window, "What are you doing standing around here?"

Maurice rolled his eyes. "Waiting for a taxi."

The officer stopped the car and stepped out. He approached Maurice, his face inches away. "You stoned? Your eyes are awfully red."

"No, officer. I'm just tired. Didn't get much sleep last night."

The cop sniffed around Maurice's body loudly. "I don't know. You smell like marijuana to me. Do you have marijuana on you?"

Maurice didn't answer. The cop pushed him toward the car. "Put your hands on the hood and spread your legs." A pat down revealed an ounce of marijuana in Maurice's coat pocket. "You are under arrest." Handcuffed, Maurice's heart started racing as the cop put him in the back of the squad car. *I cannot believe this is happening. I'm going to spend the New Year in jail. What am I going to say to Grace? She's never going to forgive me.*

They arrived at the police station, and Maurice was charged with a misdemeanor for possession of marijuana. The policemen ignored him as he continued to ask for his phone call. He almost cried when they made him take off his wedding ring. Once he was processed, they put him in a holding cell with two other men. Maurice was livid. He didn't know what to do. He paced around, eyeing the other men in the cell. A white man in rags slept on the metal bench against a wall, his stench reaching Maurice's nose. He stepped further away from the bench and closer to the young brother in jeans and an oversized t-shirt, squatting in the corner. *Who will I call? I can't call Grace.* He cursed himself a million times, pacing in a tight circle. Eventually, he tired and squatted down in the corner opposite the brother.

Sitting there seemed like an eternity, and he resigned himself to the fact that he would have to do some time. An officer came banging on the bars of the cell with a baton. "Maurice Chenault?" He jumped up and went to the door as the officer unlocked it. "You made bail. Come with me." Maurice silently prayed. *Thank you, God, for saving me. I don't know how You did it, but I'm thankful You did.*

When they brought him to the front of the station, Philippe was eating peanuts from a brown paper bag. He gazed at Maurice with cold blue eyes and shook his head. "Come on. I'll take you home." He tossed the empty peanut bag in the trash can by the door and lit a cigarette.

Head hanging down, Maurice followed Philippe to his parked black Mercedes and slid into the passenger seat. His father's gaze bore into him. "This is how you are taking charge of your life?" He snorted, started the car, and pulled into the moving traffic. "You can say thank you now."

Maurice couldn't look at him. In a low voice, he said, "Merci beaucoup."

"Hey," Philippe said, "look at me. When you are with me, please speak English. Say, thank you."

Maurice's head jerked up, and he glared at Philippe. "Thank you." After a brief silence, he continued. "They wouldn't even let me make a phone call. How did you know I was in there?"

Philippe replied, "I have a buddy at that station. He recognized you and called me. Did the cop rough you up?" Maurice shook his head.

"You need to be careful in the Quarter, especially during the holiday season. You can drink all you want, but the police are cracking down on drugs. Mostly, they're looking for heroin and cocaine, but they'll take whatever they find." He puffed on his cigarette and blew the smoke Maurice's way. "I don't envy you. Being black in this town can be a bitch. They will always come for you first. Hard." Philippe glanced at him. "Are you listening to me?"

Maurice sighed. "Yes."

"The next time you want some marijuana, just ask me." Philippe reached into his suit jacket's inner breast pocket, pulled out a plastic bag filled with weed, and tossed it to Maurice. He chuckled, "I have the best in town."

Maurice examined the bag that was thrown into his lap. His eyes widened. The weed looked high quality. "You smoke?"

"No, I import and export. It's a part of my enterprise." He threw the cigarette butt out the window. "And don't worry. I talked to the police sergeant. They're going to drop the charges."

"Thank you, Philippe." He felt like a ten-year-old child, sitting there listening to his father. "Please don't say anything to Grace about this."

"I won't," Philippe replied. "But you should. It's not good to keep secrets in a marriage."

"I will tell her. I don't want you to tell her."

"Okay. Are you going back to the Quarter tonight? Sophie said you refused her invitation."

"Yes. I'm taking Grace to my favorite dance hall for some zydeco."

"Well, please be careful down there tonight. You know it can get pretty crazy."

The car pulled up in front of the house. "Tell Grace I said hello. Be safe tonight. Happy New Year."

"Thank you again." Maurice got out of the car and stuck his head in the window. "Happy New Year."

When he walked into the house, Grace was sitting on the sofa in the formal living room with a book in her lap, waiting. "Where have you been? I've been so worried about you."

"I'm sorry. I ran into some trouble." Fear etched on her face. "I was arrested. Philippe had to bail me out." He started up the grand staircase. "I need to take a shower."

Grace trailed behind him. "Arrested for what? What happened?"

As he stripped off his clothes, he told her the whole terrible ordeal. Grace picked up the plastic bag of weed he laid on the bed. "Then where did this come from?"

"Philippe." He went into the bathroom and closed the door, hating that he had upset her. *She probably thinks I'm an imbecile. I need to do better for her.* After a moment he stepped under the steaming water. *Did Philippe set me up to be arrested so I would need him?*

When Maurice came out from the shower, Grace had a joint ready. She lit it and handed it to him. "I figured you need this now. I can't believe you got this from Philippe."

"I told you he was a drug dealer. Now, do you believe me?"

"So, it's okay for your friend to be a drug dealer but not your father?"

"Claude is not a drug dealer. He's an artist with some connections. Philippe is a professional and marijuana isn't the only drug he's selling. He must have a good relationship with the local police for them to drop the charges on his word." Maurice blew out a cloud of smoke and handed her the joint. "He reminded me that he is white and I am not. Said I need to be more careful in the Quarter."

Grace toked on the joint. "Then you should listen to him."

"I will. We will do all our smoking at home from now on." Grace passed him the joint. "Oh, I forgot. I'll be smoking alone because you will be pregnant."

"Oh, hush. You haven't put a baby in here yet."

"I think we should try right now. Why don't you take your clothes off?"

"Oh no, you have to wait until the New Year to get this cookie."

"This is the second time you've told me I have to wait. What's going on? You don't like it anymore?"

Grace put her lips on his and let her tongue tour his mouth. "Don't be ridiculous. I love it."

They made love before dressing to go out on the town. Maurice wore a black linen outfit with loafers, and Grace was stunning in her long-sleeved royal blue sequin dress. He admired how the dress clung to her sexy shape in all the right places.

Grace was animated with excitement experiencing her first streetcar ride. The French Quarter was swarming with people, and it took time to find a decent restaurant that was not packed. After dining on crawfish, gumbo, and po'boy bread, they rejoined the crowds in the street. A brass band played jazz on the corner as they turned onto Bourbon Street. They had to squeeze through the masses of people to get to the dance hall a few blocks away. Maurice held her hand tightly, refusing to lose her in the crowd. When they reached the entrance to Bayou Billy's, he gripped her waist as they pushed their way in. The club was packed, and the zydeco music was blasting. Maurice led her straight to the crowded dance floor, shouting over the music, "We'll start with the hustle, and I'll guide you through the other steps." A myriad of people danced on the floor, continuously bumping into them. The dancing continued until the music died down, and a man with a microphone started the countdown. At 3,2,1, everyone shouted, "Happy New Year!" Balloons fell from the ceiling, bouncing off their heads, and confetti filled the air. Amidst the revelry, Maurice and Grace kissed passionately on the dance floor, marking the beginning of the new year.

As the band slowed and played a love song, they swayed slowly, wrapped in each other's arms. She felt so good against his body as his hands wandered up and down her back, occasionally squeezing her firm buttocks. *I am going to love you for the rest of my life. I will do whatever it takes. I almost lost you once. I'm never going to let it happen again.*

Maurice's desire surged as the music played, and he was getting hot, horny, and hard, pressing up against her. When the song ended, he said, "Thank God I am here with you tonight instead of jail. That would have been an awful way to start the new year. Are you ready to go home?"

They walked to the streetcar, boarded, and kissed like teenagers in the back seat as they rode home. When they entered the front door, Maurice picked Grace up and carried her up the grand staircase to the bedroom. He placed her on her feet at the side of the bed. "Don't move."

Grabbing a cassette tape, he put it in the gray metal boom box on the floor near the head of the bed and pressed PLAY. Just like the first time they had ever made love, Ronald Isley's voice floated into the air. *Drifting on a memory, ain't no place I'd rather be than with you, loving you.*" Taking Grace into his arms, he pulled her close. Slowly swaying together to the music of their wedding song, he renewed his vow, whispering huskily in her ear, "I promise to love, honor, and cherish you all the days of my life." Sluggishly he pulled the zipper running down her back and loosened the sequenced dress from her shoulders. Her sweet musky scent intensified his arousal as he kissed and lightly bit her neck and shoulders. Her fingers fumbled with the buttons on his black shirt, and he took her hand and kissed it. "Let me undress you first." She stood still as he pulled the dress down and stepped out of it. Getting down on his knee, he removed her shoes and hose. Upon standing, his mouth was on hers, and their tongues danced together. Kissing her shoulders as he pulled her bra straps down, her nipples hardened when he freed her breasts and feasted on them. Running his hands over her soft silky skin, without inhibition, he was in no hurry. Her breath became more labored as he slowly kissed and lightly licked her body down to her naval. He picked her up and laid her on the bed to remove her panties. Placing her ankles on his shoulders, he slowly dragged her silky panties from her behind, past her thighs, and finally off her feet. Burying his face between her legs, he tasted her dripping wet honeypot. She was moaning, Mm yes, don't stop, that's it, oh no, oh yes. Raising his eyes to meet hers, he whispered, "You like that?"

"Yes, I love it. I want all of you. Take off your clothes."

Standing over her, she had so much passion in her eyes, burning into his own. He slowly unbuttoned his shirt without ever breaking the intense gaze between them. Licking his lips, he danced while stripping off the remainder of his clothes. The music continued, but he focused on his wife, stretched out, naked, with no inhibition at all. This woman he loved more than his life. He teased her with his hardened shaft rubbing it against her pleasure bud.

"Time to make a baby," he whispered, easing on top to slowly enter her. He started with slow rhythmic strokes, but she was so tight and wet he couldn't control himself. Grace wrapped her legs around his thighs as he increased the pace of their movements. Bursts of electricity and heat pulsed through his body as his hands gripped her hips, controlling her movements to match his rhythm. Filling her, he knew they belonged together. With eyes locked in a fiery gaze, every gyration reverberated prickly pleasure throughout his body. "This pussy was made for me," he whispered thickly, increasing the speed and intensity of his strokes. "Tell me it's all mine."

"It's all yours," Grace cried out. "Oh my god, it's all yours." Another orgasm rocked her as he continued to fill her. He was peaking, but it was too delicious. Not ready for it to end, he stopped moving and put his nose against hers, whispering, "Tell me you love me."

"I love you. I have always loved you. Don't stop."

Resuming slowly, Maurice steadily worked himself up to a second crescendo until she screamed yes, oh, that's it, and her muscles tightened further against his member buried deep inside her. A strangled growl ripped from his throat as he fiercely pumped into her and let it flow. *Grace, my sweet love.*

January 1988

Chapter 8

On Friday, New Year's Day, Maurice and Grace stayed in bed, eating, laughing, talking, and making love between calling Jacque, Anne, Beverly, and Abe to wish everyone a happy new year.

Early Saturday morning, Grace awoke with a smile on her lips. She was thrilled at their new life in New Orleans thus far. The house was grand, and Philippe proved to be a helpful ally rather than an ogre. She was grateful that he had bailed her husband out of jail. Rubbing her belly, her smile deepened. *I could be pregnant. I took my last birth control pill a couple of weeks before Christmas. Lord knows we've had plenty of sex. A baby may be growing in there.*

Maurice awakened, pulling her close. "Good morning, my love. What's the plan for today?"

"You should call Philippe and ask him to take us to the warehouse. Even with our furniture here, the house is still so empty. I want to see what we can salvage from your mother's furniture."

"Good idea. I will call him after breakfast. Let's go to the kitchen and see what we can rustle up to eat."

Putting on their robes and entering the kitchen, a white wax bag with a note was on the table. Maurice opened the bag and read the message. "Beignets from Pierre. He's the best. All we need to do is make some coffee."

Grace asked, "What are they?"

"Fancy French donuts. Here, try one." He took one of the fried dough squares covered in powdered sugar out of the bag and held it to her.

Grace nodded as she took a bite and savored the sweet flavor. "Mm, good. Let's get the coffee going." Maurice fiddled with Mr. Coffee as she finished her beignet. "I love all the different types of foods down here. I will have to get a few recipes to make at home for us."

"Marva could help you with that."

"I will ask her."

After enjoying a breakfast of beignets and coffee, Maurice arranged a meeting with Philippe for later in the afternoon. They dressed in jeans and t-shirts and agreed to set up his studio. While sorting through the multitude of paintbrushes and tubes of oil paint, throwing out some and keeping others, the doorbell rang. Grace glanced at Maurice. "Are you expecting someone?"

His brow furrowed. "No. It's probably someone selling something. I'll get rid of them."

Grace continued going through the art supplies until Maurice called her name. Upon entering the formal living room, he stood flanked by two men dressed in black suits.

"This is my wife," Maurice said to the men, putting his arm around Grace's shoulder. "My love, these gentlemen are agents from the FBI. I told them anything they have to say to me, they must say in front of you."

The tall, light-skinned man with a short afro extended his hand to her while the blond-haired man stood with his hands folded. "Hello, ma'am. My name is Rick Wolf, and this is my partner, Dennis Hayes." After shaking her hand, he reached into his pocket, pulled out his badge, and flashed it at her. Grace's eyes widened and her heart raced, hoping their visit had nothing to do with Maurice's arrest.

Agent Wolf addressed Maurice. "We'd like to speak with you about Philippe Le Coeur. You work for him, don't you?"

"No. Whatever gave you that idea?" Maurice said.

"We've noticed his interaction with you since you came to town."

Appalled, Maurice asked, "You've been watching me?"

"No, we've been watching him. We've been investigating Mr. Le Coeur for quite some time now."

Grace pulled away from Maurice to sit on the sofa. She couldn't believe what she was hearing.

Maurice folded his arms across his chest. "So what's that got to do with me?"

"He's been running illegal gambling houses and prostitutes and supplying all manner of drugs to the local dealers in this city for years. And anyone who gets in his way is silenced."

Grace started biting her thumbnail as Maurice glanced her way and looked back at the agent. "Again, I ask, what does this have to do with me?"

Agent Wolf sighed. "You must be someone significant to Mr. Le Coeur. He spent considerable time and money preparing this house for you to live in. If you don't work for him, what's the nature of your relationship?"

"Why?"

"We were hoping we could get you to cooperate with us. We need someone on the inside to bring Mr. Le Coeur down."

Maurice started shaking his head. "No. I will not help you. You both need to leave my house now."

Agent Wolf reached into his pocket, pulled out a business card, and offered it to Maurice.

Maurice uncrossed his arms and took the card. Then he went to the front door and opened it, gesturing for them to leave. The two agents walked past him silently.

Agent Wolf stopped right outside the door. "Mr. Chenault, Mr. Le Coeur is a dangerous man and a blight upon this city. He's transporting drugs into this country from Central or South America. People are dying. You think about that for a while, and if you change your mind, call me." He turned to his partner, and they walked back toward the street.

Maurice slammed the door and spun around to Grace. "You see. I told you."

Trembling, Grace asked, "What are we going to do?"

"We're not going to do anything. We are not involved in any of Philippe's business, and he promised to shield us from any fallout. I'll tell him about this when we see him later today." He sat on the sofa beside her. "Do you still want to go, or are you afraid of Philippe now?"

"Truthfully, I am a bit afraid, but I still want to go." She grabbed his hand and squeezed it. "Whatever happens, I want us to do it together."

He kissed her nose. "Good. Now let's finish setting up my studio."

She followed him back to the studio and tried to focus on getting back to work. Maurice seemed to take the FBI's visit calmly, as if he were expecting it. Her hands shook a little as she picked up a half-used tube of yellow oil paint. She was unnerved when the agent spoke about all of Philippe's activities. *People are dying. I advised him to get close to his father, and now we're under surveillance by the FBI. I can't ask him now to turn his father in. If Philippe is killing people, he should be in jail.*

"Grace, are you all right?" Concern filled into Maurice's face.

"The FBI is going to be following us now, aren't they?"

"Apparently, they've already been doing it."

She went to embrace him. "I didn't know what I was getting us into here." She looked up into his green eyes, hoping he wouldn't be upset with her.

"It's okay. We're not doing anything illegal. Let the FBI follow us. At least no one will get away with robbing us in the streets while they're watching." Maurice kissed the top of her head. "You really didn't believe me when I told you my father was a criminal. You thought I was being dramatic." *It's true. I didn't believe his father was running around killing people. I was wrong.* Maurice continued. "At first, I thought it was Philippe who set me up to be arrested, so I would need his help, but now I'm not sure. The FBI could have been the ones behind my arrest. They could have set me up to see if Philippe would come to bail me out."

"I don't know what to think," Grace said, burying her head further into his chest. "I'm scared."

"Don't be afraid, mon cheri. I won't let anything happen to you." He lifted her head to kiss her softly. "If Philippe tries to do anything to hurt you, I will turn him into the FBI."

Hearing him say he'd turn on Philippe if he had to was comforting until Maurice continued. "And if they don't take care of him, I will kill him myself." The look in his eyes told her he was serious. She didn't like hearing that at all.

"Come now, allez, we've got work to do before we meet with Philippe." Maurice went to a large cardboard box with several of his paintings. He pulled one out and held it up. "I think I'll hang this painting up in here."

Grace tried to steady herself as they continued organizing the studio. Maurice bopped around, humming with the boom box going while deciding where to hang his pictures. *I don't know how I will behave normally around Philippe today. I'm never going to see him in the same harmless way.* She tried to focus on helping Maurice and not think about Philippe anymore, but the thoughts kept creeping in.

An hour later, Maurice said, "We'd better get ready. Philippe will be here soon to pick us up." He looked at her. "Are you sure you want to come? You don't have to. I can pick a few pieces of furniture out."

Grace tried to hide her discomfort with a smile. "No, I want to go. I'm okay." They went upstairs to freshen up and get their coats.

Maurice put on his army jacket as she grabbed a gray cardigan sweater. The doorbell rang, and Maurice went down to answer the door.

Grace's heart started to race as she went into the bathroom. Picking up her brush and running it through her hair, her reflection in the mirror was panic stricken. *You need to relax, breathe, and calm down. He's not going to hurt you.* Putting the brush down, she took two deep breaths. Her face softened in the mirror. *You can do this.*

Philippe and Maurice stood in the foyer, engaged in a lively conversation, as she descended the grand staircase. The resemblance between them was uncanny. Although Philippe's skin was fairer and his eyes sparkled blue, there was no denying he was Maurice's father. The shape of their face, eyes, nose, and lips were identical, as if Philippe had birthed him all by himself. The blue eyes locked on hers.

Philippe was in a jolly mood. "There's the lovely buttercup. How are you, Grace?"

Maurice gave Philippe a scrutinizing glare. Grace reached the bottom of the stairs, only to be swept up into Philippe's embrace. Her eyes widened as she glared at Maurice, seeking help.

Maurice swatted at Philippe's arms wrapped around Grace. "Okay, enough. You can put her down."

With an amused chuckle, Philippe released Grace, a gleam of mischief dancing in his eyes. "All right. Come on, let's go."

They walked out to the black Mercedes parked on Napoleon Avenue. Grace's eyes darted around, searching for a sign of the FBI, but the street was devoid of any parked cars or people. Maurice opened the back passenger door for Grace and slid into the front seat with Philippe.

Philippe laughed as he settled behind the wheel, leaning toward Maurice. "What's the matter? You don't trust me? Grace should sit up here with me, not you." He turned around to face Grace. "You're not afraid of me, are you?"

Grace smiled, "No, why would I be?" *I hope that sounded convincing.* Maurice turned around and smiled at her. *I will look to him for strength today. Nothing is going to happen to me.* She folded her slightly trembling hands in her lap, determined to appear calm.

The ride to the warehouse didn't take long. The Mercedes glided onto Magazine Street and pulled into an empty lot adjacent to a weathered, expansive brick building. With Philippe leading the way, they followed as he unlocked the colossal wooden doors. He flipped the light switch by the door, and the overhead fluorescents flickered to life. The cavernous space was filled with cars, furniture, and towering metal shelves laden with crates and boxes.

Philippe strode down an aisle between the rows of crates. "All of your mother's belongings are near my office." Maurice grabbed Grace's hand as they followed behind him. Philippe unlocked the office door, and they stepped in. It was a small gray room with a bare metal desk and a cluster of steel office chairs. Papers littered the desk while a tall metal file cabinet stood against the wall. Photographs adorned the wall opposite the desk of a woman holding a baby and another walking with a little boy. Philippe pointed at them before rounding the desk and sitting. "Those are pictures of you and your mother." Maurice and Grace both leaned in to take a closer look. *Maurice's mother was a beautiful woman. He was such an adorable boy.* There was a resemblance between Maurice's mother and herself around the eyes and the lips, and her petite stature.

"Sit down." Philippe took out a pack of cigarettes and lit one as they each took a chair.

Maurice glanced around. "It's a mess in here, like your other office."

Philippe opened the desk drawer and took out a bottle of bourbon and a small glass. "Would you like a drink? I have more glasses."

"No," Maurice said. "Two FBI agents came to the house today."

"And?"

"They wanted me to help them bring you down, as they put it."

Philippe's eyebrow went up. "Are you wearing a wire?"

"No."

Philippe kept his piercing blue eyes on Maurice. "Is she?"

"No, of course not."

Philippe's gaze went to Grace as he smiled at her seductively. "This is very good. I'm glad you told me." He puffed on his cigarette, poured a drink, and took a sip. "The FBI started investigating me last year. In that time, do you know what I found out FBI really stands for?" He took another sip of bourbon. "Fucking bumbling idiots." He burst into loud laughter.

Maurice looked at Grace with a sour look on his face.

Slamming his glass down on the desk after draining it of bourbon, Philippe got up and went back to the door. "Come on. I'll show you where her things are."

They walked a few paces from the office, and Philippe unlocked a gated warehouse area. Peering through the links, Grace's eyes went to the large portrait of Maurice's mother. When the gate opened, Maurice went straight to it. "Here it is. The portrait I did of Nettie. What do you think, Grace?"

"It's amazing. Your mother was beautiful."

Philippe's demeanor turned somber. "Yes, she was a remarkable woman."

Maurice focused on Philippe. "You'll have it shipped to my house?"

"I told you; you can have anything you want."

Maurice wandered through the furniture, rubbing some with his hands. "Grace, come over here. It's the bedroom furniture." As Grace walked toward him, he was already off, examining what else lay hidden under the thick layers of plastic sheeting. His joy was immense, seeing his mother's belongings. It was a heartwarming sight for Grace that eased her fears.

"Some of the furniture could use a touch-up," Philippe said. "Do you mind if I have it refinished before delivery to you?"

Grace replied, "No, we wouldn't mind. Thank you."

"Now you see, that's what I like," Philippe said, gazing at Maurice. "She knows how to express gratitude." He turned to Grace. "It's my pleasure to serve you." His blue eyes were penetrating, and she had to look away. "I'm going back to my office. You two have fun here. Take the plastic off the furniture you want so I'll know what to send."

As Philippe walked out, Maurice started ripping off plastic sheets. "What do you think about this?" Overwhelmed by the massive amount of furniture, Grace loudly exhaled. *I guess this is what it takes to furnish a five-bedroom house.*

On the drive home, Philippe said, "Don't be too concerned about the FBI. They're a nuisance at best. I know they probably told you terrible things about me, but it's not the whole truth. They are a bunch of hypocrites. The government doesn't give a damn about the poor people in this city or this country. It's true, I make a lot of money, but I don't keep it all to myself. I help a lot of people, especially the poorer ones who live down in Central City. I had a community center built there with a food pantry and a daycare. I make sure they have toys at Christmas and turkeys for Thanksgiving. If the government cared about those people, they would do something about the hunger and homelessness in this city. Instead, they waste money investigating people like me who serve the community. People want to have fun. They enjoy drinking and getting high, gambling, and having someone to comfort them occasionally. I also own several legitimate businesses. Dry cleaners, laundry mats, and small groceries in neighborhoods no one else wants to do business in." He stopped a moment before continuing. "The people the government claim

I am terrorizing know me. I take care of them. In return, they are loyal to me. And the local politicians and the police are happy as long as they get their cut. No one is going to help the FBI around here. Please don't worry about them, okay?"

"We're not worried," Maurice replied.

Grace, however, was quite worried. She considered all Philippe had said, but one thought haunted her. *People are dying.*

Chapter 9

With the studio set up, Maurice started spending more time alone, striving to conjure artistic brilliance. Nothing ignited his passion. A dozen sketches of pelicans, magnolia trees, and riverscapes ended up shredded on the floor. *All of this crap with Philippe has me artistically constipated. I need something to stir me up. New Orleans always inspired me before, but now…*

Leaning back from his drawing table in his supple leather chair, Maurice recalled Grace's fear. For two weeks, he consciously tried to limit their time with Philippe. She seemed more relaxed, busy decorating the house with curtains, quilts, and throw pillows. He hoped she wasn't regretting their decision to move, that the roots they were planting were taking hold. Philippe called several times to invite them to dinner. Still, Maurice refused, saying Grace was sick, or they already had plans with Babeth. He didn't know how much longer he could make excuses.

"Are you busy?" Grace stood in the doorway, holding a different color swatch of cloth in each hand, so sexy in her form-fitting tan jogging suit.

"No, my love. I was thinking about you." Maurice extended his hand for her to come closer.

"The man who is reupholstering the chairs for the formal living room dropped off a bunch of samples." Grace held up the two swatches. "These are the two I picked out. Which color do you like better? The mint green? Or the light teal?"

"I like whatever you like." Pulling her to sit in his lap, he kissed her nose. "Can you take a break? Maybe you can help me formulate an idea worth painting."

Contemplation clouded her face as she surveyed the studio. "You could do something abstract, without form or shape, with a plethora of colors. A metaphor for our new crazy life."

"Crazy?"

"We're officially members of a crime family. It is crazy, and I haven't yet wrapped my mind around it." Grace sighed, leaning on his chest. "What am I going to tell my parents? They cannot come here. What if the FBI were to come back while they were visiting?"

Witnessing her dismay, Maurice's heart ached for her. "We will say it's a misunderstanding. The police harass innocent people all the time. C'est la vie." *She had the same droopy face last week when she realized she wasn't pregnant. I'm disappointing her. I must do better for her.* Holding her tighter, he wanted to tell her everything would be all right, but he promised he wouldn't lie. "It looks nice outside. Why don't we go out for some ice cream? You can drive."

"I like that idea." Grace jumped to her feet. "I'll go grab the keys from the kitchen." Jingling the car keys in her hand, they left through the studio door to the stone walkway leading to the driveway and the garage. "You know the way, right?"

"One thing I know is where they serve the best ice cream. It's not far from here."

Settling into the sun-baked car, the windows went down immediately to release the heat. Grace felt around for buttons and bars to adjust the driver's seat to her comfort and tilted the rearview mirror. She glanced at Maurice with a mischievous smile. "Ready?"

The Mercedes jolted forward when she put it into drive, pressed the accelerator, and slammed on the brake. They both jerked back and forth in their seats before turning to one another and bursting into laughter. "Maybe this wasn't such a good idea," Maurice said.

"I'll be fine. It's been a while since I've driven, but it's like riding a bicycle."

Maurice snickered. "Okay. Drive slowly, please."

The car cruised down the driveway smoothly on her second attempt. Maurice directed them to Jefferson Avenue and pointed at the sign. "There it is, Creole Chill Cream." The parlor was busy with patrons. They checked out all the different flavors through the foggy glass case while waiting. Maurice opted for a double scoop of Cookie Monster, while Grace indulged in a scoop of butter pecan. Cones in hand, they strolled down the street, window shopping in the small antique stores and boutiques they passed while enjoying their sweet treat.

"Mm, you were right," Grace said between licks. "This may be the best ice cream I've ever had. What does yours taste like?"

"A chocolate chip cookie. Would you like to try it?" He offered his cone for her to sample.

She eyed Maurice seductively as she slowly licked the cone. "Mm. It's good. Maybe I'll get it next time."

Laughing, he said, "You're so naughty. I love it."

Further down the street, Maurice stopped in front of a print shop. "I want to order some custom business cards. I need to let people in town know I do portraits and hopefully get a client or two." They finished their cones before going inside. Maurice sketched out a draft of his card design for the printer. The printer told him the business cards would be ready in a couple of days.

When they returned to the car, Maurice proposed they stop by Tulane University. "You could pick up a catalog and see what courses are coming up. It's right down St. Charles Avenue."

In minutes, the car pulled into the large university lot, and following the signposts, they located the administrative office. Grace went in while he waited in the car. *Going to school will give her something to take her mind off our troubles. Hopefully, there will be a class starting soon.*

Grace quickly returned to the car with the catalog. "Speaking of school, when will you start your driving lessons?"

"I was going to ask you to teach me," Maurice chuckled, "but now I think I should go to a driving school. I'll have to find one."

Grace giggled as she started the car. "That's probably best." She drove them home safely and went to the formal living room. "I'm going to read through this catalog. Are you going back to work?"

"Oui. I'll be in the studio." Maurice sat at his drawing desk, gazing out the long open windows. *What do I do about Philippe? The Art of War says, "Keep your friends close and your enemies closer." I need some way to get leverage against him, forcing him to leave us alone. I can't keep putting off seeing him. There must be a way for me to gain an advantage.* A sudden ring interrupted his thoughts.

"Philippe, how are you?" Maurice answered the call cordially.

Philippe was in a chipper mood. "I'm checking up on you. Is everything okay? Is Grace feeling better?"

"Not really. I think she might be developing an allergy. Maybe it's the magnolia trees."

"I see." A loud exhale.

"What if you and I go out tonight?" Maurice asked.

"If Grace won't mind, that would be great. I have a few things I want to talk to you about, anyway."

"Good. What time can I expect you?"

"I'll pick you up at seven. See you soon."

Maurice stared at the phone after putting the receiver down. *What does he want to talk about? Is this where he's going to make his pitch to get me involved in his business? I know it is coming.* As he walked to the formal living room, Maurice mustered up a cheerful face. "Grace, I'm going to have dinner with Philippe tonight. He wants to talk to me alone. I hope you don't mind."

Glancing up from her catalog, Grace nodded. "No, of course not. I'll be fine. There is leftover chicken I can have for dinner."

Returning to the studio, Maurice paced slowly back and forth, trying to formulate a plan. *There must be something Philippe is doing or has that he doesn't want anyone to know about. Everyone has secrets. I bet he has a big one. I need to find out what it is. I must stop shutting down around him and be my usual talkative self. Ask lots of questions and see how much he is willing to tell.* He stopped pacing and sighed aloud. "I hope it won't take too long."

He recalled Philippe saying how helpful he could be since he knew people with money to buy expensive art. *What if I painted a series for everyone to enjoy, whether they have a lot of money or not?* A smile crept across his lips as he went to find the box with his old sketch pads. He kept the ones with drawings he liked but, for one reason or another, never completed them. Rummaging through the dozens of pictures, he finally found what he was searching for and pulled it out. A sketch of Grace sitting on a stool with her bare back showing, staring at a giant human-faced scorpion draped over her shoulder. *Me and Grace. Virgo and Scorpio. Horoscopes are popular. I can do something spectacular with this. Finally, a brilliant idea.*

"Babe, I found a class I want to take." Grace carried the open catalog in her hand. "It starts next week. I need to go back to the university tomorrow to register."

"Great. We will do it first thing in the morning." He held up the sketch pad. "Do you remember this picture?"

"Oh yes, you did it while I was in the hospital. You said you weren't going to finish it. I didn't know you kept it." She took a closer look. "It's a little strange."

"I know. I was ambiguous about it at the time, but now I'm ready to finish it. It will be the first of a series."

Grace leaned up to kiss him. "I'm sure it will be wonderful."

Maurice put the sketch pad down to fully embrace her. "You are wonderful. I love you." He started kissing her slowly and got carried away, ravaging her mouth with his own. "We haven't christened the studio yet," he whispered.

Grace leaned back. "And we're not going to. There are no curtains or blinds. What if Pierre walks around back? He'll see us."

"Okay, what about our old bed in the guest suite?" Not waiting for an answer, he pulled her toward the bedroom.

"What time is Philippe picking you up?"

"Not until seven. We have plenty of time."

Maurice had no idea where Philippe was taking him. Sporting a black suit with a white shirt, he mimicked Philippe's style. After gelling his hair and combing it smoothly into a ponytail, he stared at his reflection in the bathroom mirror. *Let's see what this demon is hiding.*

Grace stood up from the sofa when he came down the grand staircase. "Wow. You look incredibly sexy. I don't know if I should let you out of the house."

He kissed her passionately. "I don't want anyone but you." The doorbell rang. "By the way, I told Philippe you have an allergy. Try to look sick." Maurice went to answer the door.

Philippe strolled in wearing a black suit and a white shirt. Smirking, he embraced Maurice. "You look good. I like it." He turned as Grace came to the foyer, holding a tissue to her nose. "Oh, poor buttercup. Sorry, you're not feeling well. I promise I won't keep your husband out too late."

Grace sniffled. "It's okay. Take your time. I'm going to go lie down in bed and probably fall asleep."

As they walked to the car, Philippe lit a cigarette. "I'm glad you dressed. We can go over to the Commander's Palace."

"You made a reservation?"

Philippe snorted. "I don't need one."

The restaurant was buzzing as usual. Several people sat at the bar and in the nearby waiting area. The maître d greeted them with a smile. "Mr. Le Coeur, so good to see you. Give me a moment, and we'll have a table for you." Philippe gazed at Maurice with a knowing smile. They were seated at a corner table by a window in minutes.

"Perhaps Grace should see a physician. She's been under the weather for weeks."

Maurice glanced out the window at the passersby. "She'll be all right. Moving from a cold climate to a hot one takes time for one's system to adjust."

The waiter came over with menus. Maurice waved him off. "I don't need one. I know what I want."

"So do I," Philippe said. "We're ready to order. Bring me a bowl of gumbo, and then I'll have the filet. Rare."

"I will have the turtle soup, romaine salad, and the grilled pork chop, please."

The waiter wrote the order on his pad. "Any wine or drinks?"

Philippe answered, "Two Weller bourbons and a bottle of Merlot."

After the waiter walked away, Maurice frowned. "I don't drink bourbon."

Philippe chuckled. "I know. They're both for me. How's the painting coming along?"

"I'm not working on anything right now. We're still getting the house organized. I ordered some business cards today. I was hoping you could pass a few around for me when they're ready. You did offer to help."

"Of course, I'd be happy to. That's actually what I wanted to talk to you about. The gallery you want to open. I have some property on Julia Street. It's been vacant for a while since the neighborhood has gone down. Maybe we could start revitalizing the area by opening a few art galleries."

Maurice cocked his head while raising an eyebrow. "A few?"

"You have artist friends, don't you? I'd be willing to sponsor a couple you deem talented and worthy."

Maurice remained suspicious. "What would you want in return?"

The waiter brought the drinks and opened the wine to pour two glasses. Once he left, Maurice slid his glass of bourbon toward Philippe.

Philippe sipped his drink. "Money, of course. I would expect this to be a profitable business within three years. We would work up terms for payback over time with interest."

"What happens if it's not profitable?"

Philippe leaned across the table. "That is what insurance is for." He winked at Maurice. "I believe it's worth a gamble. Would you like to go see the property tomorrow?"

"Yes, I would." Maurice sipped on his merlot. "I have a favor to ask."

"If it is within my power, I will do it."

Maurice feigned an innocent look. "Would you teach me to drive?"

Philippe burst into loud laughter, a playful glint in his eyes. "It would be my pleasure. Yes." He reached across the table to touch Maurice's hand. "This is progress. This is good." Draining the first glass of bourbon, he started on the second one. "We'll stop at DMV on the way to Julia Street. You need to apply for your temporary license. Also, get one of those books and read it to pass the written test. Then we'll start your lessons. I'm free on Sundays. You?" Maurice nodded as he continued, "I'm surprised you didn't ask Pierre to teach you."

Maurice chuckled. "I thought about it, but then I figured I may give him a heart attack if I'm horrible at it. Better not to risk it." He sipped his wine. "Thank you for agreeing to do it. I know you're a busy man, and I appreciate you taking the time."

Philippe nodded, gazing at him intensely. "This is very good." Once the waiter delivered the soups and salad, he said, "I have a favor to ask of you as well."

Maurice tasted his turtle soup. "What is it?"

"Mardi Gras next month. Your house is right on the parade route. It would be nice if you would host a family gathering on Fat Tuesday. I could bring Sophie and Marie. You haven't met your other sister yet. You could invite Yves and Babeth. Grace wouldn't have to do anything. I'll send a caterer to handle the food and serving."

Maurice faked a smile. "Of course. We'd be honored to host the family."

"Good. So tell me about some of your artist friends. Do you have anyone in mind who might be interested in my proposition?"

"I know several people." The conversation about the art galleries continued throughout dinner. *What did Philippe mean when he talked about insurance?*

Grace was sitting up in bed reading a book when he came home. "How was dinner?"

Maurice shared Philippe's idea with her. "I'm trying not to get excited about it, but it's hard not to. It's exciting. I can't wait to see the property tomorrow." He undressed to join her in bed. "There's one more thing. We're hosting a family Mardi Gras party. I'm sorry. I couldn't get out of it."

"When is it?"

"February 16th. A little less than a month from now."

Grace put her book down. "I spoke to Anne while you were out. Jacque wants you to call him."

"In the morning." They kissed and lay down to sleep.

The shrill ring of the phone startled Maurice, waking him. He snatched up the receiver, peering at the clock. "Who is this?"

"Cousin, are you still sleeping? You should be up."

Maurice glanced at Grace, still sleeping. "Jacque. It's five a.m. Please tell me Anne is in labor, or I'm hanging up."

"Grace said you were out to dinner with Philippe last night. What are you doing?"

Maurice dropped the phone. Exhaling loudly, he punched his pillow and laid back down. After tossing around for a few minutes, he got up, put on his robe, and went to the kitchen.

Jacque answered on the first ring. "Bonjour. I'm fine. How are you, cousin?"

"Everything is fine. I'm handling Philippe."

Jacque laughed. "Handling him? How?"

"In my own way." Maurice ran his hands over his hair. "You were right. I could not stop him from intruding, but I'm working on something."

"All this code talking. Sounds like a lot of bullshit to me. Why are you even talking to him? Hanging out with him?"

Maurice sighed. "Look, you said you didn't want to be my father anymore. I'm not going to explain everything to you and ask for your expert opinion. I am doing this myself. Everything is fine."

"Don't delude yourself. You need to cut all ties with him."

Maurice spent the next hour telling Jacque everything that had happened from the moment they touched down in New Orleans.

The art gallery proposition outraged Jacque when he heard about it. "You cannot go into business with Philippe. Please, Maurice, don't do it. I know what he meant when he talked about having insurance. If the business doesn't turn profitable, Philippe will burn it down. Then he collects the insurance and moves on. You and your friends lose everything."

Maurice's skin tingled. "How do you know this?"

"Because he's done it before. I did a little checking of my own into Philippe once you insisted on moving down there. Think about Grace. You should abandon this ridiculous mission and return to New York."

"I want to know everything you found out about Philippe. Will you help me?"

"I will send you a package via FedEx today. I have to go. Be careful."

Chapter 10

Maurice leaned into getting to know his father for the next few weeks. The documents Jacque sent were beneficial as he delved into understanding Philippe's intricate web of operations. It was extensive. The man had tentacles all over the city. From high-ranking officials to denizens of the streets, he paid for information. None of it, however, was the leverage Maurice was looking for.

A major part of his strategy was to go along with Philippe and the gallery plan, promising to set up meetings with local artists who may have an interest. Today was his third driving lesson with Philippe, another chance to get information.

Dressed in his mini-me outfit, Maurice came down the back staircase to the kitchen, finding Grace at the table, surrounded by her books and notebooks. "You have been at it since breakfast. They gave you a lot of homework to do?"

"Yes," Grace replied. "I have a ton of reading. I feel a little rusty since I took last semester off. I'm taking my time with it."

He kissed her cheek. "You'll be fine. I'm off for my lesson."

It was warm outside, and Maurice didn't want to wear a suit but had to continue his charade of wanting to be like his father. Philippe pulled up in the tan Toyota Camry. Maurice's training car, since Philippe refused to teach him how to drive in his Mercedes. He had laughed loudly, "What? You think I'm going to let you ruin my Benz?"

Maurice studied Philippe's profile as they drove to the empty parking lot of a nearby elementary school. *His secret isn't going to be found in his business. It's something more personal.* Philippe parked the car, and they switched seats. Maurice got into the driver's seat and said,

"I think I'm ready to go on the road now. How many times will you make me drive around this parking lot?"

Philippe laughed. "I was waiting for you to tell me you were ready. Let's do it." He lit a cigarette as Maurice pulled out of the lot. "You know how to get to Magazine Street? I want to stop by the warehouse."

Maurice relaxed behind the wheel. "I think so, but pay attention. I may need some direction." They rode in silence momentarily. "Remember what you said about secrets in a marriage? How could you say that? Wasn't Nettie a secret in your marriage?"

"No." Philippe puffed on his cigarette and blew a cloud of smoke out the window. "My wife, Mia, knew about Nettie and you. I told her before we married that I loved someone else, but she wanted to marry me anyway. Now that Nettie is gone, she has me all to herself."

"I can't believe your wife permitted you to sleep with another woman."

"She didn't want to divorce me. You know, Catholics."

"And she never got mad for revenge, drunk, crazy? Nothing?"

"Mia's a quiet, gentle woman. Very understanding. I treat her well. She's happy."

"What about your daughters? Surely they heard the same gossip about you and my mother as I did growing up. They never questioned you or complained?"

Philippe looked at him with steely eyes. "Did you ever question your mother?"

Maurice fell silent and focused on driving. *I am not getting anywhere with this line of questioning.*

With a little direction from Philippe, Maurice pulled into the warehouse parking lot. As they got out of the car, Philippe said, "You did well. I think you may be ready for the road test soon. Have you taken the written one yet?"

"Yes, I passed. Driving is not hard." He followed Philippe to his office in the warehouse.

As usual, Philippe had his drink before he pushed a folder across the desk toward Maurice. "Those are the contract terms for you and your artist friends for the gallery project. Read them over and let me know if you have any questions. This way, you can talk to your friends intelligently about the proposal."

"Thank you. I will. And thank you for passing around my business cards. I received two calls from potential clients, Ms. Lily Dumont and Ms. Natalie Barnes. Ms. Barnes is coming tomorrow."

"Dumont, I know, but I don't know Natalie Barnes. Guess you got that one on your own. It's good news. I'm glad to hear it." Philippe sipped his drink. "Is Grace pleased with all the furniture?"

"Yes, she is. She's very grateful. Since she started back to school, she's been busy studying. Lots of homework. She is looking forward to Mardi Gras."

"Good. I am too. Marie is bringing her new boyfriend. I haven't met him yet, as far as she knows."

"As far as she knows?"

"You don't think I'm going to allow my daughter to be running around town with any old body, do you? I've already checked him out. He seems okay." Philippe drained his glass. "Come on, let's finish your lesson. You can practice parallel parking on Magazine Street and then drive home."

Maurice came into the kitchen, holding up a bag. Grace was still studying at the table. "I brought dinner. Fried chicken and sweet potato fries."

She looked up from her notes. "You are an angel. I completely forgot about dinner. Come, kiss me."

"As you wish." He sauntered over to the table, put the bag on it, and pulled her into his arms to kiss her. "How was that?"

"Mm, good. The chicken smells good too. Where did you get it?"

As they ate, he told her about his lesson with Philippe and the last stop at Chicken Joe's. When they finished eating, Maurice asked, "Almost done with your homework?"

"I am done. I covered a lot today. I feel prepared for class tomorrow. And you have your first client. Are you excited?"

"Very." He kissed her hand. "If you're done with schoolwork, can we go to bed early?"

"Absolutely."

The next day Maurice and Grace arose early and feeling well-rested. They shared a pleasant breakfast of scrambled eggs and toast, fueling themselves for the day ahead. As Grace readied herself for her morning class, Maurice lounged on the bed in tight jeans and a red golf shirt, admiring her figure. "Your class is over at noon, right?"

Grace paused buttoning her white shirt dress to give him a curious smile. "Yes, why?"

A playful glint lit up Maurice's eyes. "I was thinking about taking you to lunch afterward. Would you like to go?"

Grace leaned in to place an affectionate kiss on his lips. "Sounds great. I love you. Got to run."

"Drive safely," he said, following her down the grand staircase and into the studio.

Maurice watched her from the window until she vanished from sight. The contract from Philippe was on his drawing table. His client wasn't due for another hour, and he sat down to read it. *There seems to be nothing fishy in here, but I'm not an attorney. Is there someone I can trust who doesn't know Philippe to look at it? Do I want to risk getting my friends involved in this? Maybe Jacque is right.* The doorbell rang.

When Maurice opened the door, there stood a stunning, captivating woman. Her skin was dark and smooth like a Hershey Kiss, with sharp cheekbones and full plump red lips. Dark cat-like eyes penetrated his own, putting him in a trance.

"Mr. Chenault?" Her voice was like music. "I'm Natalie Barnes. I believe we have an appointment. May I come in?"

Maurice snapped back into focus. "Of course. Please, call me Maurice." He stepped aside to allow her to pass. As she walked by, he took a deep breath, the sweet scent of chocolate filling his nose. Her tight white sheath dress hugged every curve of her body. His mouth watered as he began to get aroused. Natalie's beauty had a magnetic pull that he fought to break. *Think about Grace, beautiful Grace, my love Grace, Grace.* He smiled at Natalie. "My studio is this way." Heat rose in his blood as she followed him.

Natalie stopped as they passed by the formal living room, noticing the portrait of Nettie hanging prominently on the wall. "You painted this picture?" She approached the portrait before facing Maurice, flashing a brilliant smile.

"Yes. It's the first portrait I ever painted. She was my mother." Focusing on Nettie's smiling face calmed him down.

Natalie's eyes glowed. "It's stunning. I want to look like that. You can do that?"

"I would like to try. Come, I'll show you some more of my work."

A rush of heat pulsed through Maurice's body as he placed his hand on the small of her back and escorted her into the studio. Gesturing for Natalie to sit in his desk chair, he retrieved his large portfolio of portraits. Placing it on the desk before her, he leaned over her shoulder to open the book to the first page. The tantalizing chocolate scent teased his senses, and he stepped back. "Would you like a drink? Some iced tea?"

"Yes, thank you." Natalie flipped through the pages of the portfolio, stopping to study one. Maurice stood mesmerized until she glanced up at him. "Is something wrong?"

"No, no. Excuse me. I'll go get the tea. I'll be right back." Entering the kitchen, he grabbed the countertop and took several deep breaths. *What is this woman doing to me? I have got to pull myself together. I hoped for a pleasant face to paint, but this may be too much. I don't know if I can work with her and maintain control.* He paced around the kitchen before getting the iced tea. *I love Grace. She is not as beautiful as Grace.* Staring at his wedding ring, he took a few more deep breaths before returning to the studio.

Natalie, sitting with her legs crossed, swiveled around in the supple leather chair to face him. His eyes followed the curve of her long sexy legs right down to her ankles into her white stilettos. Handing her the glass of tea, his eyes went to her lips again, and he instinctively licked his own.

Taking the glass, she gazed into his eyes. "It's okay. I find you very attractive, too." Once again, she had him mesmerized.

Maurice cleared his throat and walked over to get another portfolio from against the wall. He laid it on the desk on top of the first one. "This has some more of my work in it."

"I don't need to see anymore. I want you to paint my portrait. What do you charge? How long will it take?"

Maurice avoided prolonged eye contact, tapping his fingers on the portfolio cover. "It depends. How large would you like it to be? What type of setting do you wish to be surrounded in? I can paint you in an office or outdoors in a garden. Did you have something in mind?"

"A garden would be lovely. It doesn't need to be as large as your mother's portrait. Half that size would be appropriate. It's a birthday gift for my father."

Picking up the portfolios from the desk, Maurice hauled them to their place against the wall. When he turned to face her, her glowing eyes were waiting. "It will cost you two thousand dollars. I can get it done in, say, three weeks. The first week I will need you to pose for several hours for the initial sketch, and then I will finish it. You pay me half when we start and the rest when the portrait is done. If you don't like it, I will give you all your money back and keep the portrait. Is that agreeable to you?"

"Yes, when can you start? Are you busy today? I have cash." Natalie reached into her pearl-covered clutch purse and pulled out a roll of bills. Gazing intensely into his eyes, she held it out to him. "Here's two thousand dollars. You can take it all now. I trust you."

"Uh, all right. I guess we could start now." He took the money from her hand. "Excuse me. I'll be right back." Going to the kitchen, he broke the spell with a few paces. *Grace, I love Grace.* Picking up one of the kitchen chairs, he carried it back to the studio, setting it near the window. "You can sit here. I'll get another chair, and we'll imagine it as a bench in a garden." He strutted back to the kitchen and stood looking up at the ceiling. *I can do this. She is not as beautiful as Grace.* He carried another chair to the studio and placed it beside the first one.

Natalie strolled over and sat down in a chair. Maurice suggested she lean slightly and place her arm across the backs of the two chairs. Stepping back, he visualized the final outcome. He grabbed an easel and set it up a short distance from her with a large sketch pad. "What type of flowers would you like to see in your garden?"

"I'm not sure. Maybe red roses on a trellis? What do you suggest?"

"I'm thinking something a bit more exotic. Hot pink bougainvillea on a trellis with a few bright orange tropical hibiscus flowers. A hummingbird could be sucking nectar from a blossom."

"Yes, that sounds incredible."

Standing behind the easel, Maurice started to sketch. Natalie kept gazing at him with a seductive smile. After a few strokes, he put the pencil down and went to stand at his desk.

Natalie's reflection appeared in the window behind him. "Is your wife home?"

As he turned, she stepped closer and kissed him. Maurice's eyes widened as he tightened his lips so her tongue wouldn't go into his mouth. He turned his head. "Natalie, this is not what we are here for. Please step back."

She raised her hand to touch his face, and he grabbed her wrist. "It's true. I find you very attractive, but I don't cheat on my wife. Now, please step back." She placed her free hand on his crotch and rubbed his stiffening member through his jeans. Maurice closed his eyes and suppressed a moan in his throat. Reaching down, he removed her hand, and she quickly grabbed his shirt collar to pull him in for another kiss.

The studio door opened, and Grace stepped in. "What the hell?" Her face was twisted and red.

Natalie stepped back as Maurice released her wrist. "Grace. I didn't do anything. She kissed me." Grace ran across the studio into the hall.

Natalie snickered as she picked up her purse lying on the desk. "What time should I come back tomorrow?"

Maurice took the roll of bills from his pocket and handed it to her. "Please take this and go. We cannot work together." He held the door open, and Natalie sauntered outside. Slamming the door behind her, he hurried to the hall. "Grace, I didn't do anything, I swear." He stormed to the kitchen, but she wasn't there. "Grace, where are you? Please listen to me." He walked through the empty great room and saw the door to the guest suite was closed. "Are you in there? Please come out and talk to me. She came on to me. I did not kiss her."

The door cracked open, revealing only a sliver of her face. Enough to see she was crying. "You should wipe her lipstick off your mouth before telling me you did not kiss her. I know what I saw." The door slammed closed.

Maurice banged on it. "I didn't do anything. If I was going to cheat on you, do you think I would be stupid enough to do it right here in our home? Do you really think so little of me?"

A muffled voice came through the door. "No. You think so little of me."

Her soft sobbing broke his heart. Sinking to the floor with his back against the door, he wiped his mouth with his sleeve. "I love you. I would never disrespect you or our home like this. Never." Tears welled up in his eyes. "Please, believe me. I did not want to kiss her. She forced herself on me. I was trying to restrain her."

He sat there with his head in his hands, hoping she would speak, but Grace would not say anything else. *I cannot believe this is happening. Damn it. I wanted to, but I did not do it, and she's going to punish me for it anyway.* "Grace, please open the door." Tears rolled down his cheeks. "I love you."

As he sat there, a sourness rolled through his belly. His head started throbbing as he cradled his arms around his knees. "I'm not moving until you open the door and let me talk to you. Please."

Hours later, the door slowly opened. Maurice rolled onto his knees, taking Grace's limp hand to kiss her wedding ring. "Please believe me. I love you so much. I would never do anything to hurt you. I swear it. You are my life."

Grace pulled her hand away. "Fine. I believe you."

She walked to the kitchen, and Maurice was on her heels. "You believe me?"

Grace poured herself a glass of Chardonnay. Sipping the wine, she gave him the coldest stare. "I'll be sleeping in the guest room."

"Grace, please. If you believe me, why would you do that?" He reached out his hand to her as she cringed, stepping around him.

"I believe your story. I just can't look at you tonight. I'll talk to you tomorrow."

Following her as she made her way back to the guest suite, he pleaded with her. "We should talk about it tonight. It's not good to go to bed angry."

Grace slammed the door in his face. Her muffled voice said, "Tomorrow."

Chapter 11

Grace sat on the bed, her fingers gently gripping the wine glass as she slowly sipped. Once again, the image of Maurice and the woman exploded in her mind. His eyes were wide open in a wild stare. Red lipstick smeared across his lips from the woman with a smoldering glint in her black eyes and a seductive smile. *Did he want to kiss her? Was he completely overtaken by her beauty? But how could he do it in our home? I want to believe he is telling me the truth. He knew I was coming home. I can't believe Maurice would purposely seduce a woman in front of me.*

When she opened the door to Maurice kneeling at her feet, her heart softened. The anger that had consumed her began to fizzle. His beautiful green eyes glistened with sorrow. *What can I say? Women come on to him all the time. I know this.*

For the most part, she was secure in her marriage, but secretly, she harbored a fear that, eventually, he would return to philandering. Maurice had been supportive and loyal throughout her recovery after the fire. They intertwined their lives with promises of forever. Eloping to Las Vegas was his idea, but she prevailed with a small wedding ceremony with family on Christmas Eve. The happiest day of her life. But the beautiful dream had a nagging ugly underbelly where dread lived.

Is this it? Is this the beginning of my nightmare? Did he uproot me from my family to betray me? Since moving to New Orleans, our lives have been falling further off-kilter. First, Philippe seduces us into being a part of his crime family, then Maurice's arrest and the FBI surveillance. We came here for a fresh start, but instead, we are in a dangerous, chaotic mess. And we're falling apart.

In somber silence, Grace drained her wine glass and lay down. Exhaustion tugged on her entire body, but sleep remained elusive. The image of Maurice's face, tainted by those crimson lips, kept torturing her. Tears seeped from the corners of her eyes as she squeezed them shut.

As the new day dawned, the morning sun's rays beamed through the sheer curtains of the guest suite. Awaking with a slight headache and feeling confused, Grace pulled back the covers, revealing the white shirt dress from the day before. Shielding her eyes from the bright sunlight, she stumbled from the bed. *This room needs some mini blinds. I need some coffee.*

At the kitchen table, Maurice hunched over a mug of coffee, eyes brimming with sadness. "Good morning."

Ignoring his greeting, Grace prepared her coffee before sitting at the table across from him. "Before you say anything, I don't want to talk about yesterday. I want to put it behind us." She sighed heavily. "I think we should go back to New York." *Please, please, agree with me.*

Maurice's lips pursed. "Where would we live? We don't have a place there anymore."

"It's New York. We'll find a place. If we sell this house, we can buy a house there."

"I don't want to sell this house." Getting up to refill his mug, he stood at the counter, avoiding her eyes. "This is the only thing I have left of my mother. I cannot give it up."

Shaking her head, she peered into her coffee mug. "Nothing about being here is helping us take charge of our lives."

Returning to the table, Maurice pulled his chair closer to hers. "We're spending less money, aren't we? It's true, there have been challenges, but we can be happy here. It's only been a month. We are still adjusting, settling into the new reality. Things will get better. As long as we stick together, we can do anything." His lips pressed against hers in a tender, lingering kiss, his determination seeping into her being. He picked her up, carrying her upstairs to their bedroom.

After making love, as they dressed, Maurice said, "I'm working on a way to have Philippe leave us alone for good, and once I cut the head off the demon, we will be fine."

"Are you going to the FBI?"

"No. This is something I must do myself. Philippe has a secret. Once I find it, I will use it as leverage for him to leave us alone." His tone and gaze conveyed bravado.

Her brow furrowed. "What kind of secret?"

"I believe it's got something to do with his daughters. I need to do more investigation. I must stay close to him to discover it."

"Is that why you asked him to teach you to drive?"

"Yes. I've learned a lot about him. Initially, I thought the secret would be something about his business operation. Now, I believe Sophie and Marie are the keys. And I am not doing the art gallery project with him. It's too risky. Later on, we will open our gallery together." He kissed her softly. "Thank you for trusting and believing in me. I just need a little time. If everything is still going haywire by June, we will go back to New York. Is that agreeable to you?"

Grace didn't want to agree to those terms, but she did.

"I'm going to work in the studio. Je t'aime, mon cheri."

After he left, Grace sank onto the bed, her mind swirling. *The house is beautiful, and I like the New Orleans food and culture. I could see us living here with three kids running around. Even though I know they are there, I haven't seen any sign of the FBI lately, and The Natalies of the world will come no matter where we are. I will focus on my studies. Hopefully, I'll get pregnant soon.*

Their lives seemed to settle as the city buzzed with preparations for Mardi Gras. Grace embraced her school routine, diligently working on homework, while Maurice spent most of his time in his studio. Fortunately, his next client, Ms. Lily Dumont, was a lovely, elderly woman who wanted her portrait done while holding her yappy Pomeranian pup. When he wasn't working on her picture, he was busy creating his horoscope series. Once Maurice received his driver's license, they began to tour museums in the afternoon and spent more evenings out at jazz clubs and dance halls. Mardi Gras parties were happening before the big day, and they attended a few grand ones.

On Fat Tuesday, the caterers Philippe hired arrived early in the morning at the house. The parade would begin at eight a.m., and they set up a lavish breakfast buffet in the main dining room. Jumping into the spirit of the holiday, Grace determined to enjoy this family day and the parade. Wanting to wear a Mardi Gras color, she put on an olive-green sleeveless jumpsuit and helped the catering team blow up balloons and put up banner decorations. Outside, crowds of people lined up on Napoleon Avenue. Yves and Babeth were the first to arrive, and Grace greeted them at the front door.

"There is so much excitement in the air," Babeth said, entering the foyer. Her flowy purple and white floral dress was elegant while

Yves wore a plain black suit. "Thank goodness the weather is warm this year. I hate it when it's chilly on Mardi Gras."

Yves nodded in agreement as Grace led them to the main dining room. "It's a good thing you live close enough to walk here. Most of the streets are already closed. I don't know where Philippe will park his car when he arrives."

"Don't worry about Philippe," Yves said. "He knows where to go. Is this your first Mardi Gras?"

"Yes. We've been enjoying the parties around the city all weekend. I'm excited to see the parade. Unfortunately, Pierre won't be joining us today. He left two days ago to visit a friend in Houston, Texas. Claimed he's celebrated enough Mardi Gras for the rest of his life."

Maurice, wearing tight jeans and a lime green golf shirt, escorted Sophie and Marie into the dining room. Marie, a gangly teenager, sported thick, wavy black hair cut in an angular bob. Her skintight jeans bore assorted rips, and a tie-dye tee peeked out beneath her black leather jacket. A ring adorned every finger of the hand she offered Grace. "Howdy, it's nice to meet you." A tight-lipped smile accompanied Marie's firm handshake.

As the sisters greeted Yves and Babeth, Grace asked Maurice, "Where's Philippe?"

"He's outside grilling Marie's new boyfriend in the driveway." Leaning in, Maurice whispered, "You keep an eye on Marie today. I'll watch Sophie."

Bubbling with excitement in her bright green and yellow print sundress, Sophie gave Grace a big hug. "How are you, sis? I haven't seen you since the day you came to my bar. Everything good with the house?"

"Yes, we finally have everything pretty much in order."

"Do you mind showing Marie and me around? I would love to see your interior design skills." Without waiting for an answer, Sophie strutted out of the dining room toward the great room. "Come on, Marie." Grace followed behind the two of them.

Upon entering the great room, Sophie said, "This is nice and comfy." She flopped down on the beige sofa as if to test the buoyancy of the cushions. "Why don't you have a big television in here? This would be the perfect place to sit and watch movies and football games."

"We don't own a television. Maurice doesn't like them."

"Frig what he likes. What about you? You don't like watching television?" Sophie glanced at Marie. "Who doesn't like watching television?"

Grace snickered. "He says people who watch television are being brainwashed. I don't miss it. I read a lot."

"He's probably right," Marie said. "All of those stupid commercials."

They went to view the guest suite and then back through the great room to Maurice's studio. Marie was in awe of the artwork on the walls. "Wow, he is a really good artist. Do you think he would give me one of these pictures?" She pointed to the series of abstracts that used to hang at Le Beau Riviere.

Grace smiled. "He might. You should ask him."

Approaching one of the two covered easels, Sophie began to lift the drape. "Don't do that," Grace warned. "He doesn't like for people to view a work in progress."

Sophie lifted the drape anyway. "Well, he's not here, and he won't know unless you tell him." She unveiled the painting of Grace with the scorpion on her back. "What the hell is this?"

Marie came closer to examine it. "Cool. Very cool."

Grace wanted to get them out of the studio before Maurice noticed they were in there. "Come on, I'll show you the bedrooms upstairs." As they entered the foyer to go up the grand staircase, Philippe came in with a tall, good-looking young brother dressed similarly to Marie. "Hey, hey, where are you ladies going? The parade's about to begin. Everyone grab something to eat and drink and let's head outside."

Marie went to the young man and took his hand. "Darius, this is Grace. Grace, this is my boyfriend."

"So nice to meet you. Come on, I'll show you where the food is." Everyone was around the buffet, fixing plates and pouring drinks. Outside on the front veranda, patio chairs were set in pairs with a snack table between them. A perfect place to view the parade as the procession made its way down the avenue. For a moment, Grace stood at the veranda's edge to gaze at the massive sea of people as far as the eye could see. The band's music was rhythmic and loud. Marchers and dancers wore colorful costumes with masks. Beaded necklaces of all colors, tiny toys, plastic cups, and gold coins floated through the air, tossed from enormous outrageously decorated floats into the extended hands of the crowds below. One float stopped in the block directly in front of the veranda. Colorful Zulu warriors danced to melodic drums to Grace's amazement before proceeding down the street.

"I've never seen anything like this," Grace said to Maurice.

"Biggest party of the year," he replied. "Each float is created by a group of people called a Krewe. There are about sixty different krewes around the city. They spend all year designing their float around a theme. There is a tradition as to which Krewe follows which street and the order of floats in the procession. Those gold coins they throw are called doubloons, and each Krewe has its mark stamped on them. People will fight you to collect them. I don't know why. They're not worth anything, and they throw the same junk off the floats every year."

"It's a souvenir, and it's a tradition. Everyone is having fun. I think it's fabulous." Philippe and Sophie kept jumping out of their seat, yelling and cheering with revelers on the floats and in the street. "Those two are enjoying themselves."

Maurice glanced at them, chuckling. "You think this is bad? You should see people in the French Quarter when the parade comes through. Girls stand on the balconies while guys below shout for them to show their tits, and the girls lift their shirts to give them a good look. It's pretty wild."

Grace gave him an incredulous look before returning to the parade. Later, she did a double take when some girls lifted their shirts, exposing their breasts on one of the floats. The spectacle went on for hours, a dazzling kaleidoscope of colorful entertainment. At the parade's conclusion, everyone gathered in the dining room where a sumptuous lunch awaited. In the center of the feast, there was a large, round, colorful cake.

"Maurice, make sure Grace tries the king cake." Babeth smiled at Grace. "Another one of our wonderful traditions."

Maurice snorted, before whispering to Grace, "Another silly tradition where they bake a plastic baby inside the cake, and everyone argues about who found it and whom it belongs to." He smiled at Babeth. "The king cake is always delicious."

Sophie sat next to Grace. "I'm having a party tonight at the bar. We cleared the pool tables to make room for a band and a dance floor. Would you like to come?"

Maurice leaned across Grace toward Sophie. "We can't be out late tonight. Grace has school tomorrow."

"Too bad." Sophie pouted. "I was hoping to see some of those zydeco dance steps my big brother taught you on New Year's Eve."

Maurice rolled his eyes. "Please don't call me that."

"Did you know his dance moves are legendary?" Sophie leaned across Grace toward Maurice. "Someone named Lindsay saw your business cards on the bar. Said she dated you a few years back and the two of you won a dance contest together."

"Lindsay?" Grace glanced at her husband as he closed his eyes, shaking his head.

Sophie laughed. "She's still single, but she has the cutest little boy now with dark, wavy hair."

"Grace," Philippe said, "how are you enjoying Tulane University? Are your classes going well?"

"It's only one class, but it's going well."

"And hopefully," Yves said, "she'll be coming to work with me at the bank this summer."

Grace smiled. "Yes, I'm thinking about it."

After the meal, Philippe and Yves walked to the backyard. Marie snuck off somewhere with her boyfriend, leaving Sophie, Babeth, Grace, and Maurice at the dining room table.

Sophie turned to Maurice. "So, big brother, how's the painting going? Getting any new clients?"

"Right now, I'm finishing a portrait for Ms. Lily Dumont. Do you know her?"

"Yeah," Sophie replied. "Sweet old lady. Anybody else?"

"A gentleman called me about doing a portrait of his daughter, but he hasn't stopped by yet to see my work. Who knows if he'll follow through. In the meantime, I'm working on something new. I want to have some paintings ready to sell when the art festivals start in the spring. How are things at the sports bar?"

"Do you get much business during the Mardi Gras season?" Grace asked.

"Business is booming." Sophie grinned. "I love this time of year."

Marie and Darius returned to the dining room and sat near Grace. The scent of weed floated in the air, and Marie's eyes were tinged red under droopy lids. She whispered to Grace, "Should I ask him now about the picture?"

"Maurice," Grace said, "Marie wants one of your paintings. Let's take her to your studio to show you which one."

Marie and Darius got up from the table, along with Maurice and Grace. Sophie was about to get up, but Babeth covered her hand. "Sophie, I heard you talking about the new spa in town earlier. I want to hear more." The foursome went to the studio and left the two ladies chatting about the spa.

Marie went right to the studio wall where the picture was hanging. "This is the one. I love all the colors and how they burst. So much energy. May I have this one?" She turned to Darius. "It's cool, isn't it?" Darius nodded.

"Of course you may have it. Go ahead and take it off the wall." Maurice smiled. "It's nice to know I have a little sister who appreciates good art."

"All of your artwork is really cool." Marie took down the picture and handed it to Darius. Walking closer to Maurice and Grace, she said, "Thank you," in a low voice. "I think I'm going to like having you for a big brother. But watch out for Sophie. She does not like you." Marie gazed out the window at Philippe smoking a cigarette, in deep conversation with Yves in the backyard. "And him. Watch out for him too. They call him the laundry man."

Maurice expressed his puzzlement. "Who? Yves?"

Marie nodded as Yves and Philippe began slowly walking toward the house. "Come on, let's have some more king cake," Maurice said.

Marie and Darius were cutting slices of cake when Philippe and Yves entered the dining room. "Isn't this lovely?" Philippe said. "All of my children are together for the first time." He draped his arm around Grace's shoulder. "Thank you for hosting today. You have made me a very happy papa." He kissed her cheek before moving around the table for a slice of cake.

Yves and Babeth announced they were leaving, and Grace walked them to the door. When she returned, Philippe was opening a disposable camera. He handed it to Grace. "Please take a few pictures of us." Grace took pictures of Sophie and Marie sitting at the table with Philippe and Maurice standing behind them. The camera passed around as they took turns taking pictures of one another. Once the picture-taking was done, Philippe said, "All right, crew. Let's get out of here. Thank you, Grace, and Maurice. It was a grand day. And don't worry about cleaning up. I'll send some people tomorrow to take care of it. They will clean the whole house."

As Maurice and Grace escorted them to the door, Sophie pulled Grace aside. "Babeth wants a girl's day at the new spa downtown. I'll arrange something and give you a call."

Grace hesitated. "I don't know if I can make it. I'm very busy with school."

"Oh, come on. Have you made any girlfriends since you moved here? No. You spend all of your time with your husband. It will do you good to have a day out with the girls. What days do you have class?"

"Mondays and Wednesdays."

"All right. I'll make the appointment for a Thursday afternoon. And I won't take no for an answer." Sophie grinned. "You're not going to make me go alone with Babeth, are you? She'll talk me to death."

Philippe yelled for Sophie to come on.

Grace agreed. "Okay. Let me know when you make the appointment."

Sophie hurried down the walkway to join her family, who were already down the street, out of sight. Grace waved and closed the door.

Maurice turned to Grace. "We survived the family Mardi Gras. It wasn't all bad. At least now I know whom to focus on to find Philippe's secret."

"You do? Who?"

"Marie. I need to know what she meant about Yves being the laundry man. He and Philippe spent most of the afternoon outside. I didn't know they were such close friends. I wonder if Jacque knows."

"We are not going to find out tonight, and I'm pooped," Grace said. "But I have to ask. Should I be worried about Lindsay?"

"I was with her after you married Trevor. Briefly. She was a poor substitute for you." Taking her hands, he gazed into her eyes. "But I did not father a child with her. I took precautions. And we don't worry about what happened before we got married, right? You have a past, I have a past."

Grace shook her head. "All right, I believe you." Going to the kitchen, she returned with a roll of aluminum foil. "We've been up since five a.m. Let's put the leftover food away. Mardi Gras is officially over. I hope the cleaning people don't come too early in the morning."

Later, Grace tossed about in the bed, unable to sleep. *Another part of my husband's life that I know nothing about. Lindsay. And I'm not allowed to dig into it because it's in the past. We did agree on that, but how am I supposed to ignore the past if it impacts our future? Trevor's dead, but Lindsay is not.*

Chapter 12

The kitchen wall phone rang just as Grace was closing her accounting textbook. "Hi. It's Sophie. We're going to the spa this Thursday at eleven. I booked a massage and a mani/pedi for each of us. I'll pick you up around ten-ish after I scoop up Babeth, okay?"

Just as Grace hung up, Maurice strolled into the kitchen. "Who was it?"

"Sophie. We're going to the spa with Babeth on Thursday. I'm not a fan of massages. Strangers rubbing your body. But she wouldn't take no for an answer."

Maurice snickered. "Sounds like fun. Relax and enjoy yourself."

When spa day arrived on Thursday, Grace was looking forward to it. Hours hunched over textbooks had left her neck and shoulders tense and aching. A massage would do her good. It was warm outside again today, and she opted to wear a pair of blue capri pants with a flowery blue ruffled blouse. She pinned her hair in a French roll to allow the masseuse access to her neck. Bouncing down the grand staircase, she kissed Maurice goodbye and headed outside to the street to wait for Sophie. Scanning for some sign of FBI surveillance on the street was now a habit. As usual, there was no activity on Napoleon Avenue.

Sophie's red BMW pulled up to the curb with a toot of the horn. Grace hopped into the backseat, saying her greetings. They made small talk as they drove downtown to the Serenity Spa on Bienville Street. It was a sleek concrete and mirrored building at the corner of a small strip mall. As they strode toward the entrance, Sophie and Babeth put their heads together, giggling as their colorful floral dresses blew around in the breeze.

Sophie glanced back at Grace, lagging. "We must do a shopping spree on our next girl's day. Your wardrobe could use an upgrade."

Grace was taken aback. *What's wrong with my clothes?*

A bubbly blond woman greeted them at the front desk, wearing a white camp shirt and beige khakis. "Welcome to Serenity Spa. Do you ladies have an appointment today?" Grace gazed around the spa as Sophie dealt with the young lady. The blue tones of the décor created an air of elegance and tranquility. Grace followed Babeth as the blond led them to the locker room to change. The fluffy white cotton robe and slippers the spa supplied felt like heaven, much softer than her robe at home. After changing, they settled into the waiting area, each in a white leather chair surrounded by glass tables laden with magazines and pitchers of cucumber water. Grace poured herself a glass of water and picked up a *Cosmopolitan* magazine.

"I've been looking forward to this all week," Babeth said. "This spa has been getting rave reviews since it opened two months ago. It was tough to get an appointment, but I knew Sophie could swing it. She's well connected."

A blond hunk built like a Chippendale dancer wearing navy blue scrubs entered the waiting area. "Elizabeth Benet?" Babeth waved her hand, and the man assisted her to her feet. "My name is Hans, and I will be taking care of you today. How are you?" Babeth was all smiles as her masseuse led her to a private room. *He is gorgeous. I hope my masseuse looks like that. The last thing I need is a grungy little toad putting his scaley hands all over my body.*

Sophie giggled. "That broad can't wait to have a man's hands rub her body." A moment later, an Asian woman came to collect Sophie.

Grace indulged in an article in Cosmo about ways to spice up your sex life until a man called her name. Looking up, she smiled at her very own tall, dark, and handsome Italian-looking Chippendale dancer. "My name is Davis, and I will be taking care of you today."

The private room's dim lighting, the gentle strumming of acoustic guitars, and the scent of eucalyptus created a relaxing atmosphere. Davis's skilled hands rubbed and kneaded her entire body, releasing her tension and stress. *This was a good idea. Just what I needed. Thank you, Sophie.* The hour passed quickly, and she was sorry to hear Davis say, "You may relax here for as long as you like. I hope you enjoyed your massage," before exiting the room. Her body felt like jelly as she closed her eyes. *This is the most relaxed I've been since we came to New Orleans.* After laying quietly for a moment, she remembered a manicure and pedicure to be had and returned to the waiting room. Sophie and Babeth were already there.

"Hans was incredible." Babeth squealed with delight. "How was your massage? Did you enjoy it?"

"Much more than I expected," Grace said with a smile. "Sophie, what about you?"

"Fantastic. I love this place so far." Sophie leaned over and whispered to Grace, "I think the old girl had a big O in there. She looked positively flushed when she exited her room." Grace gave Sophie a sour look. *What an extremely distasteful thought.*

The same blond from the front desk came into the waiting room. "Ladies, if you follow me, we'll go to the nail salon." As they walked, the young woman explained the room was not completely private. "There are partitions between the nail stations, but we ask our guests to carry their conversations in a low tone." Grace chuckled. *Not possible with Sophie.*

The blond stopped in front of a large display of nail polish in a multitude of colors. "Please choose your polish for your fingers and toes."

Grace selected a shimmering maroon and settled at a manicure table across from a young black woman with braided hair. "My name is Vanessa. How are you today? Are you enjoying your spa experience so far?"

Grace spread her fingers as she laid her hands on the table. "Yes, it's been lovely. Very soothing." As she examined Grace's nails, Vanessa chatted about her experience and working at the spa. The relaxing effect of the massage lingered and Grace felt serene as her hands went into a bowl of warm, soapy water. Suddenly, the tranquil mood was shattered by a loud shriek of laughter.

"Girl, stop. Please tell me that did not happen," the woman continued. Grace turned to see who was violating the 'keep your conversation in a low tone' rule. *Natalie. That loud woman is with Natalie.*

Grace zeroed in on Natalie in her white robe, silky black hair caressing her shoulders. *What is she doing here? I can't believe she is here. I wanted to never see her again.* The loud woman was of lighter complexion, with long tresses of blond highlighted brown hair cascading down her back. Her face held high cheekbones and perfectly arched eyebrows over big brown eyes. The twosome were animated as they talked, swaying and lightly swatting one another on the shoulder. Natalie strolled to sit in the booth next to her and her friend at the next one over.

Grace could not help but hear as Ms. Loud continued talking. "You said this new man of yours is an artist? What kind of art does he do?"

Grace's spine immediately stiffened, and she yanked her hands out of the warm, soapy water.

"Is everything all right?" Vanessa's face bore a concerned expression. Grace froze, listening as Natalie answered her friend.

"He's painting my portrait. He won't let me see it until it is done. But I've seen other portraits he's done, and they were spectacular. I'm certain mine will be too."

Vanessa took Grace's hands and gently wiped them with a towel. Grace attempted to focus on the nail technician, but she was lightheaded, her throat dry. *They cannot be talking about Maurice. They cannot.*

"Well, you a better woman than me," the loud woman said. "I don't have time to be messing around with no married man. I need a man's full attention. You know what I mean?"

Natalie laughed. "It won't be long before he leaves his little mouse. Now that he's tasted a real woman, he's completely pussy whipped." The loud woman joined her in raunchy laughter.

Vanessa cocked her head, staring at Grace. "Miss, are you all right? Do you need some water?"

Grace tried to compose herself, but her head was exploding. *Are they having an affair? I can't believe this. Maurice is seeing her in secret.* "Yes, some water would help, please," she said, voice trembling. Vanessa went to get the water as Grace closed her eyes and took a deep breath.

She listened as Natalie and the loud woman continued talking, but the subject changed. "We should go to the spot with the good jambalaya. What was the name of that place?"

Grace took another deep breath as Vanessa returned with a glass of cucumber water. After taking a few quick sips, she looked at Vanessa. "I'm so sorry. I felt faint for a moment. I don't know what came over me. I feel better now." The sound of Sophie and Babeth talking and laughing overrode Natalie's conversation and soothed her nerves.

Vanessa smiled at her. "No problem." Taking Grace's left hand, she began to clip and file her nails.

When are they meeting? Where? Her mind raced through a thousand scenarios of Maurice and Natalie making out. *No, he wouldn't do that. She must have been talking about someone else. Maurice is not the only artist in town.* The vision of his face with the red lipstick smeared across his lips bubbled to the surface. *I cannot believe he is seeing her again.* Heat began to rise within her. *He would not do this. It cannot be him.* Suddenly, Vanessa's voice brought Grace back into the moment. "I'm sorry. What did you say?"

"I was asking where you're from," Vanessa said. "I detected an accent."

"I'm from New York. I moved here a few months ago." Grace determined to stay in the moment and not drive herself crazy thinking about Maurice and Natalie continued to converse with her nail technician. Fingernails complete, as Vanessa led her to the pedicure station, her mind returned to Maurice. *Should I ask him about it when I get home? Would he tell me the truth?*

"It's been my pleasure to serve you today," Vanessa said as she settled Grace into a leather recliner. "Gwen will take care of your pedicure." Gwen, a slim girl with blond hair, introduced herself before directing Grace to put both feet into the hot, bubbling blue water in the foot bath.

Leaning back in the oversized leather chair, she tried to relax and calm herself, but the image of Maurice with the lipstick on his face would not leave her alone. The effects of the massage disappeared entirely. Her body tensed at the thought of Maurice being unfaithful to her. Indeed, he was capable of it, but she didn't want to believe he would do it. *Not now. We're married now. He promised, and I believe him. It cannot be him. They must have been talking about someone else.*

Grace's mind stayed in a fog of is he or isn't he for the rest of the afternoon. During the drive home, Babeth and Sophie chatted away while Grace sat in the backseat, tortured by the infidelity demons. When they arrived at her house, she bid them farewell with a wave. Taking a deep breath, she entered the front door.

Instead of going directly to the studio, she detoured to the kitchen for a glass of Chardonnay. *Should I ask if something is going on or not?* Heat rose as she nervously tapped her fingers on the kitchen table. She drained her glass and poured herself another one. After a few sips, she left the glass on the table and marched to the studio.

Maurice sat at his drawing table with a book. Swiveling to greet her, he asked, "How was the spa? Did you have fun?" He rose to embrace and kiss her softly. Grace leaned back, glaring. His puzzled look met her gaze. "What's wrong?"

She pushed his hands away. "I saw Natalie today at the spa."

Maurice looked down at his feet. "Oh."

"Have you seen her since that day? She said she's getting her portrait painted."

Maurice stared at her. "No. I told her we could not work together. There are other artists in this city."

"You're certain?"

Maurice came closer, taking her hands into his own. "I have not seen Natalie, and I have no desire to see Natalie. I don't know who is painting her portrait, but it is not me." He put his mouth on Grace's, but her heart wasn't in it. Her lip went limp. "I would not go behind your back," Maurice whispered. He tried to kiss her again, but she pulled away, walking back to the kitchen. "Grace, we're not going to rehash this again. You said you believed me." He followed her as she grabbed her wine. "I don't know what happened at the spa, but whatever she said has nothing to do with me. I have not seen her." He took the wine glass from her hand and set it on the table. Taking her by the chin, he forced her to look into his eyes. "I love you. You are my wife." He kissed her, and this time, she gave in, allowing his tongue into her mouth. *I know you do. I love you too.* The passionate kiss reassured Grace. Maurice lifted her hands to examine them. "Your nails look very nice. I can't wait to see your toes." He smiled at her. "Did you eat? I'm hungry. We could go out for a bite. What are you in the mood for?"

"I'm not fussy. Whatever you want will be fine with me."

Opening one of the kitchen drawers, Maurice combed through the menus before selecting one. "I'll order takeout from the Ragin Cajun, and I'll go pick it up."

Later, Grace monitored Maurice closely as they sat at the table eating. *He ordered jambalaya. Really? I'm being stupid. It's a coincidence.* Her eyes stayed glued on him as he shoveled huge amounts of rice, beans, and sausage into his mouth while talking. Specks of rice and spital flew out along with his words.

Slowly, she put a small forkful of rice in her mouth, pretending to listen to him. *He's talking about his horoscope paintings again. Is he even chewing his food before he swallows it? I wish he would shut up about the Aquarian woman. I've told him a million times it's fine.*

Maurice stopped talking. "Grace, are you all right?"

Blinking, she smiled faintly, putting her fork down. "Yes, I'm fine. I'm really not hungry. I'm going to go upstairs and lie down." She kissed him on his temple and went to the bedroom.

Sitting on the side of the bed, stomach cramps gripped her. In the bathroom, blood. *Damn it. Why am I not getting pregnant? We have sex all the time. The doctor said I shouldn't have any problem getting pregnant again after the miscarriage.* She exhaled loudly. *Maybe something is wrong with Maurice?* Taking out her box of tampons, she took two Pamprin for the pain. Staring at her reflection in the mirror, she did not look like she'd had a relaxing day at the spa. *My periods are heavier, and my cramps have returned since I stopped taking the pill. And I cannot get pregnant. Great, just great. Monsieur Loverboy cannot get me pregnant.* She doused her face with cold water and removed the hairpins. *It couldn't be because he's spreading himself around town, could it?*

After dressing for bed in her cotton nightgown, she went to the window to view the setting sun. *Don't lose faith. It's only been two months. I'm going to get pregnant. God knows how much I want to have a baby.* As she lay down on the bed, Maurice entered.

"Ready for bed so early? I was going to ask you if you wanted to go out. Claude called earlier. He's having a few people over." He sat beside her on the bed. "Are you all right?"

I wish you would stop asking me that. "I got my period."

"Oh. Then you should rest. You won't mind if I go out for a few hours, will you?"

"No, of course not. You go ahead." She leaned up for a kiss, and he quickly pecked her lips. "Have fun."

Maurice blew her a kiss on his way out the door. "I love you, mon cheri. See you later."

Is he going to Claude's house? He invited me to go. He must be going to Claude's.

She awoke to the sound of snoring. The clock flashed 2:00 in red. Gazing at Maurice's sleeping profile, his hair wildly splayed over the pillow, she frowned. *He needs a haircut.*

Creeping into the bathroom to not wake him, she took two more Pamprin. A pile of clothes Maurice left on the floor lay at the foot of the bed. Rummaging through his army jacket and jeans pockets, she found nothing but lint. *Why am I spying on Maurice? I need to trust him and stop this. He is not having an affair with Natalie.*

Climbing back into bed, nudging Maurice to roll him over ended the snoring, and she spooned herself against his back. *I love him, and he loves me.*

Chapter 13

For days, Maurice worked diligently on completing Ms. Lily Dumont's portrait. Standing in the center of the sunlit studio, he assessed the final product. This creation required more time to complete than initially anticipated. Getting the Pomeranian's fur to look authentic demanded enormous patience to do each tiny, detailed stroke of paint correctly.

As Grace entered the studio to peck his cheek, he covered the portrait with a drape. "I'm off to class. See you around noon."

Maurice walked her out to the Benz. "I'm delivering Ms. Dumont's portrait this afternoon. Would you like to come with me, and afterward, we can have an early dinner in the French Quarter somewhere?"

"Sounds good." Grace drove off.

Returning to his studio, Maurice uncovered his latest work in progress. A bull, drinking from a pool, as two fish converged from opposite directions to dance in the bull's reflection. *This pairing of Taurus and Pisces came out extraordinarily well. I think it's the best.* Another canvas bore the image of a male Centaur being given water by a woman at a well. Uncertain that the woman symbolized an Aquarian accurately, he contemplated modifications. *I've paired Virgo with Scorpio, united Sagittarius with Aquarius, and joined Taurus with Pisces. What should be next? I must have each sign represented in this series.* Retrieving his astrology bible to review the remaining symbols and their compatibility choices, he could not decide. The doorbell interrupted his train of thought.

Anticipating another solicitor, Maurice opened the door to an unexpected delight. There stood Marie, clad in her ripped jeans, tie-dye tee, and leather jacket. *Just the person I wanted to see.*

Today, she added thick black eyeliner and black lipstick to her attire. "Howdy. I hope you don't mind me dropping by uninvited." Her dark eyes were hopeful.

Maurice embraced her. "You are always welcome here. Come in." The chance to spend time with his little sister privately, without Philippe's awareness, brought genuine joy. "Perhaps you can help me with a decision I'm trying to make."

Following Maurice to the studio, Marie walked straight to the vivid portrayal of the bull. "This painting is awesome. The bull is frightening and gentle at the same time. How did you do this?"

"I don't know. It's a gift." Maurice glanced at the wall clock. "I'm glad to see you, but shouldn't you be in school?"

"I'm a senior. My classes end early. I could have graduated in January because I had enough credits. I took a few extra classes to stay close to Darius."

"I see," Maurice said. Marie's features tightened as she studied the picture of the bull, as though distressed. He attempted to regain her attention. "I was trying to decide the match for the twins of Gemini. Do you think they should be paired with the ram of Aries or the lion of Leo?"

Marie's pensive expression gave way. "I like the ram with the twins. They could be feeding him something like corn. What do rams like to eat?"

"I don't know. I'll have to research it." Maurice gestured for her to sit in his desk chair. Leaning in, he pointed out a paragraph in his astrology book. "You see, air signs go with fire signs. Water signs align with earth signs. This is the premise I'm working from."

"Cool," Marie replied. "Do you really believe in astrology?"

"I do, from the aspect that it is important what day a person is born. There is a divine plan behind each person's birth. But I don't let daily horoscope forecasts run my life."

Marie nodded in understanding. "Darius' birthday is this month, March. He is a Pisces. My birthday is in December. I am a Capricorn. You have the bull, Taurus, paired with Pisces. Does it mean Darius and I are not compatible?"

"No, not at all," Maurice chuckled. "Capricorn is also an earth sign, like Taurus. Pisces and Capricorns should get along very well."

A broad grin broke out on Marie's face. "Good to know, because I think Darius may be the one. I really love him."

"You are too young to be in love," Maurice said. "Give yourself time to experience more of the world. You never know what treasure you may find out there."

"How did you meet Grace? How did you know she was the one you wanted to spend the rest of your life with?"

"Grace and I met in college, and after a short time, I knew I loved her, but it took a long time for us to truly bond. She was ready to get married way before I was, so we broke up, and she married someone else. I am her second husband."

"Get out of here." Marie's eyes widened. "You two seemed so in sync on Mardi Gras. I would have never guessed something like that happened. How did you get back together?"

"Her first husband died in a tragic fire at their home. Grace almost lost her life as well, but thankfully, she recovered, and we got a second chance at love."

"That's quite a story." Marie had admiration in her eyes. Glancing away, she waited a moment before continuing in a low voice. "I like to draw too."

"You do? What do you enjoy drawing?"

"Most of my drawings are abstract, like the painting you gave me. I'm no good at drawing people. It's too hard."

I need a reason for Marie to visit me regularly so I can get information about Sophie and Philippe. "I could teach you if you want to learn. It's not as complicated as it seems. There are some basic techniques, and once you master them, you can draw anyone."

Marie perked up. "You think I could do it?"

"I know you could, with a little instruction." Maurice stood at the window, gazing out on the lawn. "I was thinking about doing a portrait of you." He turned to face Marie. "You are a beautiful young lady. I bet Papa would love to have a painted portrait of you hanging in your home." Calling Philippe Papa was nauseating. "Would you be willing to pose for me?"

Marie focused on her hands twisting around the ring on her left middle finger. "You don't have to say I'm beautiful. I know I'm not."

Maurice put his arm around her shoulder. "Nonsense. You are very beautiful to me. Let me paint you as I see you, and you will see the beauty within you."

"Okay. I'll pose. But the portrait will be a gift for Darius, not Papa."

"When it is finished, I will give it to you, and you may gift it to whomever you wish."

"When can we start?"

"What are you doing right now?"

Marie was apprehensive. "Are you certain you can make me look beautiful?"

Maurice smiled at her. "You are beautiful. I don't have to fake it. I will enhance your natural beauty in your painting, and you will shine. I'm thinking you could be outdoors in a swamp land. Everything is a lush deep green, wet, and you are in the center. Your white skin shimmering in contrast to the darkness which surrounds you."

"Sounds cool. Let's do it. Should I take my jacket off?"

"Yes. I'll reimagine your clothing into something torn and tattered, as if you're emerging from a battle. The struggle of life."

Marie took off her jacket. "Where should I stand? What do I do?"

Maurice guided her to a corner of the room. "Crouch down here. Act as if you've just killed a lion or a tiger. How does the conquest make you feel? Show me."

Marie squatted with her head down. When she lifted her head, her countenance was fierce. Maurice grabbed an easel and a sketch pad and set them up. "Oh, Marie, I love it. Do you think you can hold this position for a while?"

"I'll try."

Maurice, truly inspired, quickly began sketching her face. Marie held her pose until he could capture the essence of her spirited conquest. Putting the pencil down, he said, "You can relax now. Tomorrow, we'll work on it more if you're free to pose again."

"I can come back tomorrow."

"Good." Maurice placed a cloth drape over the sketch. "Would you like some iced tea?"

A sly smile formed on Marie's lips. "Do you have any weed to go with it?"

"Oh, sure. I can roll a joint for us." Turning on the boom box, George Michael sang, "You gotta have faith, faith, faith." *How appropriate. I'll loosen her up with a joint and get her talking.* He told Marie, "I'll be right back."

Racing up the stairs to the master bedroom, he grabbed his stash of marijuana before heading to the kitchen. After quickly pouring glasses of iced tea, he returned to the studio. Marie sat at the desk, reading the astrology book. He placed her glass of tea beside the book and sat on the floor to roll a joint. When he lit it, Marie joined him on the floor as he handed the joint to her.

"I like hanging out with you. It's too bad Sophie won't even try to get along with you."

Maurice feigned ignorance. "What do you mean? Sophie has been very nice to me."

"Don't be fooled. Sophie pretends a lot. And I could tell from how you looked at her on Mardi Gras that you don't like her either."

Maurice frowned. "Did it show?"

"Uh, yeah," Marie said. "At least Darius and I noticed it. I don't know if anyone else did." She held the joint up. "Do you want me to give you a shotgun?"

"Okay." Maurice held his open mouth near Marie as she put the lit end of the joint in her mouth and blew the smoke his way. He inhaled the thick smoke as Marie took the joint from her mouth. "Was it good? Did you get it?"

Maurice nodded as he kept the smoke in his lungs. When he blew out a cloud of smoke, he said, "You do that very well."

"I have a thing for shotguns." She handed Maurice the joint. "Give me one."

Maurice had never given anyone a shotgun before. He imitated Marie by carefully placing the lit end of the joint in his mouth, praying he wouldn't burn his tongue. Blowing into it, Marie inhaled the stream of smoke, which appeared until her lungs couldn't take in any more. She held it for a moment and then blew it out, first coughing and then laughing. "I'm glad I came here today. I wasn't sure how you'd react."

"I'm glad you came too." He sipped his iced tea, and Marie got up to retrieve her glass from atop the desk.

"Do you know what I don't like about Sophie?" Maurice blew out a cloud of smoke. "She's abrasive, talks too loud, and is very aggressive. I prefer a softer woman."

"She hates you because she thinks you are Papa's favorite."

"Why would she believe such a thing? Philippe hardly knows me."

"He knows more than you think. Papa talked about you a lot once Yves told him you were moving here. You're his only son. No matter what Sophie does, she cannot change from a daughter to a son. She wants to take over Papa's business and thinks you'll take it from her."

"I have no interest in Philippe's business."

"You should tell her that. I don't know if she'll believe you, but you should try. It might make her feel better."

Maurice puffed on the joint. "I've told Philippe. He can tell her."

Marie gave him a skeptical look. "Do you think he will? Because I don't. You should tell her yourself."

Maurice considered Marie's comment as he handed her the joint. "Maybe I will."

Marie focused on the drape concealing Maurice's sketch of her. "Can I take a peek at what you drew?"

Maurice frowned at her. "I don't think you should. I don't want to spoil the surprise of how it will look when it is finished."

"Please? I won't judge. I just want to see it."

"Okay, go ahead." Maurice waited for her reaction.

Lifting the drape, Marie's eyes widened. "This is so cool. I can't believe you did this so quickly. It really looks like me."

"I'm glad you are pleased. It will be really cool when it's finished."

As Grace entered the studio door, her eyes focused on the siblings. "Hi, Marie. I didn't know you were coming over today."

"She popped by for a spontaneous visit," Maurice said. "We started work on her portrait. Have a look."

"Ooh, what a ferocious expression. I like it." Grace turned to Marie. "What do you think?"

"He is an amazing artist. He's going to teach me how to draw people."

Grace's eyebrow went up, gazing at Maurice. "Is he, now?"

Marie checked the wall clock. "I better get going. Darius will be going to lunch soon, and he only has one class after that. Thanks, Maurice. I'll see you tomorrow."

Maurice rose to escort her to the front door. "Remember, you can stop by anytime. Okay?"

Marie waved before walking to the street and disappearing.

When he returned to the studio, Grace was staring at the painting of the bull. "I like this one a lot. Where's Ms. Lily Dumont?"

Maurice uncovered the portrait, and Grace stepped closer to examine it. "Oh, she is going to love this. Look at little Peppy. You truly brought him to life. He appears to be yapping."

"Because he is," Maurice laughed. "That dog was the noisiest, most obnoxious little beast I've ever had the displeasure of meeting." He kissed Grace. "I hope she likes it because this is one portrait I do not want to keep. I need to find my camera to take some shots of it for my portfolio before I give it to her. I had planned to do it earlier, but when Marie dropped by, I got distracted."

"Did you find out anything?"

"I did. Sophie hates me because she thinks I want to take over Philippe's business."

"What?"

"Sophie plans to take over the business and thinks I want to usurp her position. Marie suggested I tell Sophie I do not want it."

"Are you going to talk to Sophie?"

"No. I'm certain Philippe already told her. I will continue to pretend I like her, just as she is pretending with me." He went to the bookcase, searching for his camera. When he found it, he held it up for Grace to see. "Voila. I will take a few pictures, and we can deliver the portrait to Ms. Lily and Peppy."

Chapter 14

Not wanting to be late to class, Grace hurried from the university parking lot to Woldenberg Hall. Maurice ravaged her body in the early morning hours, and afterward, she fell back asleep. Fifteen minutes before class commenced, she woke up startled, threw on clothes, and raced to the car. The drive from home to school was only eight minutes, and she prayed to reach it before Professor Collins closed the door. He was notorious for embarrassing students who were tardy by saying something witty and cleverly debasing.

Breathing a sigh of relief, she took her usual seat in the second row on the right side of the room. As she removed her books and notes from her tote bag, a young brother approached her desk. "Hi. My name is Xavier. I'm transferring into this class, and Professor Collins suggested I get the last notes from another class member. Do you think you could help me?"

Before she could answer, Professor Collins stormed into the room, slamming the door behind him. Xavier slid into the seat next to Grace as the professor began his lecture. "Today, we will complete our lesson on financial statement preparation. Next week, there will be an exam."

Grace stole a glance at Xavier, his muscular biceps bulging from his white golf shirt sleeve. She studied his rugged facial profile and the sparkling diamond stud in his ear. *He must be an athlete. Quite the hottie, like Michael Jordan.* Xavier glanced at her with a big grin on his luscious chocolate face. *Ooh, the whitest teeth. What a beautiful smile.* Her lips unconsciously curved upward. She turned her attention back to Professor Collins, unable to disregard the aura of Xavier's presence beside her. *There are fifteen people in this class. Why would he ask me for help?* She evaluated her classmates, whom she hadn't paid much attention to since the beginning of the course. The majority were young, preppy white boys. There were three white girls, two of whom seemed to be friends, and two other black students in the class, who behaved as a couple. No one had been friendly, and it hadn't concerned her. She wasn't there to make friends but to complete her CPA requirements. After reassessing the class makeup, she guessed she was the logical choice for Xavier to approach for help.

After assigning homework, Professor Collins ended the lecture, and Xavier leaned over to Grace. "I'm sorry. I didn't even get to ask your name before." She told him. "Grace, would you mind sharing your notes with me?"

"No." Grace smiled. "Are you free now? We could go to the library, and I'll review what I have with you. I'm not sure you'll understand my chicken scratch if I just give you my notebook."

"I bet it's not too bad. I don't want to hold you up if you have somewhere you need to be." Xavier's bright white smile was disarming. "How about you give me the notes, and I do the best I can with them. If I have any questions, I'll ask you next class." He admired Grace's manicure. "You've got pretty hands. I bet you write beautifully."

Grace reached into her tote to remove a notebook and slid it toward Xavier. "All right, take this one. It covers the first five chapters. You'll have a lot of reading to do, too, to catch up."

"I can handle it. Thank you, kind lady." He put the notebook in his backpack before strutting out of the classroom. *He's got a sexy walk, too.*

Grace's stomach growled as she walked to the car. *I didn't even have time to eat breakfast, thanks to Maurice. I hope he's cooked something. Maybe we have some leftovers.*

"Mrs. Chenault?"

Agent Wolf stood by the Mercedes, casually dressed in a gray t-shirt and jeans, his feet clad in work boots.

"My husband does not want me talking to you." Her hand went to the car's door handle.

Agent Wolf put his hand flat on the car door. "Did you hear about the murders at the port last night? You must have seen it. It was all over the news." His eyes revealed inner pain and agony. "Three people shot dead, numerous others injured over a drug deal gone wrong. One of the victims was an undercover agent. My friend."

Grace shook her head, looking downward. "I'm sorry you lost a friend. I did not see it on the news, and I don't know anything about it." She looked the agent in the eye. "I'm truly sorry, but I need to get home."

"You could help us. We know Philippe Le Coeur is behind this latest massacre. I saw your face the day I came to your house. You were shocked to hear what your father-in-law has been up to." Grace's eyes widened. "Yes, we know your husband is Mr. Le Coeur's son. It took a while to connect the dots, but we got there."

The agent's hand went from the door to Grace's. She pulled her hand away from his as if it burned. "I cannot help you. Please move. I want to go home."

Agent Wolf persisted, repositioning himself to not allow her to open the car door. "Please, talk to your husband. Neither of you is safe. We can protect you."

"Hey, Grace. Everything all right over here?" Xavier came strolling up beside Agent Wolf. "What's up, bro? You bothering this nice lady?"

Agent Wolf stepped back away from the car door. "No, we know each other. Just having a friendly conversation is all."

Xavier looked at Grace and then opened the car door before turning back to Agent Wolf. "Looks like the conversation is over, man. Later." Grace got in the driver's seat, and Xavier closed the door. Agent Wolf slowly walked across the parking lot.

Rushing around the front of the car, Xavier jumped into the passenger seat. "You're upset. Who is that dude? Was he threatening you?"

"It's okay. He knows my husband." Putting her hands on the steering wheel, she attempted to steady herself.

Xavier placed his hand near hers. "You're shaking. You shouldn't try to drive like this."

Grace discerned that he was genuinely worried about her. "I'm fine. I don't live far from here." She gave him a weak smile after taking a deep breath. "Thank you for stepping in."

He withdrew his hand from the steering wheel. "Okay. Please, be careful." Stepping out of the car, he knocked twice on the outside of the door. She started the engine and drove home.

Upon entering the studio door, Grace found Maurice intently sketching Marie, crouched in a corner. "Bonjour, mon cheri. We'll be done in a moment."

Swiftly kissing Maurice as she passed him and went to the kitchen, Grace dropped her tote on the table. Reaching into the refrigerator, she seized a Chinese food container. *Beef and broccoli from when?* After sniffing the container, she prepared a bowl to heat and eat. *I didn't want to bring up the FBI in front of Marie. I don't know how much she knows about her father's business.*

Maurice escorted Marie to the front door as she put her empty bowl and fork into the dishwasher. "See you later. And feel free to bring Darius back with you tonight."

Grace intercepted him on his way back to the studio. "What is happening tonight?"

"I hope you don't mind. I invited some people over tonight. Artist friends of mine to discuss the gallery project. I'm meeting with Philippe tomorrow, and I need to tell him no one is interested in his proposal."

"I'm confused. You said you weren't doing the gallery project with Philippe. Why would you invite people over here to discuss it?"

"Because I don't know who is watching. I don't want to lie to Philippe. I will talk to my friends and tell them to think it over. Then I will suggest something I know they will be interested in. An entirely new proposal for the buildings down on Julia Street. A cultural arts center."

"What?"

"The buildings are in a great location. I can legitimately buy the buildings from Philippe rather than have my friends sign his stupid contract. We, artists, can form a nonprofit to fund the center ourselves."

Grace put her head in her hand. "The FBI stopped me in the school parking lot today." She relayed the incident, leaving out the part about Xavier. "Please, don't do anything with Philippe. What makes you think he will sell you the buildings, anyway? He wouldn't even let you buy the car. How's this any different?"

"A car is nothing to him. Property, I think, will be different. If Philippe cannot get us to do his long-term deal, I think he'll settle for some immediate compensation. He can still have a hand in the center, but only through me. I think he'll go for it." Maurice wiggled his eyebrows. "After all, I am his favorite child."

Grace shook her head. "I think you're delusional. Have you eaten today?"

"I did, Merci. I ordered a bunch of food from Ragin Cajun for later tonight. We can use the great room. Or maybe the dining room will be better? Our guests will arrive at seven. Marie has shown an interest in the arts, so I invited her to come back with Darius." As he walked back into the studio, Grace followed him.

"How many people? And when did you decide to plan this event?"

"It's something I've been meaning to do for weeks. When I started talking to Marie about my idea for a cultural arts center, I thought, why not tonight? I called Claude and some other friends you haven't met yet. Everyone was free. C'est tres magnifique?"

Grace frowned. "Hm. Magnificent. How come I haven't heard about this wonderful idea? I thought we were going to wait to open an art gallery together. Me and you."

A big grin filled Maurice's face as his hands gestured wildly. "After you left, the idea for the cultural arts center struck me this morning like a lightning bolt. Don't worry. You will be very much a part of this project. We'll need a good accountant to take care of the bookkeeping for the nonprofit foundation."

I would like to strike you like a lightning bolt right now. "I wish you had spoken to me before you planned this evening. I don't see how this is any different from doing the art galleries with Philippe. He's still involved."

He took her hands. "You are right. I'm sorry. I just got so excited about the idea." He kissed her nose. "Forgive me." He kissed her softly on the lips. "If the buildings are in my name, Philippe is not involved. His name will not be included in the nonprofit foundation."

"He is not going to sell you those buildings. How would we pay for them, anyway? Did you forget the reason we are here? All the money we lost? We cannot afford to make a massive investment right now."

Maurice's grin faded. "It's true." He folded his hands and put his index finger beside his nose. "Maybe I didn't think this idea through thoroughly." He threw up his hands. "C'est la vie. I'll fly the idea by them tonight and see what happens. At least you'll get to meet all of my artist friends. Parties are always a good idea."

"Not on a Wednesday night." Grace left him standing in the studio and headed for the stairs.

"Why not? You don't have school tomorrow."

Grace marched to the master bedroom, took off her jeans, and lay on the bed. *He was not the least bit concerned about the FBI stopping me to tell me his father is murdering people. And this crazy idea of his will only get us in deeper with Philippe. I don't get it. Why would he think Philippe would sell him those buildings? He won't do anything unless he can be a part of it.*

"What if we form the nonprofit first?" Maurice came in and sat on the bed. "Then we could purchase the property as a group. Philippe doesn't have to know I'm involved."

"He would know. All he needs to hear is 'artist', and he will know. Philippe is not stupid. And there is still the money issue." *You are the one being stupid right now.*

Maurice mumbled, "You're right." He began pacing around the room. "There has to be a way."

"Did you find out anything else from Marie today? About Sophie or Philippe?"

"No, but it's okay. I really like her. She's a good kid."

"I'm happy you're bonding with your sister." Grace shifted to her side, no longer facing him. "I'm getting a headache. I'm going to try to take a nap."

"All right. I'll check on you later."

She truly was getting a headache. *This is not my home. I want to go home. I miss my mother and father. I miss Anne. He said we'd go back to New York in June, but I don't know if I can wait that long. I'm afraid Maurice is going to get us killed messing around with Philippe. He is not thinking clearly. We should go back to New York right now.* Xavier's face popped into her mind with his brilliant smile. *Thank goodness he showed up when he did. That agent had me rattled badly. At least he cared, unlike my husband.*

"Grace," Maurice whispered, lightly tugging on her shoulder. "Are you up? Our guests will be arriving soon."

For the second time in a day, she sat up, startled. "What time is it?"

"Six thirty. I tried to let you sleep as long as I could. You should get dressed." The doorbell rang. "That's probably the food. Please, my love, get ready." He left to answer the door.

Grace dragged herself from the bed into the bathroom to freshen up. Then she stood before the closet, grappling with what to wear. *I am not in the mood for a party. Lord help. Sophie said I need a wardrobe upgrade. She may be right, but it ain't gonna happen tonight. Just pick something.* Opting for a denim skirt and a white peasant blouse, she quickly dressed. Pinning her hair in a French roll, she applied light makeup to her face before forcing a smile in the mirror as the doorbell rang. *Showtime.*

As she descended the grand staircase, the doorbell chimed once more, and Maurice raced to answer it. "Raymond, Sid, come in. How are you?" He glanced to see Grace coming down the stairs. "This is my wife, Grace." Taking her hand, he led everyone to the dining room.

Four people were already seated having wine. The only face Grace recognized was Claude. Maurice introduced her to everyone in the room as the doorbell rang again. After greeting everyone, Grace went to the kitchen to see what food he ordered. The covered tin pans felt slightly warm. Preheating the oven, she put the food in to warm further. Grabbing two bottles of wine from the refrigerator, she returned to the dining room. All their guests seemed to be old friends, engaged in lively conversation.

Maurice returned with three more people, plus Marie and Darius, in tow. The atmosphere was relaxed, with a few joints making the rounds as introductions flowed. Grace couldn't ignore the beautiful woman whose name escaped her. Her radiant skin was the color of whipped butter. Blond and brown braids jumbled around her head, and her gaze flashed almond-shaped hazel eyes. Maurice had his arm around her waist, and the woman was smiling in his face. She turned to Grace. "I don't know how you did it. I thought Maurice would never settle down.

He was my boyfriend in high school, and he vowed never to get married to anyone." *High school? I thought he was away at boarding school.*

"Tara was never in love with me," Maurice chuckled. "She only spent time with me that summer to get my help with her painting technique." *Tara.* "Now that everyone is here, I want to tell you about a proposal I received regarding opening several art galleries on Julia Street as part of an effort to revitalize the neighborhood." Maurice went through his presentation and passed around the contract Philippe had drawn up. He told them he didn't like the terms and that it was too risky for them as individuals. When he launched into his nonprofit idea, eyes lit up around the room. One man said he knew a potential benefactor he would contact, and another started talking about having a fundraiser. They all seemed to think creating a cultural arts center would be magnificent, just as Maurice had said.

Returning to the kitchen, Grace removed the trays from the oven. *Thank God we have a dishwasher, since we have no paper plates.* She took every plate they owned to serve everyone, along with all the forks and spoons she could find. Returning to the dining room, she announced hot food in the kitchen. Several men got up for a plate, but Tara and Maurice remained huddled together in conversation. Grace bristled, returning to the kitchen to supervise the men.

Marie approached her, with Darius by her side. "This is a great party. Thanks for inviting us."

"Glad you're enjoying yourself," Grace said. *I'm not. I cannot believe these people are buying into this cockamamie idea. And Tara clinging to Maurice as if she owns him.*

Grace entered the dining room and drained her glass of wine. She refilled her glass, watching the twosome laughing and smoking a joint, before approaching Maurice. "Can I join in?"

"Of course, my love."

Maurice handed Grace the joint as Tara stood up. "I'm going to get something to eat."

Grace sat in the chair Tara vacated. "High school girlfriend, huh? You never told me about her."

"It was a summer fling. Nothing worth mentioning. Give me the joint. I want to give you a shotgun." Maurice put the joint in his mouth, blowing a stream of smoke her way.

Grace leaned back, perplexed. "What are you doing?"

"You're supposed to inhale the smoke when I blow it to you. Marie taught me how to do it. Come on, try it again."

"Lovely." She inhaled the smoke and started coughing. "That's too much."

Marie came over. "Give me one." Maurice blew the smoke to her, and she gave him a thumbs up when her lungs were full. She took the joint from him as she blew out a cloud of smoke and gave him a shotgun in return. Next, Darius took a turn, and Grace could not decipher how they were not burning their tongues. Suddenly, the phone rang, and she went to the kitchen to answer it. After a few quick words, Grace hurried to the dining room. "Maurice, Jacque is on the phone. I think Anne is in labor."

Maurice went to the phone, speaking in French. After hanging up, he announced, "Baby Benet is on the way." Most of the men knew Jacque, and they started giving Maurice high fives, saying congratulations. Grace sent up a silent prayer for Anne to have a healthy baby. *Lord, am I ever going to have one?* As Tara embraced Maurice, planting a kiss on his cheek, Grace squirmed. *Oh, Tara was definitely in love with you, and I think she still is. Now you'll be working together. Great, just great. Magnificent.*

Chapter 15

The ringing phone jolted Maurice awake, and he grumbled as he answered.

"It's a boy. I have a son." Jacque was elated.

Maurice held the receiver to his chest. "Grace, are you awake? It's Jacque. Anne had a boy." Grace sat up, rubbing her eyes as he told Jacque, "Congratulations, Papa Bear. How's Anne doing? Wow, eight pounds? I'm glad everything went well, and you have a healthy son. Okay. Later."

"I'm so happy for them." Grace yawned. "Did they name him yet?"

"Guess not. He didn't say," Maurice replied, ducking back under the covers. He playfully pulled her closer, but she resisted.

"I'm still tired. I'm going back to sleep." She turned her back to him.

"It would be a good time to try again for our baby. I'm already hard." Leaning over, Grace had her eyes shut. "I know you're not asleep." He massaged her buttocks and breasts while lightly kissing her shoulder. "You'll sleep better after I give you a dose of this." He rubbed his member against her backside, but she scooted away.

"Not now. Maybe later."

"We cannot have a baby unless we do it."

"We do it all the time, and we do not have a baby." She sat up. "Why do you think that is?"

"I don't know. These things take time. If we keep trying, it will happen." He rubbed her back. "Lie back down and let me make love to you."

Grace got up and went to the bathroom.

What is going on with her? She was cranky last night and now again this morning. He stared at the ceiling. *Maybe the FBI visit frightened her.*

She returned to bed, leaving plenty of space between them. Maurice stretched his arm out to touch her on the hip. "You know I would not let anything happen to you, right? I'm sorry if the FBI frightened you. I should have been more comforting when you told me. I was so focused on the party that I neglected your feelings. I'm sorry."

"It's okay. I'm going to sleep."

"It's not okay. Please, forgive me." He inched closer to her. "Let me show you how sorry I am."

"Really?" Grace sat up, glaring at him. "You're apologizing so you can have your way? Unbelievable." Getting out of bed, she put her robe on. "I may as well make coffee, since I'm not going to get any more sleep."

Maurice got out of bed as she stormed from the room. *What the hell is wrong with her?* He went to shower and then dressed in jeans and a black NYU sweatshirt.

In the kitchen, Grace stirred pancake batter. She glanced at him. "You're not wearing your uniform. I thought you were meeting your father today."

"I decided to be myself today." He poured himself a cup of coffee and sat at the table.

"Have you thought about getting a haircut? You would look even more like him."

"The last time I cut my hair, you said I shouldn't do it again. You've changed your mind?"

"I have. Not that it matters what I think."

"Of course it matters. Why would you say that? I care very much what you think."

The skillet sizzled as Grace poured the batter into it. She retrieved bacon from the oven and grabbed syrup from the pantry, all the while averting her eyes.

"I have apologized for having a party without discussing it with you first. I apologize for not comforting you after your incident with the FBI. What else have I done? You are upset with me about something. What is it?"

"I want to go home."

"This is your home."

"No, it's not. It is your home. Your family, your friends. I have no one."

He stood behind her. "You have me. I am your family. I am your best friend. I love you."

"I don't think I can wait until June. There's no point in staying in this big house. We're not going to have any children."

Taking her by the waist, he made her turn to face him. "Please, don't say that. We're going to have a family. Have some patience. It will happen."

Grace turned back to the stove to remove the pancakes from the pan. "Maybe you should see a doctor. I know there is nothing wrong with me."

Dropping his hands, he returned to the table. "There is nothing wrong with me. Okay?"

"How do you know? You've got someone pregnant before?"

"Not that I know of." He looked at her. "But I am healthy. What could be wrong with me?"

"I don't know. A doctor could tell us if there is something wrong." She put a plate of pancakes on the table before him and returned to the stove to put another batch in the frying pan. "Will you at least think about it?"

When she returned to the table with the plate of bacon, he said, "Remember, you agreed to wait until June. If you're not pregnant and are still unhappy, we will go back to New York as you wish, and I will see a doctor."

"Do you promise?"

"I do." He started eating even though this conversation had caused him to lose his appetite. "I know you don't think I'm getting anywhere with Philippe, but I am making progress with him. Today, I will talk to him about Sophie and how we don't like one another."

Grace sat down with her plate and another one filled with pancakes. "What for?"

"He needs to know we are not bonding as a family as he had hoped. Perhaps if he shows her more attention than me, she will come around to liking me." Maurice went to pour himself a glass of milk.

As he sat down, Grace asked, "And what will make you like her?"

Maurice snorted. "Nothing. She's like sandpaper."

Pierre came into the kitchen. "Good morning, all. Thanks for calling me, Grace."

"Of course, Pierre. Come join us."

Pierre sat down and helped himself to some bacon. "I have to tell you something." They both stopped eating to look at him. "I'm going to be moving out. I have a lady friend, and she's been asking me to move in with her. I decided now would be a good time. You all don't need me. You both are driving, and you can get anyone to trim hedges and mow the lawn."

"Pierre," Maurice said, "You sly devil. Good for you. We will miss you, but please do whatever will make you happy."

Grace smiled. "You will be missed, but I'm happy for you. Where does your lady friend live?"

"Next town over, Metairie. You'll still see me on occasion. I have already started packing. Hopefully, I'll be done and moved out by next week."

"Let me know if you need help with anything." Maurice finished his plate and went for more coffee. "Even though you are leaving, I will continue to pay you."

"You don't have to do that," Pierre said. "I've got some money tucked away."

"I want to," Maurice replied. "You have dedicated your life to this family. Please let me do it for you."

"Okay. If you insist. Can I have a cup of coffee, please?"

Maurice poured a cup for him and set it on the table as the phone rang. "Yes, Philippe. I am ready now. You can come early if you like." He turned to Grace and Pierre as he put down the phone. "I need to put on some shoes. Excuse me."

Philippe sounded anxious on the phone. First Grace, now him? Merde. He slipped on his sneakers and then his eyes fell on the music box Jacque had given them for their anniversary. The soothing notes of their wedding song played as he opened it. The doorbell rang, snapping him out of the trance. He closed the box before heading down the grand staircase.

Philippe stepped in, giving Maurice a once-over. "Slumming today, are we?"

Maurice snorted before yelling, "Grace, I'm leaving."

"Not so fast," Philippe said, heading for the kitchen. "I want to say hello to my buttercup."

"She is my buttercup." Maurice trailed behind him.

Philippe made a grand gesture of opening his arms for an embrace when he entered the kitchen. "Grace, how are you?" He pulled her into a bear hug and her eyes widened as she gazed at Maurice.

"Okay, enough with the hugs." Maurice swatted at Philippe's arm, and he released Grace.

Philippe swung around to Pierre. "How are you, my friend? We missed you at Mardi Gras."

"I was telling Maurice I'm moving to Metairie."

Philippe patted Pierre on the back. "About time you gave Debra her wish. Good for you. Let me know if you need any help moving."

Pierre stood up. "I will. I'm going to go get back to packing. Thanks for the breakfast, Grace." He left through the kitchen door.

Philippe looked at Grace. "Nice bathrobe. It's too bad you're not dressed. I wanted you to see the present I bought for your husband."

Grace narrowed her eyes. "What is it?"

"Well," Philippe said, "if I tell you that, it will ruin the surprise. I'm sure he will tell you all about it later." He glanced at Maurice. "You ready? Let's go." He winked and smiled at Grace. "See you later, buttercup."

As they left the house, Maurice bristled. "Why must you flirt with my wife? It's extremely disrespectful."

"Stop being so serious. I'm having fun with her. She likes the attention. All women do."

They stepped onto Napoleon Avenue, where the sole vehicle parked along the street gleamed like a pearl - a white Porsche 911 Carrera with the convertible top down. Maurice gazed down the road. "Where is your car?"

Philippe opened the door to the Porsche and slid into the driver's seat. "This is my car. After you learn to drive it, it will be yours."

Maurice's face broke into a broad grin. "Are you kidding?"

"No. Get in."

Maurice hopped into the passenger seat. Philippe held the stick shift in his hand. "Once you learn how to handle this baby, then you can say you know how to drive." The engine roared to life as they pulled away from the curb. He drove to the elementary school parking lot to find it full of cars and school buses. "Shit, I forgot, it's not Sunday." He spun the car around. "Guess we'll have to take this baby out on the open road."

As Philippe cruised toward the highway, Maurice fidgeted in his seat. *What is he up to? Why is he giving me this expensive gift?* Once on the highway, Philippe sped up. It was exhilarating riding with the wind whipping his hair. "This is amazing. How fast can it go?"

"Over 150 miles per hour, but you should never drive it that fast. You'll lose control."

In minutes, they were near the airport. Philippe found a parking lot with only a few cars and stopped to talk to the man at the payment booth before pulling in. "You ready to give it a try?" They both got out of the car. As Maurice slid into the driver's seat, Philippe explained how to use the clutch pedal and stick shift. "Take your time. Go slow." He lit a cigarette as he watched Maurice jerk the car around the lot a few times and eventually smoothly transition into higher gears. He zoomed around the parking lot several times before pulling up beside Philippe. "You're a fast learner." He dropped his cigarette as he walked around the car and sat in the passenger seat. "Flat ground is easy. Hills are a bit more difficult. We'll save that lesson for another day. Put it in reverse. Let's see how you do going backward."

Maurice slowly backed the car up and then applied more throttle. The car spun around. "Holy smokes. I see what you mean about losing control. Sorry."

Philippe laughed. "It's fine. Better to lose control out here than in traffic." He gazed at Maurice. "You like the car?"

"I do, but I cannot accept it." Maurice took his hands from the steering wheel, letting them fall in his lap. "Grace will not be happy about this. It's a sports car. We're trying to have a baby and this would not be appropriate for a family."

"What's the problem? Why isn't she pregnant?"

"I don't know." Maurice threw up his hands in frustration. "It's only been a few months, but she has no patience. Jacque and Anne just had a baby boy, and I think it's making her even more anxious. She blames me for not getting her pregnant. This morning she suggested I see a doctor."

Philippe snorted. "You don't need a doctor. What you should do is stop smoking weed. It slows your whole system down. And stop wearing those tight jeans and tighty whitey underwear. You should wear boxer shorts. Your balls need to hang freely for healthy production."

Maurice stared at him. "How do you know what kind of underwear I'm wearing?"

"I can see your johnson all knotted up between your legs. With those pants, everyone can see it. Do you even have room for a hard-on in there?" Philippe reached over and felt Maurice's stomach. "When's the last time you worked out? You're getting a bit of a pooch there."

Maurice swatted his hand away. "Why are you examining my johnson and my stomach?"

"Hey, I'm just trying to help. If you do as I say, Grace will get pregnant. Drinking some ginseng tea may help as well. So when's the last time you've been to the gym?"

Maurice thought about it. "Not since we moved here."

"I've got some workout clothes at my office downtown. We'll stop and pick them up and go to my gym. A good workout will help pump blood to all the right places. I'll drive." They switched places. "Hold on." Philippe put the car into gear and sped to the exit. He said, "Thanks, Joe," as they left the parking lot and hit the open road again. In minutes, they were pulling up to Philippe's office in the French Quarter. "You wait in the car. I don't want to have to put the top up. I'll be right back."

Maurice glanced at the people walking the streets. When he opened the glove compartment, a handgun was lying there. He quickly shut the compartment door. *What the hell?* He nervously looked around again, hoping no one else saw it. He breathed a sigh of relief when Philippe returned to the car with a gym bag.

"What's the matter? You look like you just saw a ghost." Philippe threw the gym bag into Maurice's lap.

"It's nothing. I'm fine. Do you have an extra pair of shorts in here for me?"

"Of course. And yes, they are clean." Philippe ignited the engine and eased into the traffic. As they passed the elegant entry to the Hotel Monteleone, Natalie strolled with a man toward the revolving door.

"That's her." Maurice banged his hand against the glove compartment. "Stop the car. Stop the car. That's Natalie." Philippe pulled over in the first available space on the street.

Maurice jumped out of the car before Philippe could finish parking. He ran up to the hotel entrance, through the revolving door, into the lobby. *Where is she? I know she came in here.* There were overstuffed beige sofas and large floral arrangements on glass tables around the lobby, but no one was sitting there. Two customers waited at the check-in desk for their rooms. He went down the corridor with elevators, but no one was waiting. Another hall led to the entrance to the Carousel Bar and Lounge. Standing in the doorway, he scanned the room. Natalie and a tall white man with dark hair stood near the carousel, chatting, as the patrons drinking and laughing on the colorful carousel spun around.

Philippe came up behind him. "What the hell are you doing? Who's Natalie?"

"Natalie Barnes." Maurice leaned back to look at his father. "My first client. She's trying to create problems between Grace and me, and I want to know why."

"Where is she?"

"The beautiful dark-skinned girl with the white guy. On the other side of the carousel. They're waiting for a seat."

Philippe stepped closer to the bar. He turned around, tapping Maurice on the shoulder. "Come on. Let's go." Philippe headed out of the bar.

Maurice snorted. "No, I'm going to talk to her."

Philippe grabbed his arm. "No, you're not. Her name is not Natalie. Please, come with me."

Maurice pulled his arm from Philippe's grasp. "You know her?"

"In the car, I will explain everything. Please, come with me."

Reluctantly, Maurice followed Philippe back to the car. Philippe pulled into traffic. "What is going on between you and her?"

"Nothing. Natalie Barnes was my first client. Remember, I told you. You said you didn't know her."

"Her name is not Natalie Barnes. Her name is Carol Brown. But she is known by the name Cocoa. She's one of Sophie's girls. High-class hooker." Philippe glanced at Maurice. "Now, will you tell me what is going on, please?"

Maurice put his head in his hand as he chuckled. "Cocoa. How appropriate." *I cannot believe she is a hooker. My chocolate dream is a damn prostitute.*

Philippe hit him in the arm. "What the hell happened? How is she causing problems between you and Grace?"

"She came to my studio for a portrait. I have to admit, she was intoxicating, but I didn't make a move on her. She made a move on me. Kissed me just as Grace was walking through the door. It was a complete shit show. Thank God Grace believed me when I told her the truth of what happened."

Philippe glanced at him. "Thank God. She's very understanding because most women I know would not forgive that easily."

Maurice lost his composure and threw up his hands. "What are you talking about? Your wife permitted you to sleep with my mother."

"Anyway," Philippe said, "Is that all that happened?"

"No." Maurice looked out the side of the car as the shops blurred by. "Sophie took Grace to the spa, and they just happened to run across Natalie. Natalie said she was having an affair with an artist who is painting her portrait. Naturally, Grace assumed it was me, but I convinced her it was not." Maurice turned full face to Philippe. "Sophie is trying to sabotage my marriage. You do know that she does not like me. Hates me, in fact, according to Marie."

"I detected an inkling of animosity, but I assumed it was natural for a bit of sibling rivalry. I had no idea Sophie was playing games like this with you." Philippe glanced at Maurice. "I will talk to her. I will take care of Sophie." He pulled into the parking lot of Jack LaLanne Fitness Club and parked. Maurice held the gym bag as Philippe put the convertible roof on the Porsche.

Once done, Philippe slapped him on the back. "Come on, let's sweat out the stress. We can talk about the art galleries while we exercise. Later, we'll stop at the store on the way to your house and pick up some boxer shorts. Everything will be fine with you and Grace. She'll be pregnant in no time."

Chapter 16

Loud music greeted Maurice when he stepped into the foyer. Following the sound to the great room, he found Sophie and Grace on the sofa watching television. "Bonjour."

Grace didn't even turn her head. "Hey, babe."

"When did we get a television?"

"It's a gift." Sophie grabbed the remote control and paused the show. "I couldn't believe it when she told me you didn't have a TV, so I brought it over today, along with a VCR. You can watch movies now whenever you like. Right now, we're watching *The Color Purple*." She turned to Grace. "It's great, isn't it?"

"It is." Grace pointed to the remote. "Start it again."

With a stride forward, Maurice reached behind the television and pulled the plug from the wall. The screen went black. "You may take it back. We don't watch television."

"Don't be a jerk," Sophie said. "Plug it back in. At least let Grace finish watching the movie." She gave him a toothy grin. "What's the matter? You didn't have fun with Papa today?"

Maurice focused on Grace. "May I speak to you a moment? In the kitchen."

"Not now." Grace sighed. "Plug the TV back in so we can finish the movie. Please."

Reluctantly, Maurice put the plug back into the electric socket. The screen came to life as he stalked out of the great room. *She is in there fraternizing with the enemy, and she doesn't even know it. I have to tell her about Sophie and Natalie.* He headed for a shower. Dressed in his new white boxer shorts, black sweatpants, and a red t-shirt, he returned to his studio. Sitting at his desk, loud noises from the great room tortured him. *Why would she allow Sophie to bring that idiot box into this house? How long is the movie going to go on?* He took out his sketch of the Gemini twins to work on. An hour later, the noise ceased and Grace said goodbye to Sophie. A moment later, she entered the studio.

"Why were you so rude?"

Maurice snorted. "You know I hate televisions."

"Well," Grace said, "It's in the great room, and you hardly ever go there. You don't have to watch it. And don't worry, using the VCR means I didn't see any commercials. I have not been brainwashed." She approached his desk. "I didn't know Sophie was coming by today. She just showed up with a man who set up the television and VCR. I thought it was very nice of her to do it."

He went back to sketching. "Sophie is not your friend. You shouldn't have accepted her gift."

"What did Philippe give you?"

"A sports car." Maurice raised his voice, glaring at her. "A gift I told him I could not accept because it is not a family car. You should be glad right now that you are not pregnant. You and Jacque were both wrong about the criminal gene. It does exist, and Sophie has it. She is a criminal. I want you to stay away from her."

Grace's mouth dropped open, her eyes widening. "Why are you shouting at me?"

Maurice jumped up to pace around the room, waving his hands wildly. "Because Natalie is not Natalie. She is a prostitute named Cocoa, who works for Sophie. Sophie arranged for her to come here pretending to be a client, and I'm certain she made sure you saw Cocoa again at the spa to hear her lies."

He halted in front of Grace. "She is trying to destroy our marriage. What Marie said is true. Sophie hates me and is doing her best to make me miserable."

Grace ran from the studio up the grand staircase. He followed her as she flung herself onto the bed, sobbing. Maurice took a deep breath to calm down.

"I'm sorry, mon cheri, please don't cry." Seating himself beside her, he attempted to soothe her by rubbing her back. "I'm not angry at you. I'm angry at Sophie. I didn't mean to shout at you."

"Just go away."

He sighed and recounted how he uncovered the truth about Cocoa. "I know you didn't know. But now that you do, please stay away from Sophie. Philippe said he would talk to her, and I will too, to make it clear to her that I do not want Philippe's business. She can have it." He rubbed her back again. "I don't know how she knew I hate television, but I'm certain it is the only reason she brought it here. She wasn't being kind to you."

Grace turned to look at him with wet eyes. "I told her you hate television. On Mardi Gras." She rolled back over. "I guess you should have accepted the car, since you don't want to have a baby anymore."

"I didn't say that." Lying down on the bed, his arm encircled her. "I do want us to have a baby. We will just have to keep a close eye on him or her, is all." Gently, he kissed her neck. "How old do you think a child is when they start showing their criminal intent?" She turned to gaze into his eyes. "I'm kidding." Covering her mouth with his own, he devoured her tongue. "I want to try again for a baby right now." He stood up to pull off his t-shirt and sweatpants. "Take off your clothes."

Grace stood up. "Where did you get those shorts?"

"Philippe bought them for me. He says they're more comfortable, so I'm giving them a try."

She giggled. "You look like a grandpa with those on."

Removing the boxer shorts, he lay on the bed. "Get your naked butt in this bed, and we will see who is a grandpa."

After making love, they snuggled together under the covers. A smile played on Maurice's lips. "I was thinking about what you said about having a friend. I think Tara would be a good friend for you."

Grace wrinkled her nose. "You want me to be friends with your ex-girlfriend, who is still in love with you?"

Maurice snorted. "Tara is not in love with me. She is happily married with two children. Her husband, Guy, is also an artist. He's into body paint and tattoos."

Grace glanced at him from her comfortable spot under Maurice's arm. "Body paint?"

"Yes. The artist paints on a human body instead of a canvas. Needless to say, it gets him into all sorts of trouble with Tara all the time. Painting naked people can lead to all sorts of crazy situations."

"I never heard of such a thing."

"It's trendy, and Guy is wildly successful. Between tattooing half of the military people who pass through this city in his shop, he also gets a lot of modeling and commercial work." He kissed her nose. "We could invite them to dinner, and you two could get to know each other better. You were very cranky the night of the party, but Tara told me she thought you were nice."

"I was not cranky." Grace playfully pinched him.

"Ow. Okay, you were not very cranky," he chuckled, "just a little bit. Only I noticed. So what do you think? Can I call them tomorrow and see when they're free for dinner? We could go to the Commander's Palace."

"All right, but I am not having the fried seafood platter again." She placed a gentle kiss on his chest. "You didn't tell me what Philippe said about the buildings. Is he going to let you have them?"

"He liked the idea of having a cultural arts center. Still, he needs to consult his accountant to see if he could donate the buildings to the nonprofit and get a tax deduction or something."

"Really? I'm surprised."

"I was too. He even suggested we name some part of the center after my mother."

"What a nice idea. Oh, I almost forgot. I spoke to Anne today. She is doing well, and the baby's name is Jackson."

"Jackson? I like it. It's a good name. Babeth and Yves are heading to New York this weekend to meet their grandson. I'm sure they will return with tons of pictures, and we will see the baby. While they are away, it may be a good time to visit Marva and get some of those Creole and Cajun recipes."

Grace yawned. "I will call her." A few minutes later, she was asleep.

While Maurice worked in his studio, Grace spent most of the next day studying for her upcoming exam. He finished his sketch of the Gemini twins with the Aries ram and was busy assessing it when Grace arrived. "What do you want for dinner?"

He held out his hand to her. "Come, take a look at this."

She came closer to examine the picture of twin girls in flowing tunics with long braided plaits, kneeling on either side of a large ram with enormous curled horns. Each girl held out a handful of grain for the ram to eat. "I love it. Magnificent." She kissed him. "Are you hungry?"

"I am. Let's order something. You choose." He put the sketch back down and started making changes to it.

"What are you doing? It's perfect now."

"I have to fix his nose. His nostril's not right." He glanced up at her. "Go order the food, and I will be done in a minute."

When he walked into the kitchen a half hour later, two pots were on the stove as Grace read her textbook at the table. "I found some sausage and tomato sauce. When you're ready, I will make the pasta."

"I am ready." He sat at the table, and she got up to boil the pasta. "I called Tara. She said a Sunday brunch would be best while her mother takes her girls to church for a few hours. We'll meet her and Guy at a restaurant called Arlene's in the Quarter. Brunch starts at ten."

"Works perfectly. I told Marva I would visit Sunday afternoon." Grace stirred her sauce.

"Tomorrow, I would like to take you downtown. We can go shopping, and I will get a haircut."

She stopped to stare at him. "Seriously?"

"Oui."

The phone rang as they were finishing their spaghetti dinner. Maurice answered and had a quick conversation. "Philippe is stopping by. He needs to talk to me."

After putting the dishes in the dishwasher, Grace poured herself a Chardonnay. "Okay. I'm going to watch television."

Maurice shook his head as she headed for the great room. "Make sure you watch a movie on the VCR." He poured a glass of wine. *I could use a joint about now.*

Philippe arrived shortly after and followed Maurice to the kitchen. He offered Philippe a glass of wine.

Philippe snorted. "It will do if you have nothing stronger. I spoke to Sophie. She shouldn't give you any more trouble."

"What did you say?"

Philippe glared at him. "I took care of it." Sipping the wine, he made a sour face. "Tastes like chilled piss. How do you drink this?" Guzzling the remaining wine, he placed the empty glass on the table. "I spoke to my accountant. He said I can get a nice tax deduction by donating the buildings. You may begin to form your nonprofit foundation for the cultural arts center."

"Thank you," Maurice hugged Philippe. "Thank you so much." He sat in the chair next to him. "I truly do appreciate this. It's a very generous gift that will benefit the entire city."

"I agree with you. I haven't done anything nice in a while. Not since the community center, actually." A thoughtful expression crossed Philippe's face. "I want you to go to the center with me next week. I think the children there would enjoy a painting lesson."

"Of course," Maurice said. "It would be awesome to work with the kids." Maurice patted Philippe on the back. "I must admit, you are full of surprises. I did not expect this."

Philippe put his hand on his cheek. "I told you, I'm not a bad guy."

When the doorbell rang, Philippe said, "That's for me." Taking a set of keys from his pocket, he handed them to Maurice. "I parked the

Porsche in the driveway. We'll trade it next year for a minivan. You need two cars now. Okay?"

Maurice took the keys and followed Philippe to the front door. "I'll call you when I set the date for our visit to the center." A tall, dark-skinned man was waiting outside the door. "Say hi to Buttercup for me." Philippe walked to the street with the man and disappeared. Maurice stood in the foyer after closing the door. *I'm starting to like him. He is not who I thought he was.* A grin broke out on his face as he hurried to the great room. "He's going to donate the buildings."

Startled, Grace looked up from the sofa. "He is? I can't believe it."

"I know. It's amazing. Turn off that stupid television. Come with me." He grabbed her hand as she reached for the remote control. The television went off as he pulled her to the studio and out the door to the driveway. "This is the car. He insisted I take it and said we could trade it for a family car next year. Come on, get in. I'll take you for a ride."

Grace stood with wide eyes, gawking at the car. "You can drive this?"

"It will be a quick trip. To the university and back."

Respecting the speed limit, they arrive at the university parking lot. It wasn't packed with cars, and Maurice seized the opportunity to zoom around the lot several times. Grace was laughing, calling him crazy. *I'm glad she is happy. This is the best time we've had together in a while. I will make sure we have fun shopping tomorrow too. I hope she gets along with Tara.*

When they got home, they went upstairs to the bedroom. It elated Maurice that his vision for the cultural arts center was beginning to manifest, but he wanted to focus on Grace. He didn't want to hear her say she wanted to go to New York again. "Philippe took me to a nice gym yesterday. We can stop by there on our way downtown tomorrow. They have state-of-the-art equipment and an Olympic-sized pool. We could go swimming together like we used to at the Y."

"Philippe is being very nice, but it doesn't change the fact that he's killing people." Grace looked at Maurice. "You remember, right?"

Maurice glanced away. "People are being killed by all sorts of atrocities. Starvation, disease, war. What will we do about it?"

Grace pulled on his arm. "Are you giving him a pass on murder?"

"No. Killing is wrong. But I cannot stop him. At least he is doing some good in the community, too. I will be a part of the good he is doing."

"You asked me to stay away from Sophie because she is a criminal. So is Philippe. I'm sure he taught her everything she knows. What happened to cutting the head off the demon?"

Sitting on the bed, Maurice put his head in his hand. "Grace, he is my father. I cannot sever that bond."

Shaking her head, Grace objected. "I don't like it. Philippe should not be a part of our lives."

Maurice took her hand and pulled her to sit beside him. "He, unlike Sophie, has not tried to harm us. And he said she shouldn't give us any more trouble." Pulling her closer, he kissed her softly. "I know this isn't going how I planned, but the cultural arts center will be fully independent of Philippe. Our relationship with him will be personal, not business."

"And you believe it is safe?"

"I do. I promise I won't let anything happen to you." He kissed her again.

Saturday morning, Maurice made omelets for breakfast before driving to the gym. With Grace's approval, he purchased memberships for them before heading to the Quarter in the Mercedes. They stopped at Sak's Fifth Avenue and spent a few hours buying new outfits. At The Gentlemen's Barber, a familiar face greeted them. His old barber, James, was still there.

"Look what the cat dragged in," James said upon seeing Maurice walk through the door. He was graying around the temples, but was still an energetic man. Maurice introduced him to Grace and took a seat in his chair. "I hear you're a famous painter now."

"I'm not famous, but I do all right. My wife insists I get a haircut."

James whirled around to Grace. "I know. It's a miracle you got him in here. I don't think I've put a hand on this head since 1970. His mother used to drag him in."

Grace smiled. "I like his hair, but he needs a more mature look." Maurice rolled his eyes.

James chuckled, "Don't worry, baby, I'll take care of him." Grace picked up a newspaper from the pile next to the waiting area chairs to read while James cut Maurice's hair.

James left a nice amount of thick wavy hair on the top while closely trimming the sides and back. Maurice admired his new look, and from the smile on Grace's face, she liked it too.

As they walked back to the car, she said, "You look incredibly sexy. I mean, you always look sexy to me, but this haircut is working for you. And it is nothing like Philippe's haircut. I love it. Does this mean you will continue being yourself and stop the mini-me routine?"

He ignored the question. "I'm happy you are happy." He started the car. "Let's go to Bourbon Street and have lunch. Then we have one more stop to make before we go home."

"Where?"

He winked at her as he drove. "It's a surprise."

Maurice parked the Mercedes on a side street, and they walked to Bourbon Street. They ate seafood platters at Felix Restaurant and Oyster Bar. Afterward, they strolled down Bourbon Street, window shopping in the antique stores and clothing boutiques. At the corner, Maurice stopped at Marie Laveau House of Voodoo. "This is it. Our last stop."

"What are we buying in here?"

"Some fertility herbs. And a voodoo doll to stick pins into. We will name her Sophie."

They laughed as they went inside.

Chapter 17

Grace and Maurice arrived at Arlene's before Tara and her husband. She felt overdressed as they stood in line with the other customers waiting to be seated. Her new black A-line dress adorned with delicate white printed roses wowed Maurice when she modeled it for him. Most of the other patrons in line wore jeans and tees. *I should have saved this dress for a more momentous occasion. At least I know I will look better than Tara, and my husband's eyes will be on me. He looks so handsome with his haircut and new black suit. He is all mine.*

The restaurant décor had the flavor of a country kitchen. The blue checkered table cloths matched the wooden chair cushions and ivy dripped from the ceiling amongst plates and platters on the walls, showcasing roosters and cows.

Grace squeezed Maurice's hand, and he gazed into her eyes. "You look so beautiful." He gave her a peck on the lips before glancing around. "I've never eaten here before, but it smells good." Once seated at a table, Maurice draped his arm around her shoulder. "We will give them a few minutes. Otherwise, we will start without them. I'm hungry. Are you?"

Grace giggled. "I am, but we should wait." The waiting line for seating disappeared, and patrons descended on the long buffet tables in the center of the dining room. Maurice bit his lip as the plates piled with delectable dishes went by.

Finally, Tara stepped into the restaurant. "I'm sorry we're late. Guy is parking the car. The girls were fussing. They didn't want to go to church. What a morning." Tara's braids were hanging down, cascading over her shoulders, and her beige cotton wide-leg pants with a matching oversized shirt flowed around her. Maurice stood to kiss her cheek and pulled out a chair for her to sit across from Grace.

Grace greeted her. *Tara is glowing in her bohemian chic. Why didn't I buy an outfit like that? She looks amazing.* A moment later, another guest arrived at the table, a tall, strikingly handsome man. Sun-kissed tan with a thick blond ponytail and colorful tattoos down one arm. Grace looked up and fell into the ocean of his deep blue eyes. Her jaw dropped as he spoke.

"Bonjour," Guy said as Maurice embraced him, and they launched into a conversation in French.

Tara pounded on the table with her fist. "Boys, speak English, please. Guy, say hello to Grace. Sit down."

Grace could not take her eyes off Guy as he leaned in to kiss her cheek. "Bonjour, Cher." *I may faint.* His relaxed attire, the baggy jeans and snug t-shirt featuring Betty Boop seemed effortlessly cool. A little blond stubble traced a path along his lips and jawline, adding to his rugged charm. "A pleasure to meet you."

"Don't sit down," Maurice said. "Let's eat."

Grace could barely choose from the buffet because Guy had her full attention. His arm muscles rippled under the tight shirt as he reached to fill his plate with food. He ignored Tara as she fussed at him about his buffet choices.

Maurice tapped Grace's shoulder. "There is nothing on your plate. I thought you were hungry." The plate in his hand held scrambled eggs, waffles, and gobs of bacon.

"I am." She took her eyes off Guy long enough to put scrambled eggs, home-fried potatoes, and sausage on her plate before following Guy back to the table.

A few blond strands escaped the ponytail, floating around his gorgeous face. *Is that a snake on his arm?* Grace's eyes met his, and he stopped eating. "I see you," he said, a smile playing on his lips. "Do you like my tattoos?"

Grace's heart pounded, looking down at her eggs. "I do." *Oh, my god. He has the sexiest smile ever.*

Tara sat across from Grace and examined Guy's plate. "Do not complain later about your stomach hurting. Every time you eat mushrooms, you get a stomach ache. Why must you do it?"

Guy waved around a giant mushroom on his fork before putting it in his mouth. "Because they taste delicious."

Maurice returned to the table with his plate piled high with food. Grace stared at him. "You are going to eat all of that?"

"Yes, and then I will have some more." Tasting a piece of waffle drowning in butter and syrup, he nodded his approval. "Mm, very good."

Tara and Grace looked at one another and laughed while shaking their heads. "I'm glad you invited us out today. How are you enjoying New Orleans?"

"I love the city. Mardi Gras was amazing." She talked about the house and her classes at Tulane. Maurice and Guy returned to conversing in French as Tara chatted about her two daughters and artwork. *She is nice. Maurice was right. She is not in love with him. Why would she be? She has Guy. Gorgeous Guy. I think Tara and I will be good friends.*

"While the girls are in school, I can get out," Tara said between bites. "We should have a girl's day. Have you been to the new spa? I hear it's wonderful."

"I have," Grace said. "It's nice, but I don't want to go back. We could do lunch, and maybe some shopping. I love your outfit. Where did you get it?"

"A little boutique in Central City. I'll take you there."

The morning passed with good conversation and lots of laughter. As they walked to their cars, Tara promised to call Grace to firm up their plans.

Once in the Mercedes, Maurice leaned over to kiss her cheek. "You liked Guy. I saw you watching him. You were supposed to be focusing on Tara." He chuckled. "Did you have a good time?"

"I had a wonderful time. You were right about Tara."

Upon returning home, Grace changed into her jeans and a light blue t-shirt. On her way through Maurice's studio, she gave him a sweet, lingering kiss. "I'm going to see Marva. Walk off some food."

Stepping out into the balmy, sunny day, she strolled to Prytania Street. Marva was a delight, discussing the fine art of cooking Creole food. On her way home, laden with a large container of gumbo and several recipes, Grace basked in the moment. *If only we could get rid of Sophie and Philippe, everything would be fine. I do like New Orleans.*

After putting the gumbo away, she went to the studio to find Maurice studying a photograph of a lion in a large book alongside his sketch pad on the desk. "Marva said you must stop by for a visit. She sent you some gumbo."

"Marva is the best," he said. "I'm glad you had a good day today."

"Me too. I'm going to study. I have a big exam tomorrow."

"Have some of the fertility tea I brewed. It's in the refrigerator."

As the night stretched on, Grace diligently studied. Early the next morning, she prepared for the looming exam, slipping into jeans and a soft pink pullover. *Feels a bit chilly this morning.* After brushing her hair, she did a final check in the bathroom mirror. *I'm ready. I should ace this test.* Beneath the covers, Maurice slept soundly.

Downstairs, Grace prepared breakfast before reviewing her notes one last time. Glancing at the clock, she checked the time. *I could go a little early. Xavier may be there with my notebook.* Maurice was waking as she came to say goodbye. "I'm leaving for school." She planted a tender kiss on his lips. "I left you ham and grits for breakfast."

"Good luck with your exam." He sat up to stretch. "I know you'll do great."

Xavier was standing in the hallway outside the classroom, wearing denim overalls with only one strap fastened over a snug purple t-shirt. He flashed his award-winning smile at her as she approached. *He is way too cute.* "Hey, Grace. How you doing?"

"I'm good. I thought you may have some questions about the notes, so I came early."

With a sly grin, Xavier leaned closer. "Great minds think alike." Slinging his backpack from his shoulder, he retrieved the notebook for her. "Thank you for this. I got most of it, but I do have a few questions. Can we go in and sit down?"

Inside the classroom, they took their seats. When he leaned over, his musky, sweet scent tickled her senses. *Lord, he smells good, too. I don't know if I should sit beside him when I take this test. I need to focus.*

Opening the notebook Grace laid on her desk, Xavier located the page he wanted to ask about. "I didn't get the difference between the debt-equity ratio and the debt-asset ratio." Grace examined his hand as he pointed out the paragraph. *Big strong hands.*

"The difference is which one you use as the denominator." She did not want to look into his eyes as she answered. "Debt-asset ratio uses the total assets, and debt-equity ratio uses total equity."

Xavier opened his own notebook and scribbled in it. "Makes complete sense." He leaned over again and flipped a few pages to another section of Grace's book. "This here," he said, pointing. He continued going through the notebook, and she answered his questions until Professor Collins entered the room. Everyone cleared their desks as the professor distributed the exam papers. The room quieted except for pencils scratching against paper.

Grace studied the first few questions on the paper. *What is wrong with me? I am married to the most beautiful man in the world, lusting after these other men like a hungry lioness. Think about Maurice. Focus on these numbers.* She took her pencil to start to work on the exam, but she couldn't help herself, occasionally glancing over at Xavier. His presence couldn't be ignored. *Why is he so attractive to me?* Xavier was busy working on his exam, not paying her any attention. Her mind went to Guy, and she flushed, getting warm. *He was extremely hot, too.* She closed her eyes to envision Maurice's face. *He is a good husband. I love him.* Determined, she went back to work on her exam.

An hour later, Xavier turned in his exam to the Professor and left the classroom. Looking down, Grace stared at an entire page of questions to answer. Putting her head down, she stayed focused and completed the exam. Her eyes widened when Xavier was standing in the hallway as she exited from the room. "You waited?"

"How do you think you did?" he asked.

"I aced it. You?"

"I think I passed. There was a lot of information to cover." A broad grin crossed Xavier's face. "Thanks to your notes, I got most of it down. I wanted to ask if you would let me buy you lunch after class on Wednesday. As a thank you for your help."

Her chin dropped as she blushed. "You don't have to do that. I was happy to help."

"I know I don't have to, but I want to. You're a nice lady. Can I walk you to your car?"

Remembering Agent Wolf, she conceded. "Yes, please."

As they headed toward the Mercedes, Xavier said, "So, what about lunch? Nothing fancy. A burger and fries. There's a greasy spoon right down the road that makes the best burgers in town."

"Probably not. My husband will be expecting me after class." They stopped at her car.

"This is a nice Benz." Xavier opened the car door for her. "What's your husband do?"

"He's an artist. A painter." She slid into the driver's seat.

"Nice. Well, ask him if it's okay if we go to lunch." Leaning down, he placed his face close to hers. "If he says yes, we'll go. If not, I understand."

Grace met his gaze. "I will ask him. Thanks."

"Drive safely." Xavier closed the door and knocked twice on the outside of the door. She drove home, her mind swirling. *I would like to go to lunch with him, but I shouldn't. I know I wouldn't like it if Maurice went to lunch with another woman. Forget about lunch with Xavier.*

When she pulled into the driveway, Marie stood outside the studio door, puffing on a joint. Grace got out of the car, lugging her tote. "Why are you smoking out here?"

"Howdy." Marie stubbed the end of the joint out against the wall. "Maurice said you guys were taking a break from smoking, so I came out here to take a few hits."

She followed Grace inside the studio. Maurice was standing at an easel, working on Marie's portrait. "Today is the last time Marie has to pose. I will finish the rest." He stopped to give Grace a loving peck on the lips. "How was the test?"

"I think I did well. Did you eat lunch?"

"I brought some beef po'boys," Marie said. "They're in the kitchen. I'm going to go meet Darius. See you." She hugged Maurice before heading out the studio door.

"Everything all right with her?" Grace asked.

"Yes," Maurice said, still sketching. "She is fine. Happy with her portrait so far. And I was right about Sophie and the television. The first thing Marie wanted to know was how angry I got when I saw it." He turned around to face Grace. "How long are you going to keep it?"

"Forever." She turned to go to the kitchen. "It's not bothering you. What's the big deal?"

Two wrapped whole sandwiches were on the kitchen counter. A third one lay open and half eaten. Grace took one of the whole ones, unwrapped it, took a bite, and poured herself a glass of Maurice's fertility tea. *I wonder if this will help. I guess it can't hurt. It tastes good with the honey and lemon he added.*

Maurice came into the kitchen and picked up the half-eaten sandwich. "We should donate it to the community center. I bet they could use a new television." He bit his sandwich and stared at her as he chewed. When she didn't respond, he continued after swallowing. "Did I tell you I'm going to the center with Philippe? He wants me to give the kids a painting lesson."

"No, you didn't tell me, but it's a great idea. When are you going?"

"Wednesday at eleven. I don't know how long the lesson will be, but I will probably be gone until late afternoon."

"The kids will love it, I'm sure. And you will too." *And I can go for lunch with Xavier.*

Maurice poured himself a glass of his fertility tea. "I'm glad you're drinking the tea. It's good, right?" He sat down at the table across from her.

"Mm, very good. I hope it works."

"It will. Have faith, my love."

Maurice made quick work of the sandwich and grabbed another whole one from the counter. He was wearing a pair of baggy jeans like Guy had on at brunch.

"Nice pants," she said. "You bought them at Sak's?"

"Yes, and I'm glad I did since you admired Guy's outfit so intently yesterday."

She giggled. "Oh, hush."

Maurice sat back down to eat his sandwich. "I think I'm done working today. Would you like to go for a swim with me at the gym?"

Gazing into his beautiful green eyes, she melted. "Yes. I would love it." *I am not going to start sneaking around with Xavier. I love Maurice too much. I'm not going to lunch with Xavier.*

Chapter 18

Standing a few feet from his easel, Maurice assessed the lion he'd drawn. *His mane should be grander. I don't like the way his paw reaches for the scale. Maybe it should be on one side of the scale with gold bars balancing the other side.* Picking up an eraser, he began removing the paw.

"Nice lion," Grace said, coming up behind him. "I'm off to school. Have fun at the community center." She kissed him on her way to the door.

"Have a good day." Maurice refocused on his artwork. *To put the paw on the scale, I must redraw the Queen Scale to be closer. Or I could extend her arm.* The phone rang, interrupting his musings.

"Hey, what's up?" It was Claude. "We haven't spoken since the party. Are we doing the arts center or not?"

"Yes. I was planning on contacting everyone to set up another meeting. Now, you can help me. We can meet here at my house again." Remembering the need to notify Grace he was having a meeting or, as she would call it, another party, he asked, "How is Friday for you?"

"Good. I guess you want me to help by calling everyone else?"

"Please. I'm on my way out for the rest of the day. Call me tomorrow morning and let me know if we are on, and I will take care of everything else. Later."

The doorbell rang. Philippe was in a chipper mood. "I like the baggy jeans you're wearing." He ruffled Maurice's hair. "Nice haircut," he said as they walked to the street to his car. "First stop is the art supply store to pick up whatever you need. I'm expecting about thirty kids, seven to ten years old. School is out this week, so the center needs some additional activities. If all goes well, maybe you could do it again tomorrow."

Maurice grinned as he put his easels and sketch pads into the back seat. "No problem. I'm looking forward to giving a lesson."

They stopped at an AC Moore and bought all the store's watercolor paint kits and drawing pads. Arriving at the community center, Philippe parked in the back of the building. It resembled a small single-level elementary school with a red brick exterior, green roof, and trim. Maurice helped Philippe carry all the supplies into the gymnasium. Children of all sizes reveled in play while a trio of middle-aged women attempted to supervise. With efficiency, Maurice arranged his two easels with a pre-drawn picture on each one, eager to begin the lesson.

Philippe introduced Maurice to Hazel, Gladys, and Mary, the women overseeing the session. Amidst clapping hands, the children gathered around Miss Hazel, who patiently waited until everyone was quiet. "Today, we are in for a special treat. A painting lesson with Mr. Maurice." He waved to the kids as they all cheered with approval. Miss Gladys and Miss Mary had tin cans already half filled with water. After each child found a seat on the floor, the ladies passed out the paint kits, water cans, and pads. To his amazement, Philippe got down on the floor in the middle of a pack of girls with his own supplies, ready to paint. Maurice instructed them on how to paint the first scene and then the second, filling in his sketches with watercolor paint. "You choose which one you want to paint. Ready, set, go." At first, it was quiet as everyone focused on their paper, trying to copy the paintings on the easels. Then the giggling and whispering became out-and-out talking and laughter. Walking around, Maurice monitored everyone's progress and assisted. Most girls painted the picture with the house, trees, and a big blue bird flying under the sunny sky. The boys favored the river scene with giant alligators and colorful flowers on lily pads beneath a bright yellow sun.

The little girls surrounding Philippe took great interest in his painting, offering their help. Smiling and laughing, he teased each one, and they squealed with delight. *I never imagined him being this playful. He is really good with children.*

Everyone was enjoying the lesson, and the time passed quickly. Afterward, Philippe offered to show Maurice the rest of the center. A large kitchen and, behind it, a storage area served as a food pantry. It was fully stocked with a variety of canned and boxed goods. Off the kitchen was a dining area to seat about fifty people at long cafeteria tables with attached seating.

Philippe explained the dining room doubled as a classroom. "You did a great job teaching the children today. Marie said you offered to teach her to draw. How's that going?"

"We haven't officially started yet," Maurice said as they returned to the gym to collect his easels and sketch pads.

"Let's get something to eat and discuss the plans for the cultural arts center." They packed his equipment into the car's back seat, and Philippe lit a cigarette as they drove.

Maurice studied Philippe as he puffed a cloud of smoke out the window. "Do I have other family? Are my grandparents alive?"

Philippe glanced at him. "You might. My father was a mean, disgusting drunk, who beat me, my mother, and my brother for whatever, whenever. The day he left was the happiest day of my life. I suppose he could still be alive, but I doubt it." He puffed on his cigarette. "My brother, Frank, took off to join the military the following year, and I haven't heard from him since. I guess he could be alive somewhere. I was left alone to care for my poor mother. I was sixteen, thinking I would have to drop out of school to take care of her. I started working on the docks after school. Your mother, she was the only one who cared about me." Philippe glanced at Maurice with a smile. "Schools were segregated back then. I rescued Nettie from a bully one day when she wandered through my neighborhood alone. Beat that kid bloody." He chuckled at the memory. "Nettie, she had this dream of being the next Josephine Baker. After school, she'd feed me her uneaten lunch, and while I walked her home, she listened to all my problems." Philippe's tone turned somber, staring at the road ahead. "Some days, that lunch was all I had to eat. My mother drowned herself in booze, mourning my shit father, and died right after I graduated high school. I was so happy when Nettie told me she was pregnant. We were going to get married and be a family. But her father wouldn't allow it. He forced her to marry that soldier and shipped her off."

Maurice stared at Philippe, his heart feeling heavy. *I had no idea he had such a tragic beginning. No wonder he is the way he is.*

The last drag of Philippe's cigarette was followed by its flick out the window. "Life kept moving, and so did I. A fellow on the docks, Mia's father, took me under his wing. He had a side gig running with a bunch of roughnecks, dealing in gambling and whore houses. He brought me into the business. Seeing how upset I was about losing Nettie, he introduced me to his daughter. And the rest is history."

They pulled into the parking lot of the Chophouse Restaurant on Magazine Street. Maurice was mulling over what his father said as they entered the steakhouse. *He got his criminal start with Sophie's grandfather. Maybe that's why she has the criminal gene, and I don't. But Marie doesn't seem to have it either.*

Once seated, they both ordered the filet with baked potato and creamed spinach. As Philippe sipped his bourbon, Maurice asked, "How is it Marie is so much younger than me and Sophie? You must have been sleeping with your wife and Nettie at the same time."

Philippe gave him a stern look. "Not everyone learns about love and sex the right way. Something terrible happened to Mia when she was young, but her father knew she needed a husband to support and protect her. I took that job. Understand?" Shifting in his seat, a smile came to his lips. "After your grandfather died in that car accident, Nettie returned to the city a widow. The second happiest day of my life, because I finally saw you. My son. You were already walking and talking up a storm. Anyway, Nettie and I had our fights like any couple. Once, we had a real nasty one, and she vowed never to speak to me again. Now, I can't remember what the argument was about. After a month of her silent treatment, I slept with my wife, and that's when Marie popped up." His eyes met Maurice's. "That's how I know you will get Grace pregnant. You've got good, strong genes." Laughing loudly, he finished his first drink before starting the second one.

"I still have difficulty believing your wife was so understanding. Clearly, Sophie is not."

"Do not worry about Sophie." Philippe reached across the table to touch Maurice's hand. "She'll come around eventually." Quickly, he withdrew his hand. "I'm glad you and Marie are getting along. Why is she coming to your house if you're not teaching her to draw?"

"I'm painting her portrait. For Darius."

"Ah." A smile played on Philippe's lips. "You must show it to me when it's finished. I bet it will be brilliant, like your mother's."

The waiter brought their food, and Philippe brought up the cultural arts center. "I want you to contact my lawyer, Blaze, about the paperwork for setting up the nonprofit." Reaching into his pocket, he pulled out a business card holder. He handed Maurice a card. "He is expecting your call. Now, what's your vision for the center?"

Maurice elaborated on how the center would combine the displays of sculpture and paintings with art history related to New Orleans and the various local artists who would display their work. "It will be an educational experience as well as an aesthetic one. We will also offer workshops for up-and-coming new talent and showcase their work to the public." Suddenly, a beeping interrupted him. "What's that noise?"

Philippe reached into his inner jacket pocket. "It's my pager." Looking at the small screen on the black device, he frowned. "I need to make a phone call. I'll be right back."

Maurice continued eating. In a few minutes, Philippe returned with a reddened face. "The buildings on Julia Street are on fire. We have to go now."

After terse words with the waiter, they rushed to the car. Philippe sped down Canal Street. Hitting his hand against the steering wheel, he cursed and mumbled as they waited at the traffic light. Maurice's heart began racing. *I cannot believe this is happening. He couldn't have done this. He's too upset.*

Firetrucks were on the scene when they arrived at Julia Street, blocking their view of the buildings. They parked and ran to get a closer look at the damage. The half-crumbled three attached buildings were black and smoldering, but most of the fire was out. Firefighters continued dousing the buildings with water hoses. Philippe's face was like stone as he talked to the fire chief.

Maurice's heart sank. *My dream is going up in smoke. This is Sophie, I know it. Philippe was too shocked to have done it.*

Silently, Maurice followed his father back to the Mercedes. Philippe didn't say a word as he lit a cigarette and started driving, and Maurice didn't want to say what he was thinking. When Philippe pulled up in front of Sophie's sports bar, he knew he didn't have to.

"Wait in the car. I need to speak to her in private." Philippe almost snatched the door off the hinges of the restaurant when he entered. Maurice sat in the car for a moment and then got out. Walking around the restaurant, the back door to the kitchen was open. The staff was washing dishes, and chaotic food preparation was going on. No one paid him any attention as he walked through and entered the darkened game room. Quickly maneuvering around the pool tables, he passed the entryway to the main dining room towards Sophie's office. Philippe was shouting.

As he put his ear to the door, Sophie calmly said, "I went with the original plan we had for the buildings."

"After I told you not to. This is unacceptable." Philippe continued to rant. "I am the one in charge here, not you. You do what I tell you."

"I don't recall you saying plans had changed. If I had, I wouldn't have moved forward. What were you planning to do with the property?"

"That is not your business. It is mine. You will suffer consequences for this, young lady."

Philippe continued to shout as Maurice backed away from the door and hurried back to the car.

In five minutes, Philippe stormed out of the restaurant. Sliding behind the wheel, his jaw tensed. "I am sorry, but we will still move forward with the nonprofit. The land is still good." Gazing at Maurice, Philippe touched his hand. "We can build a new building. It will be even better than renovating the old one. You'll see." Starting the engine, Philippe drove Maurice home. "Your sister is getting beside herself. She needs some serious correction."

Once home, Maurice took his equipment from the back seat. "Do you still want to go to the center tomorrow?"

"No," Philippe said. "Thank you for a great job today, but I will let the ladies know we will not be back tomorrow. I need to take care of a few things. You should still meet with the lawyer. I'll call you soon."

He does not have Sophie under control. Not by a long shot.

He entered the great room after putting his easels and sketchpads back in his studio. Grace was lying on the sofa watching television. Sitting up, she shared a frightened look. "There was a fire on Julia Street. I saw it on the news."

Maurice took the remote from her hand and turned off the television. "I know. It was our buildings. Philippe and I drove there as soon as we heard."

"How bad is it? Can it be salvaged?"

"No, but he said we can build a new one." Sitting beside her on the sofa, he enveloped her in his arms. "Sophie did it. She burned it down."

Grace leaned back, puzzled. "How do you know it was her?"

"Philippe went straight to her bar, and they argued about it. Sophie pretended she didn't know he had plans for the buildings."

Grace's hand went to her throat. "What? What will he do to her?"

Maurice snorted. "Not enough. She is not going to stop this relentless campaign she has against me. I don't know what to do. Philippe cannot stop her."

"Maybe you should talk to her. Tell her we don't want anything from her or Philippe."

Maurice hesitated. "I don't think she will believe me." Looking down, his hands twisted between his knees. "I'm more concerned about what she will do next. Setting a fire is far more than I ever imagined her doing. She's dangerous." He glanced at Grace. "Maybe you should go to New York and visit your mother."

"You should come with me. We should leave."

"I won't let her run me out of town." Jumping up, Maurice started pacing, waving his hands. "I have as much a right to be here as she does. I don't understand why she sees me as such a threat. I know Philippe has told her I do not want any part of their business." He stopped to focus on Grace. "You should go. I cannot let anything happen to you."

"I will do nothing but worry about you if I go. I'm not going anywhere unless you come with me." Grace extended her hand to him, and he sat beside her. "Nothing is worth all of this trouble. We can go back to New York, get a smaller place, and manage until our finances improve. We don't have to stay here. Keep the house if you don't want to sell it. But please, let's go home."

Maurice stood. "I will think about it." He left her and went to his studio. Staring out the windows from his desk chair, he took several deep breaths. *What could I say to Sophie to make her stop this madness? I cannot put Grace in danger. If she tries to hurt Grace, I will have to kill her and Philippe. Maybe Grace is right. We should leave. But I want to do the arts center. I want to live in this house.*

Rising, he removed the drape from Marie's unfinished portrait. His mind swirled, staring at her fierce expression in the drawing he'd started to paint. *Maybe she knows something to help me fight against Sophie. How much does Sophie confide in her?* Taking up his supplies, he began painting details of Marie's face. Focusing on his work calmed him down. *Marie isn't likely to stop by. I told her she no longer needed to pose. But I did offer to teach her to draw. Hopefully, she will come by for a lesson. I need to speak with her. Marie will help me. Perhaps she can warn me about what Sophie is planning to do next.* He froze. *What if she tries to burn this house down? I cannot put Grace through that again. I almost lost her.* Putting down his paintbrush, he paced around the studio. *I must protect Grace.*

"I was going to order Chinese food." Grace stood in the doorway, waving the menu around in her hand. "Is that okay with you?"

Looking at her, dressed in jeans and a red crewneck shirt, he sighed with relief. *She is so beautiful. She is the most important thing in my life.* "Chinese is fine. Please ask them to deliver it. I'm working." Once she left, he sat at his desk. *I have to put her first. If I can't convince Sophie to stop, we will have to leave.*

Returning to the easel, he resumed painting the details of Marie's face. *I will tell Claude and the others the cultural arts center will not happen.*

Later, when the doorbell rang, he assumed it was the food. His heart leaped when he heard "Howdy." Marie stood in the doorway. "I heard about the fire. I'm so sorry."

Maurice embraced her. "I'm glad you came by. Did you know what Sophie was planning to do?"

"No, I had no idea." Marie sat at the desk. "She was ranting the other night about Papa giving you the property, but she never said anything about burning it down." Marie's eyes pleaded, "You must try to talk to her before she does something even worse."

"What else was she ranting about?"

"The Porsche. At first, she was excited when Papa brought the car home and took each of us for a ride. Maybe she thought it was a gift for her, but she exploded later when he gave the car to you."

Maurice paced around. "I will give it to her. I will try to talk to her and give her the car."

Marie shook her head. "She won't take it. Papa will have a fit of his own if she does."

Grace came into the studio. "The food is here. Marie, are you going to stay for dinner?"

"No, I'm meeting Darius. I just stopped by for a hot minute." Rising, she hugged Maurice. "I'll let you know if I do hear anything. See you," and left through the studio door.

Maurice turned to Grace. "You go ahead and eat. I'm not hungry right now." Sitting at his desk, he loudly exhaled. *I will try to give Sophie the car and talk to her. Grace and I will leave New Orleans if she doesn't listen to reason.*

April 1988

Chapter 19

After eating alone, Grace returned to the great room to watch television. *I hope Maurice is now convinced we should go back to New York. Who knows what Sophie or Philippe will do next? As much as he threatens, Maurice is not a killer, but they are.*

Trying to focus on the episode of *The Jeffersons* didn't work. Her mind was elsewhere. Unexpectedly, Professor Collins announced there would be no class next week. Spring break had arrived, and Easter Sunday was imminent. *Xavier was very understanding when I told him we could not go to lunch today. I'm glad because I want us to remain friendly. I hope he passed the test. At least I have a few days off from school. I haven't heard from Tara about our shopping date. I wonder what she and Guy are doing for Easter. Probably a family day for them, full of Easter egg hunts and stuffed bunnies. Lord, will we ever have children?*

Switching off the television, she went to the master bedroom. Opening the lid of the china music box, she lay on the bed, entranced by the melodic soft bell tones of their wedding song. *I know he asked me to go to New York to protect me, but why would he not want to come with me? Since we got married, we have done everything together. I cannot leave him here.* Closing the lid, she called her mother. She felt terrible, lying to her mother, saying everything in New Orleans was great. Beverly chatted about the corn dish she was preparing for the Maundy Thursday church dinner and her plans to attend the Good Friday service. Her mother loved Easter and described in detail her new outfit with a matching hat for the main event on Sunday morning.

Inspired by her mother's banter, Grace planned to celebrate with Maurice. *I would like to go to church. I'm certain Maurice doesn't miss our Sundays with Mom and Dad, but I miss it.* In the kitchen, searching through the pantry and refrigerator, Grace made a list of what to purchase for a special Easter dinner. *A succulent leg of lamb with new potatoes and asparagus. I could also bake a cake.* The containers of beef and broccoli and chicken with snow peas were still undisturbed on the table. Entering the studio, Maurice was immersed in painting. "Are you going to eat?"

He didn't turn around. "Later."

After putting the containers in the refrigerator, she prepared for bed, and picked up her romance novel, reading until sleep claimed her.

Upon waking the next day, Grace realized Maurice had never come to bed. She put on her robe and went down to the studio. He was still standing at the easel, painting, Marie's portrait coming to life. Understanding this was his way of working off stress, she left him to his work and went to make coffee. *I miss Pierre. It would be nice to have someone to eat breakfast with.* The aroma of bacon was intended to lure her husband out, but she sat alone at the kitchen table, eating her fried egg and bacon sandwich. *He's got a lot of paintings going. Next, he will work on the horoscope pairings. This could go on for days. What will I do? I don't even have to study.* She sighed. *I don't have any friends to go out with.* The phone rang.

"Hi, Grace, it's Tara. I didn't forget about you."

Grace brightened. "I figured you're busy with your daughters. Are you coloring eggs for Easter?"

Tara laughed. "How did you know? We're doing an Easter egg hunt on Saturday because Sunday is a full day at my mother's house. Are you free on Tuesday? We could shop and have lunch. The girls will still be out of school, but my mother said she would babysit."

"Tuesday sounds great. Do you mind picking me up?"

"No problem. I'll be there around eleven. Have a Happy Easter."

Energized, Grace dressed in her tan jogging suit before picking up her list to head to the supermarket. Walking through the studio, Maurice barely noticed her. "I'm going to the store for a few things. Would you like anything special?"

"No. Be careful, please."

She drove to Rouse's supermarket, and it was buzzing with activity. Shoppers swarmed the aisles, preparing for their Easter feast as well. She found a nice, small leg of lamb and checked off the other items on her list. Once home with the groceries stored away, she decided to work out at the fitness center. Again, Maurice hardly spoke to her as she passed him in the studio on her way out the door.

The gym was less crowded than the supermarket. Without Maurice, swimming was no fun, so she tackled the exercise equipment circuit. Her arm and leg muscles were burning after completing it. *I'll do a half hour on the elliptical, and then I'm done.*

"Hey, Grace." Xavier stood there in gray shorts and a matching tank top. "I didn't know you worked out here."

She stopped the machine and climbed down from the elliptical. "Hi. I'm a new member here. This is my second time."

"Is your husband with you? I'd like to meet him." He flashed his brilliant smile.

"No, he's busy working." Grace swiped at the sweat on her brow. "Since we have a few days off and I'm all caught up with my homework, I decided to come here to work off some stress."

"What are you stressed about?" Xavier chuckled. "You always seem so together at school. Like your life is perfect."

"Hardly. It's family stuff, is all. Do you work out here regularly?"

"Yeah, but not on Thursdays. I'm only here today because of spring break. I normally have another class on Thursday."

"Well, good for you. I'm about done here. I guess I'll see you in two weeks."

As she started to leave, Xavier followed. "If you're not in a rush, maybe we could get a coffee or something. I still want to do something to thank you."

Pausing, Grace turned to see his big, beautiful smile. *Maurice is working. Why rush home to be alone? But...* "I'm all sweaty."

"Don't worry about it," Xavier said. "There's a coffee shop right around the corner. They're used to serving sweaty gym rats."

"Okay. Let me splash some water on my face in the locker room. I'll meet you out front in five minutes."

"Great. I'll go get my gym bag and meet you in five."

Examining her reflection in the mirror after putting cold water on her face, she tried to pull herself together. Seeing Xavier with such few pieces of clothing on was quite a rush. *Make sure you keep your hands to yourself, Missy. Don't enjoy yourself too much with Xavier.* Running her hands down the front of her tan jogging suit, she took a deep breath before walking out of the locker room toward the exit doors.

Xavier was waiting. *Thank God he put on a jacket to cover those beautifully sculpted arms.* "We don't even need to drive. We can walk." He pointed across the parking lot. "It's right over there."

They chatted about the nice weather as they walked. Once inside the Black Cat Coffee House, they sat at a table towards the back of the café. It was cozy, capable of hosting a minimal number of patrons amongst a few wooden tables and chairs.

"How do you like your coffee?" Xavier asked.

"With sugar and cream."

Xavier chuckled. "Light and sweet. Just like you." He went to the counter and ordered the coffee. While waiting, he viewed the sweets in the bakery case. He turned to Grace. "Do you like bear claws? They make delicious ones here."

Before she could answer, he ordered two bear claws to go with the coffee. She couldn't help but return his big smile when he came to the table with their goodies.

Taking a bite, she said, "Mm. This is good. I don't think this is what one should eat after a workout."

Xavier grinned. "Special occasions call for special treats." Holding her gaze, he took a big bite from his bear claw.

"What's special?" Grace asked, before taking another bite of her own.

"Being here with you. I'm glad you allowed me to do this for you."

A warm flush washed over her as she chewed the yummy dough. She didn't know how to respond, so she kept chewing.

"It's not every day a man meets a beautiful lady like you. Beautiful outside and inside. Most pretty girls act stuck up and want to be served. They ain't trying to help a brother out. You're different."

"That's quite a compliment." Grace met his gaze. "Thank you."

"No, thank you. I would have never gotten through those chapters without your help. I appreciate it." His hand slid across the table and gently rubbed the back of her hand.

Grace slowly removed her hand, dropping it in her lap. "Are you working now as an accountant?"

"I'm helping my sister on a part-time basis. She's a CPA and the one who talked me into taking these courses so I could get my certification. She wants us to go into business together."

"Wow, that's great. I used to work for Ernst and Young when we lived in New York. I bet your sister treats you better than they used to treat us on the job. Endless stacks of tax returns for businesses and individuals were just the tip of the iceberg."

"Ernst and Young? That's one of the big firms. You must have a lot of experience." He took another bite of his bear claw. "One day, I may get into one of the bigger firms." He winked at her and then sipped his coffee. "I'm surprised your husband isn't with you. You said he was an artist. Don't they set their own work schedules? If I were your husband, I would have taken the time to come work out with you."

"Well, when he's inspired, Maurice gets wrapped up in his painting to the point of obsession. He's determined to finish a portrait he's working on."

Xavier chuckled. "That's his name? Maurice?" He leaned in closer with a serious gaze. "I don't know him, but Maurice sounds like a fool. I could never get so obsessed with anything if I had a woman like you."

Heat flooded Grace's cheeks, and she wasn't sure if the coffee or Xavier was the cause. "I don't mind. When he's not on a painting mission, Maurice is very attentive." She finished her coffee. *I need to get out of here. I'm melting.*

"Once classes start again, would you like to form a study group?"

"Who else would be in the group?"

"I guess it would be more like a study couple. It would be just me and you. Unless you think one of those other weasels in our class would want to join us."

Grace giggled. "Weasel is a strong word to use to describe them."

"No, no." Xavier chuckled. "It's accurate." He glanced at her empty coffee cup. "You done? You ready to go?"

"I probably should get home. I still have to cook dinner."

"What? Good looking, and you can cook too? Girl, Maurice better watch out. Come on. I'll walk you to your car."

Grace could not stop smiling as they walked back across the parking lot. Xavier was easy to talk to and even easier on the eyes. "Thanks for the coffee and bear claw. I enjoyed it."

"Good, me too." He opened her car door for her.

"Why do you always knock twice on the car door after I get in?"

Xavier displayed his brilliant white teeth. "That's the signal to let you know the coast is clear. I know you didn't grow up in the hood. But that's what we do." Grace got into the car, and Xavier leaned down with his face close to hers. "You think about the study group and let me know. Okay? Drive safely and enjoy your Easter."

Xavier closed the car door, and Grace started the car. He knocked twice on the outside of the door, and she gave a little wave. As she drove, the words Xavier had said tumbled around her brain. *Is Maurice neglecting me? Should I be concerned?*

Upon entering the studio, she stopped to admire Marie's finished portrait on the easel. Heading upstairs for a shower, the sound of running water greeted her. Shedding her clothes, she entered the bathroom as Maurice turned off the shower water. His naked form gave her body a case of tingles with a surge of heat. Upon seeing her, Maurice restarted the water, holding out his hand for her to join him in the shower. Under the soothing spray, his kisses traced her neck and shoulders. Grace melted like butter on a hot piece of toast.

"Did you enjoy your workout?" He asked as he soaped her arms, breasts, and stomach with a washcloth.

Grace giggled. "Not as much as I'm enjoying this." He spun her around, hands gliding over her soapy skin, electrifying her senses.

"Good." He handed her the cloth. "You finish while I give myself a quick shave."

She reached up, feeling the stubble on his chin. "Good idea. I'll meet you in bed?"

A grin spread across his face. "In five minutes."

She watched him take his electric shaver from under the sink and start working on his facial hair. *Xavier has no idea what he is talking about. Maurice is not neglecting me. I love him.* She quickly finished washing and stepped out of the shower.

Maurice gazed at her through the reflection of the mirror. "Please, do not wear that wet towel to bed." Grace rolled her eyes and went into the bedroom to dry herself off. Dropping the towel on the floor at the foot of the bed, she hopped into bed, snuggling under the covers.

When Maurice entered, his evident arousal couldn't be ignored. She shifted her gaze from his desire to his eyes. "Did you eat?"

"Nope, but I'm ready to right now. I'm starving." He pulled back the covers to expose her nakedness. "I'm going to start with this honeypot." His hand slipped between her legs, his touch a seductive massage. "Open up. You're not hiding something in there, are you?" He widened her legs and put his mouth where his hand had been.

Her fingers went right into his hair. "Let me know if you find anything." A minute later, she was moaning. "You found it. Oh my god, you found it."

After making love, Maurice cradled Grace in his arms. "What's for dinner?"

"The Chinese food you never ate last night. I saw the portrait. Marie is going to love it."

"You think? I could have done a better job on the swamp. It's a bit murky."

Grace giggled. "Swamps are murky. The portrait is magnificent. Please, don't try to fix it."

Maurice chuckled. "Okay, I won't. But if she does not love it, I will blame you." Getting out of bed, he put his robe on. "Will you join me for some Chinese, please?" He tossed her robe onto the bed. They headed to the kitchen, warming up the food and uncorking a bottle of Chardonnay.

"I'm going to try to talk to Sophie tomorrow. I will offer her the Porsche. Marie said she had her eye on it. Hopefully, it will help ease her anger toward me, and we can reach a peace agreement."

"And if she doesn't want peace, then what?"

"Then we will leave for New York. I will not put you in danger."

A wave of relief washed over her. *Thank God he's finally come to his senses.* "Did you know Sunday is Easter?"

He chuckled. "No. I don't even know what day today is."

"I think we should go to church on Easter. Where did you go to church when you lived here before?"

"You don't want to go there. It's a catholic church."

"I don't mind going to a catholic church. They have elaborate holiday services. All the incense waving around and the priests speaking in Latin. I used to enjoy attending a catholic church on Christmas Eve when I was younger. I bet Easter is just as nice."

Maurice didn't say anything as he continued to eat his chicken and snow peas. Two forkfuls later, he said, "As you wish. I will take you to St. Leo's for Easter. But I'm warning you, the church will be packed."

"Churches are always packed on Easter, as they should be. If people never go to church any other time of the year, they go on Christmas and Easter." She sipped her wine. "Some prayer might help right now. Maybe you should talk to Sophie after Easter once you've discussed it with God."

"Believe me, I have prayed about Sophie. There's no need to wait. Either she will cooperate, or she won't."

Chapter 20

Maurice woke up early Friday morning but did not want to get out of bed. *I have to talk to Sophie today. I don't want to. What am I going to say? And I must call Claude. I'm sure he heard about the fire and is wondering what is happening.* His gaze shifted to Grace, sleeping peacefully beside him. *I must reason with Sophie. I don't want to leave New Orleans, but I must keep Grace safe.* He closed his eyes and tried to go back to sleep, but his mind kept racing. *I don't even know how to approach her. Should I continue the charade that I like her? Will Sophie ever stop pretending with me? I hope she will tell me what it is she wants.*

Throwing off the covers, he went to shower. There was no point in putting off the confrontation any longer. After dressing meticulously in a black suit paired with a crisp white shirt and black loafers, he stood before the bathroom mirror. Applying gel to his hair and combing it back, he nodded approval to himself. *Looking more like Philippe may help me gain some sway with her. I'm willing to try anything at this point.*

With a sense of unease churning in his stomach, he went to the kitchen to brew the coffee. Although it was barely eight in the morning, he grabbed the phone and dialed. "Claude, we need to talk."

"What's going on, man?" Claude's voice was groggy. "I heard about the fire. That totally messed up our plans. What are we going to do?"

"For now, the arts center project is on hold. I've got some other family stuff going on, and I may need to leave New Orleans soon."

"What? You can't leave now." Claude sighed. "Why don't you come over later, and we can talk about it? I'm still in bed, man."

"I'm sorry for waking you. I'll call you later and stop by."

Glancing at the clock, it was too early to go to Sophie's. With a freshly brewed cup of coffee, he went into the studio. Removing the drapes from the covered easels, he surveyed the horoscope series. The painting of Leo and Libra remained incomplete.

The last painting will be Capricorn and Cancer. How am I going to unite a crab with a goat in a loving manner? Retrieving his camera, he photographed the four finished paintings. *Virgo and Scorpio, Sagittarius and Aquarius, Taurus and Pisces, and Gemini and Aries. I will have posters printed of these first and see how interested the public is. Spring festivals will be starting soon, and I'm not ready to participate in any of them. I could at least sell some posters.*

He also took photos of Marie's portrait. *It captures her personality. I hope she likes it. Thank God she is in my corner.* Returning to the kitchen, he picked up the keys to the Porsche. *If I have to give it to Sophie, I may as well enjoy one last ride in it.* He drove to the camera shop in Central City. After turning his roll of film in for development, he bought a few new rolls of film and headed to Jackson Square.

People were already filling the park as Maurice strolled up the walkway to the statue of Andrew Jackson on his horse. Merchants sold their wares from small tables with umbrellas scattered around the plaza. T-shirts, purses, hats, and posters of various famous paintings were among the offerings. A few people were selling their original art, but nothing was exquisite. Nothing like his paintings. Pulling out his camera, he captured the beauty of pink blossoms before sitting on a bench to observe the crowd. *I could do well out here, selling posters. I could start by printing one hundred posters and see how they sell.*

Returning to the area where predominately artists hawked their wares, he noted the prices they were charging. Walking back to the car, a plan took shape in his mind.

Arriving home, Grace was at the kitchen table in her robe, eating cereal. "Bonjour, mon cheri."

"Where did you go so early this morning?"

"The photo shop to drop off some film and to Jackson Square for some pictures." He held up the camera case for her to see. "I'm going to sell some posters of my horoscope series there this spring. The park is already buzzing with activity today."

"It's Good Friday. There are a lot of people who have the day off today."

"I forgot Sunday is Easter." His expression turned serious. "I'm going to see Sophie now. If she takes the Porsche, I will call you to pick me up. Okay?"

"No problem," Grace said, getting up from the table. She kissed him. "Good luck. I hope you make peace with your sister."

Making his way to the studio, he dropped off his camera and then headed for the Porsche. As he drove, his mind was engaged in practicing what to say. *Sophie, let's be honest with one another. We don't like each other, and it's okay. All I want is to live in peace with my wife. I will give you anything you want. Please, tell me what will make you happy.* He glanced at his reflection in the rearview mirror. *She's not going to go for that speech. What should I say?* He concentrated on the road for a few moments. *Sophie, we are family. We must try to get along for the family's sake. Ugh, no.* As he turned into the bar's parking lot, he settled on a new angle. *It would make Philippe happy if we could find a way to get along. I'll start with that.*

The restaurant was empty when he came in. Nick was setting up glasses at the bar. "Hi, is Sophie here?"

"No. She's gone away for the Easter holiday. Won't be back until Tuesday."

Maurice thanked Nick and returned to the car. *Merde. Now I have to think about Sophie for four more days.* Starting the engine, he steered toward Claude's apartment. He stopped at a bakery and bought beignets before parking on Claude's street. Claude answered the door in a casual gray sweatsuit.

"What the hell is going on? Why are you leaving New Orleans? Are you coming back?"

Maurice handed Claude the bag of beignets. "Please tell me you have coffee to go with these."

"I got instant, man." He followed Claude to his small kitchen and sat at the round wooden table tucked in the corner. The kettle whistled, and Claude poured two cups of coffee and placed the beignets on a plate.

"The buildings cannot be salvaged, but Philippe said he would build a new one," Maurice said. "I have no idea how long it will take."

Claude munched on a beignet. "We could scout out another location. Plenty of spots in the city need revitalization. Our center doesn't have to be on Julia Street."

"True." Maurice sipped his coffee. "But I've got a personal matter to handle. I may have to move back to New York. For good."

Claude's eyes widened. "Oh, come on, man. This was your idea. You can't leave now." He took another bite and asked, "Is it something I might help you with?"

Maurice shook his head. "No." Giving Claude a weak smile, he continued. "You can do this without me. I have the name of an attorney who will work with you to set up the nonprofit."

"Moe, I know how much this means to you. Let's set up another meeting to get firm commitments from the other artists and work on moving forward. You already have the attorney contact. Please call him and let us know what we need to do to get the ball rolling. If you cannot stay, we'll go on without you. Deal?"

"I will call him right now." Fishing the business card from his pocket, he dialed using Claude's kitchen wall phone.

Blaze answered after one ring. "I was hoping to hear from you today. Philippe is eager for me to meet with you. What are you doing now? Can you come by my office?"

Maurice told him he was on his way. He looked at Claude. "Want to come with me and meet the lawyer?"

"No way, man." Claude finished a donut, shaking his head. "Lawyers give me the creeps." He shuffled alongside Maurice to the car. "Damn, man," he said, eyeing the Porsche. "This is you?"

"It was a gift to me, and I'm about to give it away."

"Who's the lucky winner?"

"My sister. I hope." Maurice slid into the driver's seat. "I'll call you later."

Blaze's office was not far from Claude's place in the French Quarter. It was elegantly decorated in rich dark woods atop beige carpeting. Blaze, a stout, middle-aged Creole man with a balding head,

217

was decked out in a beige seersucker suit. Maurice sat in one of the cushioned wing chairs facing Blaze's enormous mahogany desk.

"Your father is very excited about creating an arts center," Blaze said, shuffling a stack of papers on his desk. "I must say, seeing you dressed like this, the resemblance between you two is truly remarkable." He stopped and folded his hands atop the desk. "Do you have a name for the nonprofit?"

"The New Orleans Cultural Arts Foundation. Currently, there are eight artists in the group. Philippe is not going to be a member of the foundation. He is only donating some property."

"Oh," Blaze said. "Does he know that? I got the distinct impression he plans to play a larger role."

Maurice leaned forward, glaring at Blaze. "He is not."

"All right." Blaze assembled a packet of papers into a folder. "Take these forms and fill in as much information as possible with the other participants. They do require the disclosure of some personal information. Will you be the chairman of the foundation?"

"Probably not. I need to meet with the others and decide with them." Maurice picked up the packet from the edge of the desk.

Blaze reclined in his leather chair. "Well, do you at least have a business plan?"

Maurice's eyes widened. "No. I didn't know I needed one."

"You do." Blaze got up from his seat and leaned against the edge of his desk in front of Maurice. "I suggest hiring a professional to help you compile a thorough business plan, including your funding sources and expected operating expenses."

"My wife is an accountant," Maurice replied. "She may be able to help me create a plan."

"An accountant is a good place to start," Blaze said. "So, I understand you are living in your mother's house. Are you enjoying being back here in New Orleans? I still miss your mother. She was always such a delight to be around. So dazzling."

"Yes, I miss her as well." Maurice stood up to leave, extending his hand. "Merci beaucoup, Monsieur Blaze."

"Any big plans for all the money you will inherit?" Blaze asked, shaking his hand.

"Unfortunately, the stock market crash has taken quite a bit of my fortune," Maurice answered. "Hopefully, I will recover in time."

"Believe me, your future looks very bright. In time, you'll have more money than you will know what to do with." Blaze winked at him. "I'm off for the Easter holiday. Let me know when you've got a business plan, and we'll complete the paperwork."

Maurice walked back to his car carrying the packet. *What the hell is Blaze talking about? What's he got? A crystal ball? How does he know how much money I'll have in the future?*

At home, he found Grace in the kitchen stirring batter in a bowl at the counter.

"Hi. I decided to bake a cake."

"You're not putting any plastic babies in there, I hope." Maurice kissed her cheek. "Sophie is away for the Easter weekend. I won't be able to talk to her until Tuesday." He laid the packet from Blaze on the counter. "I'm going to need your help with this paperwork."

"What's it for?"

"To set up the nonprofit, I need a business plan."

"Oh." Grace poured the batter into two round cake pans and put them into the oven. She grabbed a bottle of apple juice from the refrigerator and poured herself a glass. "Why are you working on it? If we're going to New York, shouldn't Claude or one of the other artists be doing it?"

"New York is not definite yet," he said. "May I have some juice too?"

She poured another glass and joined him at the kitchen table. "You believe Sophie is going to make peace with you?"

He cocked his head as he gazed at her. "I'm hopeful."

Grace chuckled. "I'm not."

"The weather is beautiful outside. It's supposed to be nice again tomorrow. We should plan a day trip." Maurice didn't want to discuss his sister any further. "There's an intriguing new exhibit at a museum in Baton Rouge featured in one of my art magazines. It showcases paintings and sculptures inspired by the galaxies. It could be a good fit for my horoscope series. Perhaps I could speak to the curator and get in on it."

"I would love to go to Baton Rouge. It's a date." She finished her juice and went to the refrigerator, taking out ground beef and onions. "I'm going to make a meatloaf for dinner. Unless you prefer hamburgers."

"Meatloaf is fine. I'm going to change to work in my studio." After putting on comfortable jeans and a t-shirt, he called Claude to brief him about the meeting with Blaze. "We can set up a group meeting for Wednesday night. Creating a business plan is going to be a lot of work. We may need to hire someone to help us. Someone will have to be in charge."

"We should wait until you've decided whether you're staying. If you stay, you should be the chairman," Claude said.

"Raymond has a big ego and thinks he knows everything," Maurice replied. "Perhaps he'll be willing to take charge. Anyway, I'll make my decision soon."

"Whatever you're going through," Claude said, "I hope you work it out and stay."

On Saturday morning, the sun kissed the sky as Maurice lowered the top of the Porsche. He was about to check if Grace was ready to leave for Baton Rouge when a blue Buick pulled into the driveway, stopping abruptly and blocking him in. A brown-skinned woman with shoulder-length black hair and thick hips jumped out of the driver's seat. "Maurice Chenault. I need to talk to you."

"Lindsay?" Maurice's body stiffened as his eyes grew wide. "What are you doing here?"

Lindsay tugged on the bottom edges of her hip-hugging denim mini skirt and strode around to the passenger side of the Buick. Opening the door, she lifted a small boy out of the car and set him on his feet. "I decided you should meet your son."

Grace stepped out from the studio door as Lindsay walked the denim-clad toddler up to Maurice, standing by the Porsche. He looked down at the boy with thick black hair. "Excuse me? What?"

"I heard you were back in town," Lindsay said. "Silly me, thinking you'd come to see me. Or at least call. Since you didn't, I figured I'd pay you a visit."

Grace stood by Maurice's side as he draped his arm around her shoulder. "This is my wife. Grace, this is Lindsay. An old friend."

Lindsay's eyes widened as the little boy hugged her thigh. "Grace? The girl who dumped you? How's that?"

Grace smirked. "I took him back."

"Ha," Lindsay said, shaking her head. "That man you married must have been a real jerk if you left him to go back to this snake."

Maurice's face twisted up. "Snake?"

"Yes, snake." Lindsay pointed a finger at Maurice's nose. "That's what I call a man who slithers out of town without a word to his woman."

"Whoa, let's be clear. We had some fun, but you and I were never exclusive."

"Maybe you weren't, but I was. And now you're going to help me raise our son, Dante."

Maurice threw his hands up, stepping closer to Lindsay. "Why do you keep calling him my son?"

"Because we had sex, and I got pregnant."

"That was years ago."

"Yup." Lindsay's head continued to bob. "And your son is about to turn three."

Maurice raised his voice. "He is not my son."

Grace stepped between the two of them. "There is a simple way to resolve this. Maurice will take a paternity test." She turned to Lindsay. "Will you agree to that?"

"Take a good look at this boy," Lindsay focused on Maurice. "He looks just like you. There's no doubt in my mind. He's yours."

"Then a paternity test won't hurt, will it?" Grace asked, trying to get her attention.

Lindsay let out an exasperated sigh. "Fine. I know someone who works at Tulane Hospital, so it'll be simple to arrange." Turning back to Maurice, she continued. "I'll call you with the appointment information, and you better show up." She scooped up the boy, placing him on her hip, before heading back to her car. "And when that test proves you're the daddy, boy, you are going to pay. You are living in this big house, driving these fancy cars. Oh yeah. You are going to pay." After putting the boy back in the passenger seat, Lindsay eyed Grace before getting behind the wheel. "I'll be calling y'all." Jumping into the driver's seat, Lindsay revved the Buick's engine before backing out of the driveway toward the street.

Grace strode back into the studio with Maurice on her heels. "When I asked you about Lindsay, you said she wouldn't be a problem."

For a moment, Maurice couldn't speak. His mouth fell open as he shook his head. Grace put her hands on her hips, waiting for an answer. "Apparently, your relationship with her was more serious than you said."

Maurice looked at his feet. "No, no, it wasn't. He is not my child."

"You do realize that nothing is one hundred percent effective," Grace said. "If you slept with her, that could be your son. Although, to me, he doesn't look like you."

Maurice turned to gaze out the window. "I can't believe this is happening. Why would she wait so long to tell me? I bet Sophie put her up to this."

"My guess is Lindsay couldn't find you. I assume you left her to return to New York when you found out I was in the hospital?"

"I did. But Lindsay knows Claude is my close friend. If she wanted to find me, all she had to do was ask him. Our relationship was never serious as she is making it out to be. I know I wasn't the only one Lindsay was messing around with."

"How do you know?" Grace asked.

"Word gets around." Maurice started pacing. "Men talk."

Smirking, Grace replied. "Men lie about their conquests all the time."

Waving his hands in the air, Maurice stopped closer to her. "She is lying. Lindsay knows I am not that boy's father. Sophie must be paying her to say these lies." Not knowing what else to say, he walked to the window to gaze at the lawn. After moments of silence, he looked back at Grace. "Thank you for suggesting the test. I'm surprised you aren't angry with me."

"How can I be angry?" Her hand went to her forehead. "I married Trevor and almost had a baby with him. I can't blame you for being with her or anyone else. If he is your son, we will have to figure out a way to take care of him."

Stepping closer, Maurice took her hands. "I'm glad you said 'we.' I don't want this or anything else to come between us. I love you."

Grace gently kissed his lips. "I love you too. We'll work it out together. Besides, I agree with you. He's not your son. After all, I have sex with you all the time, and you've not gotten me pregnant yet." She walked to the hallway. "I don't feel like going anywhere now."

Maurice took the drape off of one of his works in progress as she left the room. *A perfectly good day ruined. That boy is not my son.*

The early morning sun streamed through the blinds, casting a warm glow on Easter Sunday. Maurice awoke to water running in the shower. He briefly lifted his head and then fell back on the pillow. *I promised to take her to church today, but I am not looking forward to it. It will be hot and crowded as well as long and boring.* After joining Grace in the shower, they both dressed. He admired Grace's blue floral sundress as they descended the stairs. They had a quick breakfast of coffee and toast before driving to St. Leo the Great Parish church.

Glancing up at the ornate white moldings adorning the large gray brick church, Maurice cringed. The last time he was here was for his mother's funeral. A horrible day. They arrived before all the pews were taken and sat in the middle of the church.

The congregation was a sea of ornate dresses and extravagant hats worn by the women, while most of the men donned dark suits. Before the service even commenced, hand fans were in motion, trying to beat back the heat. Grace marveled at the priest, waving the incense holder, spreading the sweet, musky scent as he marched to the altar. Maurice begrudged the aerobic workout between sitting, kneeling, and standing. Eventually, he stayed on his knees, ignoring the priest's instructions. Folding his hands, he prayed silently. *God, I know I haven't talked to you in person in a while, but I know you are everywhere, and I know you see me. I don't ask you for much, but I need your help now. Please let the paternity test prove that I am not the father of Lindsay's baby. Please, God, help Sophie to see reason and allow us to stay here in New Orleans. Please show me Philippe's secret so I can get rid of him too. I don't want to move back to New York. I want to stay here and live in my mother's house. And please, please let Grace get pregnant soon and bless us with a healthy baby. Please bless my upcoming poster project too. I don't have any exhibits coming up, and I need to make some money. I promise to donate some of my money to the church if you help me. In Jesus' name, amen.* He made the sign of the cross over his chest before getting off his knees and sitting down.

Grace smiled. "Feels good, right?"

"Oui." *Smoking a joint right now would help me feel even better.*

After church, they drove to Jackson Square and toured all the merchant tables while Maurice explained his plan to sell posters there to Grace, his words filled with energy and enthusiasm.

Chapter 21

The lamb came out perfectly medium rare, and Grace was very proud of the Easter meal she prepared. Maurice gave his full approval, telling her everything was delicious. The cake she had baked was already half eaten, but there was still enough for them to enjoy dessert.

"Thank you for going to church with me today. It meant a lot to me."

Smiling, Maurice replied, "I will do anything you ask to keep you happy."

"Not anything," Grace said. "You know, I don't feel safe here."

"God assured me, He's taking care of everything. We'll be fine."

After Maurice helped Grace clean up the kitchen, she asked, "Are you ready to watch our movie?"

Maurice chuckled. "The lengths I will go to keep you happy. Yes, I'm ready."

On the way home from Jackson Square, Grace spotted a Video Works store and pressured Maurice to stop. "Please, we can pick out something we will both enjoy watching and have a cozy movie night at home. Make our own popcorn. It'll be fun."

Maurice frowned at her. "We shouldn't even have a television or a VCR. How long are you going to keep it?"

"If we try it out tonight and you still absolutely hate it, we will donate it to the community center. I promise." Grace poked her lip out. "Please? It will help keep our minds off of Lindsay and the impending test."

After a playful debate over love stories versus silly comedies, Grace got him to agree on *Star Trek IV: The Voyage Home*. "Even you

227

know about Kirk and Spock." Grace formed the Vulcan sign with her fingers. "Live long and prosper." Maurice laughed, and they rented the video and bought two packets of microwave popcorn.

"You make the popcorn while I go set up the movie," Grace said as she headed for the great room. Excited that Maurice agreed to watch a movie with her, igniting hope he would enjoy the experience and want to do it again. *I like having a TV. I didn't realize how much I missed it. But it's not the end of the world if we don't keep it. I kind of agree with him about the brainwashing. He just takes it too far, as is his way.*

The room was dim after closing the blinds on the windows. Grace cued up the movie on the VCR and got comfortable on the sofa. The remote was in her hand, ready to press play. *It should take three minutes to make popcorn. What is he doing?*

Ten minutes later, Maurice came carrying the bowl of popcorn. "I'll be right back." After placing the popcorn bowl on the table, he left and returned with two glasses of iced tea. He looked at Grace. "What? I had to melt extra butter to put on the popcorn. It was painted yellow, but it tasted dry. And we didn't have any tea left, so I had to make more. Go ahead, start your precious movie."

They enjoyed the voyage back in time with the crew of the USS Enterprise to save the world along with humpback whales. Grace ran her hand over Maurice's hair and kissed him on the cheek. "Did you enjoy the movie?"

"I did." He turned to give her a passionate kiss. "Let's make our own movie in the guest suite."

"Let's go upstairs so we don't have to get up again."

"I like our old bed. The king bed is too large, and you always manage to squirm away from me."

"That is not true." Grace tugged his arm. "We are going upstairs to our room." As they got ready for bed, she asked, "Can we do it again?"

"We haven't done it the first time yet."

Giggling, she threw a pillow at him. "Not that. I mean, watch a movie. Can we keep the TV and VCR?"

"For now," he said, settling into bed. "Only for movies, mind you. Yves and Babeth are coming back tomorrow. She will want us to come for dinner to see all the baby pictures."

"Ooh, I can't wait to see little Jackson." Grace snuggled under Maurice's arm. "Who do you think he's going to look like? Anne or Jacque."

Maurice laughed. "I don't know, and I'm not trying to guess. We will see him tomorrow."

Babeth called a little after noon the next day, excited to share the details of their trip and baby pictures. "You must come to dinner. Marva is preparing shrimp creole and dirty rice. The food in New York was terrible." Babeth laughed. "Be here by seven."

Grace found Maurice in the studio, engrossed in painting a fierce lion, and shared their dinner plans.

"C'est bon," he said without turning around. "I should be done with this painting by then."

"I'm going to take the video back to the store."

"Do not rent another one. You will pick something sad and mushy."

"No, I won't." Grace retrieved the videotape from the VCR. She passed by Maurice on her way out. "Be back soon. I love you."

Not sure how to get back to the Video Works, she followed the signage, giving directions to Jackson Square. Spotting the store along the way, she pulled into the parking lot. Walking up and down the aisles, she couldn't decide what movie to rent next, not wanting to hear Maurice complain. While holding *Aliens* in one hand and *The Princess Bride* in the other, someone tapped her on the shoulder. She turned to see Xavier standing there with his beautiful white smile, wearing jeans and a green Tulane t-shirt.

"This is getting kind of eerie," he said. "I keep running into you in all my hangout spots. Do you think it's fate? Destiny?"

"I don't know," Grace replied. "But you're right. It is getting a bit eerie. How are you?"

"Enjoying the days off from school, but I'm still working with my sister. I rented a movie yesterday and figured I'd pick up another one today."

"Me too. We watched the Star Trek movie."

His eyes went to the movies in her hands. "You should rent *The Princess Bride*. It's terrific. Way better than *Aliens*. You know, the sequels are never as good as the first one."

With a laugh, Grace placed the horror movie back on the shelf. "I'll take your advice. But if my husband hates it, I will kill you the next time I see you. He will never trust me to choose another movie again."

Xavier chuckled. "It's nice you have someone to watch movies with. I wish I did."

"I'm sure you have plenty of lady friends to choose from," Grace said with a skeptical look. "Don't think I feel sorry for you because I don't."

Xavier gazed into her eyes. "Guess he was too busy painting to come with you?"

Grace looked away. *He is starting to get me warmed up.*

"Your husband is a real busy guy." Picking up a movie from the shelf, he read the description on the back. "Did you think about our study group?"

"No, I haven't. I don't see why we can't share information. It doesn't need to be formal. After all, it is just the two of us." She smiled at him. "Enjoy your movie. I'll see you next week."

Sitting in the car, Grace contemplated their meeting. *This is getting very weird how I keep running into Xavier. I can't believe it's all a coincidence. Is he working with the FBI? Is he following me? Maybe I should tell Maurice about him.*

Maurice was still painting when she came home. He stopped to view the videotape in her hand. "That was the best movie you could find?"

"I have it on good authority that it's a good movie."

Maurice chuckled as he returned to work. "Whose authority?"

"I ran into one of my classmates at the store. His name is Xavier."

Maurice stopped painting and put his brush down. "Xavier? Why have I not heard his name before?" After wiping his hands on a cloth, he took the movie from her hands and flipped it around in his own, gazing at the video cover.

"Because it wasn't important. Xavier sits next to me in class, and I helped him with a few questions. That's all." She glared at him. "Kind of like you and Tara. And you and Lindsay. Not worth mentioning." Taking the movie from his hands, she asked, "Did Lindsay call?"

Maurice shook his head, and she walked to the great room, placing the tape near the VCR.

Unexpectedly, Maurice stood behind her when she turned. "Do you think I'm withholding information from you again? Is that why you're keeping things from me?"

"I am not keeping anything from you. I am an open book. You know everything about me. You, on the other hand, have all kinds of secrets."

"What secrets, Grace?"

"I don't know because you don't tell me everything." Stalking out of the great room, she went to the kitchen, expecting Maurice to follow her, but he didn't. *I wasn't supposed to start an argument. I was supposed to tell him Xavier might not be who I think he is.* She took out the Chardonnay to pour herself a glass. Carrying her glass to the great room, she flipped on the television.

When the six o'clock news came on, she turned the TV off and stuck her head into the studio. "We need to get ready for dinner with Babeth."

Maurice came into the bedroom as she came out of the bathroom. "I am not keeping secrets."

"Forget I said it. I don't know why I said it. I guess I'm still in shock over the Lindsay thing." She kissed him before slipping on the black dress with the white roses she'd worn to brunch.

"You are getting awfully fancy for dinner at Babeth's house," Maurice said as he pulled on his baggy jeans.

"Babeth always has a pretty dress on every time I see her. Today, I want to wear one too."

"Okay." Maurice laughed. "You look beautiful. I'll proudly walk down the street with you on my arm." He kissed her nose. "I'll be ready in ten minutes."

Heading downstairs to the kitchen, a wave of nausea swept over Grace. Holding on to the counter, she steadied herself. *What is going on?* Drinking a glass of water helped a bit, along with sitting and a few deep breaths. *I hope I'm not coming down with something.* After a few minutes, the nausea ebbed away. By the time Maurice joined her, the dizziness also subsided as they embarked on their walk to Prytania Street.

Babeth and Yves had at least one hundred photographs of Jackson. After enjoying Marva's delicious dinner, they sat in the living room, looking at every single one. Grace's heart swelled as she studied the pictures, captivated by Jackson's endearing tiny features and his head full of black hair.

"He is absolutely adorable," Babeth said. "I didn't want to put him down. Such a good baby. He hardly ever cries."

"Is Anne breastfeeding?" Grace asked while gazing at Maurice. He was strangely quiet, absorbed in the photos.

"Yes, and she said Jackson took right to it." Babeth leaned in closer to Grace. "You know, some babies don't take to the teat readily. Jacque was like that. Very fussy." She shook her head before smiling at another photograph of her grandson.

The pictures got Grace longing for her own baby. "I think he looks like Anne."

"Oh no," Babeth said. "Jacque looked just like this when he was a baby. Jackson is going to look just like his papa."

"I agree with Babeth," Maurice said. "He definitely looks like Jacque."

"Grace," Yves said, "Have you thought about coming to work at the bank? I lost another good person today. We could use someone with your experience."

"I'm pretty busy with school right now. Maybe in the summer, I could start working." Yves droned on about the various positions open at the bank that she may be interested in as she nodded her head. Grace had no intention of working with Yves. Looking into his dull brown eyes through the round eyeglasses, a flash suddenly went off in her brain. She turned to Maurice. "I'm getting tired, babe. Are you ready to go home?"

They thanked Yves and Babeth for a lovely evening and started down the walkway.

"I figured it out," Grace said. "The laundry man. They call Yves that because he's laundering Philippe's dirty money. Cooking the books on Philippe's legal businesses to make the criminal money disappear."

Maurice stopped, his eyes growing wide. "Oh, my god. That must be it. It would explain why they have so much to talk about. Yves is up to his eyeballs in Philippe's business." Taking Grace's arm, they started walking again. "We need to call Jacque when we get home."

"Please don't tell him. It won't do any good. There's nothing Jacque can do about it, and it will only cause him to worry." Grace glanced at Maurice. "Let him enjoy his time with his son."

"You're right. I won't call him."

Settling into bed later, Maurice sighed. "Tomorrow is Tuesday. Sophie will be back."

"Good luck with that. I'll be shopping with Tara. She is picking me up at eleven."

Maurice raised an eyebrow. "Did I know about those plans?

"Yes, you did. Maybe you don't remember me telling you, but I did."

He gently tugged on her nightgown to pull her nearer. "I think I do remember." He kissed her gently. "I know you're not keeping secrets from me."

Grace bit her lip. "There is something I want to say." She gazed into his eyes. "About Xavier. I think he may be working with the FBI."

Maurice wrinkled his nose. "Why? What has he done?"

"He keeps showing up whenever I'm alone. The day I went to the gym, he was there. And again today, at the video store."

"Why haven't you told me this before? Is he making passes at you?"

"Not really. Xavier's very nice to me, and he always asks about you. He says he wants to meet you." She sighed. "I don't quite know what to make of it. It can't be a coincidence he keeps popping up."

"Well," Maurice replied, "I'm glad you're talking about me." He kissed her, his tone lightening. "I don't think it's anything to worry about. If he is an agent, you're not doing anything illegal. He'll keep you safe." He pulled her on top of himself. "Now, if he gets fresh with you or touches you, you better tell me." Covering her mouth with his own, his tongue danced around hers. "I will have to add his name to my hit list."

"It's getting to be a very long list." She started massaging his body. "Oops. I think I found your secret weapon."

"Be careful. It's loaded."

In the middle of the night, Grace awoke and couldn't fall asleep. The pictures of Anne's baby had her wondering again when her moment would arrive. Gazing at Maurice, soundly sleeping, her mind raced. *I hope there is nothing wrong with him. I want to have his baby. I'm probably being impatient, as he said. It's probably not happening because of all the stress.* Getting out of bed, she crept to the kitchen. After warming a small mug of milk in the microwave, she sat at the table, sipping her drink. *If Lindsay's boy is Maurice's son, then at least I'll know he can get me pregnant. But then, I'll never get him to leave New Orleans. He won't want to leave his son, and this nightmare with Sophie and Philippe will never end. I wish my mother was here. I miss her so much. All of my family. My dad was right. This move was a huge change, and I was not prepared for it.*

Finishing her milk, she returned to bed and finally fell asleep.

Chapter 22

With a steady hand, Maurice slowly outlined the lips of Queen Libra in black on his painting. Putting his brush down, he stepped back. *She is magnificent, perfect for King Leo. It is finished.* Wiping his hands on a cloth, he sat at the drawing table to stare at a blank sketch pad. *Now for the final painting. The crab and the goat. Cancer and Capricorn.* Going to the bookcase for his oversized wildlife photography book, he flipped through the pages and found a picture of a large white Billy goat. *The giant crab's claw could be gripping his beard. Very romantic. This will keep me busy until it's time to see Sophie.* Placing the open book on his desk, he began sketching.

Grace came up behind him, offering a steaming mug of coffee. Stepping closer to the easel, she examined the painting of Leo and Libra. "I know I said Taurus and Pisces was my favorite, but this one is truly amazing." Placing her arms around his neck with a big smile, she planted a passionate kiss on his lips. "You are a great artist. I love it."

"Merci beaucoup," Maurice said. "Let's hope the last painting comes out as well." He pointed to the picture of the goat in his book. "He is going to meet a lady crab."

"How will we know it's a lady?"

Maurice chuckled. "I haven't figured that part out yet. Maybe she'll wear a hat?"

Grace giggled. "You are so silly. I'm glad you're in a good mood. I thought you'd be miserable thinking about your sister and the lovely conversation you're about to have."

"I'm trying not to think about it at all. I got tired of thinking about it two days ago." He shook his head. "Either she will stop or she won't. And if she doesn't, we will leave."

Grace turned to leave the studio. "I'm going to get dressed. Have fun with your goat."

After studying the photo for a few minutes, Maurice began sketching. Lost in time, it surprised him when Grace came to say goodbye. She studied his sketchpad. "Nice goat. I'm going out front to wait for Tara. Shouldn't you be getting ready to leave? It's almost eleven. You want to catch Sophie before the lunch crowd comes to her place."

Glancing at the wall clock, Maurice replied, "You're right." He kissed her as she headed out the door. "Have a good time with Tara." Putting down his pencil, he went to the kitchen to get the Porsche keys. Looking down at his jeans, he contemplated changing into his black suit. *Screw it. It will not make a difference to her what I am wearing.*

The phone rang as he was about to walk out to the car. "Bonjour, cousin."

"Jacque, I'm on my way out. I'll call you later," Maurice said.

"I expected to hear from you last night after you saw the pictures of my son." Jacque ignored Maurice's desire to end the conversation. "Is he not amazing? Adorable as hell, too."

Maurice sighed. "Yes, Jackson is a most incredible baby. I'm on my way to see my sister. I need to go."

"What is going on? You haven't kept me in the loop. Tell me now. Why are you meeting with Sophie?"

"She is the source of my problems, not Philippe." He updated his cousin on the Cocoa incident and the fire at Julia Street. "I know she is not my biggest fan, but it's getting dangerous. She's committing arson, and Philippe cannot control her. I need to stop her before she does anything else. She may try to burn my house down next. I cannot put Grace in danger."

"You should cooperate with the FBI and turn her in," Jacque said. "Her, Philippe, the whole lot of them."

Maurice snorted. "Including your father?"

"Excuse me?"

"It's true. Yves is deeply involved in Philippe's business. As Grace put it, he's in charge of money laundering, cooking the books."

"It cannot be. How do you know?"

"Marie told me his nickname is the laundry man. What other explanation could there be for that title? If I turn Philippe and Sophie in, everyone goes down with them. You know how many people are linked to his criminal enterprise. From judges to shop owners, lots of people will go down if I go to the FBI. I cannot do it."

Jacque fell silent before conceding. "Good luck with Sophie. Please call me and tell me what happens. Au revoir."

Driving to Sophie's bar, Maurice mentally rehearsed the opening statement he'd settled on two days ago. *Sophie, I know you don't particularly care for me, but I know it would make Philippe happy if we could find a way to get along. I have no quarrel with you. Please tell me, how can we coexist peacefully?* He repeated it several times to himself. Parking in the sports bar lot, he collected himself in the rearview mirror. *I've only got one shot at this. I have got to get her to tell me what she wants.* Taking a deep breath, he walked into the sports bar.

Sophie was laughing loudly behind the bar with Nick. Her long black hair fell across her shoulders in the bright orange dress as she slapped a laughing Nick on the arm. Her lively demeanor waned as her gaze locked onto Maurice, standing at the bar. "Hello, big brother. I wasn't expecting to see you today."

"Sophie," Maurice said, "May I speak with you? In private. It's a family matter."

Sophie's eyebrows went up. "A family matter? Sounds serious. Sure, let's go to my office." After whispering in Nick's ear, she emerged from behind the bar.

Maurice followed Sophie to the office and asked, "Did you enjoy your Easter holiday?"

Turning back, she gave him a big, toothy grin. "Yes, I did. I went to visit a friend in Baton Rouge. Had a great time." Upon entering the office, Sophie sat behind the desk while Maurice took a wing chair. "What's the family matter you want to discuss?"

Maurice went totally off-script. "I know you burned down the buildings on Julia Street. Why?"

Cocking her head, Sophie glared at him with cold green eyes. "Well, let's get right to it. I don't want you to have a cultural arts center." Placing her elbow on the desk, she cupped her chin in her hand. "That's why I burned it down. And I will burn down any other property Papa attempts to give you."

"Why? I am not trying to take anything from you. Philippe's business is yours. I don't want any part of it. All I want to do is live my life in peace. Have an arts center that will benefit the entire city. Philippe said he had no use for the property. Why would you be against it?"

Laughing loudly, Sophie leaned back in her chair. "You think I need you to tell me Papa's business is mine?" Sitting up, she slapped her hands down on the desk. "This is not about the business. You are stealing from me. You have been stealing from me all of your life, and you will not take one cent more."

Maurice shook his head. "I don't need your money. I have repeatedly told Philippe not to do anything for me or buy me anything." Taking the Porsche keys from his pants pocket, he laid them on the desk. "Marie said you wanted the car. It is yours. What else do you think I have stolen? I will give it to you."

Sophie stood up to lean toward Maurice. "You cannot repay all you have stolen from me. You and your bitch whore of a mother."

Maurice's eyes widened as his mouth dropped open. *She did not just say that about my mother. Why is she bringing my mother into this?*

"She stole my father from his family. My family. Me, Marie, and my mother." Strutting from behind the desk, Sophie paced around the office. "All the money Philippe gave her, which went to you. The grand house in the Garden District. Le Beau Riviere. Furniture, clothing, jewels, cars." Sophie stopped in front of Maurice, head bobbing. "Your private French boarding school education. Your college tuition. Your studio in Greenwich Village. You are going to pay me back for all of that?" Maurice leaned back as she put her face closer to his. "What about all the embarrassment and shame I endured being harassed by the other girls at school? When they called my father a nigger lover and a piece of trash. Called me trash and said my father didn't love me or my mother. You're going to pay me back for that?"

Maurice glared at Sophie's reddened face, resembling a mad dog with spittle on her lips. "I didn't have anything to do with that. What happened between my mother and Philippe is done. It's history." He softened his tone. "I'm sorry you have suffered. But I never intentionally took anything from you."

Sophie laughed loudly as she started pacing around again. "You think I don't know why you moved back to New Orleans? Oh yeah, I know all about you and your genius cousin, Jacque, losing all that money playing in the stock market. You came here because you needed more money. And you knew Philippe would give it to you."

"It's not true." Maurice shook his head. "I mean, I did lose money, but I came here to live in my mother's house and have a family. That is all."

"You are such a liar." Going back behind her desk, she sat and leaned back in her chair. "I don't understand why a nice woman like Grace would even give you the time of day. You are a whore, just like your mother." She leaned forward with her hands on the desk. "Did you enjoy screwing Lindsay and Tara after your mother died? It was very convenient that Tara and Guy had broken up for the millionth time as you mourned your mother."

Maurice looked down at his hands twisting between his knees, his heart pounding. *I am going to strangle her. She is completely insane. I cannot believe she is saying these things to me.* He glanced at her. "You think I'm a whore? Is that why you sent one to my house? I'll have you know I didn't touch Cocoa. Your plan backfired."

Sophie chuckled. "I heard you were ready to fuck her until Grace interrupted you. How did you get out of that one? She must really love you. I've sent a tempting cookie her way more than once, but Grace has not taken a bite. For some reason, she is loyal to you."

Maurice's head was shaking uncontrollably. "Leave Grace alone." He stood up to lean over the desk toward her. "If you do anything to her, I swear I will kill you."

Suddenly, Sophie pulled a handgun from under the desk and pointed it at his nose. "Don't get any stupid ideas. Sit down."

Slowly backing away, Maurice sat back down in his chair. *She is totally nuts. She is going to kill me right here, right now.* "Please, Sophie. Grace and I will leave New Orleans. I cannot pay you for your losses, but we don't have to be enemies. I will leave, and we can each live and let live, right?"

"I'm sorry, but that's no longer an option." Sophie waved the gun around in the air. "You should have never come back here. You had it right the first time when you refused to speak to Philippe and left for New York. It saddened him after you left, but he got over it."

Walking back around to stand in front of Maurice, she continued. "When Yves told him you were moving to New Orleans, Philippe lit up like the sun. He's never looked at me like that. Not once."

"I am sorry," Maurice mumbled.

"After he spent thousands renovating the house, buying a new Mercedes, he did something else." Sophie pointed the gun at Maurice's head. "Do you know what he did?"

"No. I have no idea what he did."

"He changed his will. All the money Marie and I should inherit now must be shared with you. Millions of dollars I worked for, not you."

"It is money I worked for, and only I will decide who gets it." Philippe stepped into the office and slammed the door behind him. "Put the gun down, Sophie."

Walking behind the desk, she opened a drawer and placed the handgun inside before closing it. "Hello, Papa. My big brother came to discuss family matters."

Staring down at Maurice, Philippe shouted. "Why are you here? I told you I would talk to her." Picking up the Porsche keys sitting on the desk, he handed them to Maurice. "Leave. Now."

Staggering out of his seat, Maurice went to the car. The keys jingled in his shaking hands as he sat behind the wheel. *She is completely unhinged. She was going to shoot me. I can't believe this is happening. She is full of rage and extremely dangerous. Grace and I need to leave immediately.* Taking a deep breath, he started the engine. He didn't want to go directly home. *How am I going to explain any of this to Grace? Sophie wants to kill me and moving to New York won't stop her.* Taking a detour onto Tchoupitoulas Street, the road running along the Mississippi, there were barely any cars. Maurice sped up as he passed the low warehouse buildings lining the riverbank, his heart racing. *I cannot believe her. I had no idea Philippe even had a will. How is it possible that I am the secret Philippe has been hiding? Why would he put me in his will? I don't want anything from him. Why would he tell Sophie and not me?*

The wind whipped around his hair as his mind exploded with a replay of Sophie pointing the handgun in his face. Suddenly, a wobbly work truck pulled out from a side street right in front of the Porsche. Maurice slammed on the brakes, but the car did not slow down. Honking the horn, he swerved around the truck. Fortunately, there were no oncoming cars. Repeatedly, he pressed the brake pedal, saying, "No, no, no," as the car continued to speed down the road. Shifting the car down to a lower gear, the Porsche bucked, squealed, and began to slow as he entered a more residential area.

A man stepped out of his house as Maurice sped by, yelling at him to slow down. A gray sedan was moving slower in front of him, and

Maurice attempted to downshift again as he approached it. The Porsche fishtailed, and the back end hit a parked car. Jerking the steering wheel back and forth, he straightened the car enough to pass the driver in front of him.

Suddenly, a red pickup truck headed directly toward him, and he swerved in the opposite direction to avoid a head-on collision. *God, please. You didn't let her shoot me in the bar. Please don't let me die now.* Downshifting to second gear, the Porsche fishtailed again, testing his driving skills. A young woman in billowing white stepped into the street, and Maurice pressed hard on the horn, attempting to avoid her. Pulling the steering wheel hard to the right caused the Porsche to spin and slam into the trunk of a giant magnolia tree.

Chapter 23

The first stop on Grace and Tara's shopping tour was the little boutique in Central City. Grace reminded Tara of the outfit she'd admired at their brunch. "Everything I own is sort of conservative. I'd like to see how I look in some bohemian chic."

"You will find it here," Tara said as they entered the shop. "They have an incredible range of styles."

A dark-skinned woman dressed in an African print dress greeted them. "Welcome, ladies. Can I help you find something today?"

"Just browsing for now," Tara replied.

Grace ran her hand along the rack of gauzy boho V-neck printed tops in shades of blue, green, and red. Nearby, another rack held elegant boho dresses. Selecting a blue-toned dress, Grace held it against her body and checked the mirror. "How do you like this one?"

Tara smiled. "I like. You should try it on." Today, Tara wore printed jeans with a white and blue peasant blouse that playfully exposed one shoulder. *Tara has such a cool sense of fashion, unlike me.* Grace gazed down at her plain jeans and Tulane Green Wave t-shirt. *Shopping with her can help me upgrade my style.*

Choosing a pair of casual purple printed baggy leg overalls, Grace disappeared into the fitting room to try them on, along with the dress. She and Tara agreed the overalls were way cuter than the dress.

Their next stop was the mall, closer to the French Quarter. They spent several hours going from shop to shop, selecting fashionista bargains while laughing and talking. *I really like Tara. I am having a great time shopping with her.*

"I don't know about you," Tara said, "but I'm about shopped out. How about we stop for a coffee or a bite to eat?"

"It's your town," Grace replied. "Where should we go?"

"There's a spot a block from here. We can sit outside and people-watch while we eat."

At Ruby's Café, a comfortable spot awaited them since the lunch crowd subsided, giving them room to relax. Iced tea and a delectable basket of fried shrimp and french fries were set on their table outside the glass pane window of the café. Pedestrians slowly strolled back and forth near their table as they shared laughs, making jokes about distinguished passersby.

"Lord," Tara said, glancing at a woman in a tight red mini dress, "Her dress is so short if she has to bend over for anything, we are going to see her coochee."

Grace shook her head, giggling. "Let's pray it doesn't happen. I don't want to see it." Peering down, three large shopping bags filled with dresses, shoes, fancy underwear, and her overalls were at her feet. *This was a great shopping day. I can't wait to model my new outfits for Maurice.*

"Look, Bliss, my brother's wife and ex-mistress having lunch together." A smiling Sophie in a bright orange dress, alongside the loud woman from the spa, saddled up next to their table. "Isn't this cute?"

Bliss laughed loudly in her hot pink sundress. "Adorable. How does he do it?"

"Hello, Sophie, Bliss," Tara said, glaring at them with her hazel eyes. "How're tricks?"

Sophie chuckled. "Business is good. Thanks for asking. So is this the first meeting of the I Love Maurice club? Or is it Whoops, I married a Male Ho?" Gazing at Tara, she asked, "How is Guy?"

"Guy is fine. What do you want?"

"I wanted to tell Grace what a great chat I had with her husband today." Sophie leaned down, placing her face near Grace's. "You should probably be home packing."

"What happened?" Grace asked. "You two didn't make peace?"

Sophie stood up, laughing. "We did reach an agreement." She turned to Tara. "Are you sharing the details of all the comfort you gave Maurice after his mother died with her? Grace is going to need to comfort him later when she sees him. I'm sure you can give her some expert tips after all the time you spent together." Sophie looked at Grace. "He was all warm and fuzzy by the time he left for New York."

"You are disgusting," Tara said. "If you're done spewing your bullshit, you can move along now."

"Next time you and Guy break up, tell him to give me a call," Bliss said with a big smile. "He's definitely worth a repeat." She tucked her arm into Sophie's elbow. "Come on, Cher." They strolled down the street.

Grace blushed as she watched Tara's face redden. "What she said. Is it true? Did you comfort Maurice when his mother died?"

"Not the way she is insinuating. It's true. Guy and I have a complicated relationship. We fight, we break up, but we always get back together." Tara sighed. "I did see Maurice during one of our breakups. But we did nothing but talk. I cried on his shoulder about Guy. And he cried on my shoulder about you. How he screwed up your relationship. Maurice was completely brokenhearted because you were marrying another man." Tara reached across the table to touch Grace's hand. "I swear to you on my children, I have never slept with Maurice. When I said he was my boyfriend in high school, not even then did we ever sleep together. He helped me with my painting, nothing more. Maurice has never been anything but a friend to me."

Pulling back her hand, Grace reached down to collect her shopping bags. "I should get home and talk to him about Sophie. Would you take me home now, please?"

They were both silent on the ride to Grace's house. As Tara pulled her yellow Volkswagen Bug up to the curb on Napoleon Avenue, she said, "I hope you're not going to let Sophie spoil our friendship. I like you, and I enjoyed our day today. I would like to do it again."

"Thank you." Grace got out of the car. "I would too. We'll talk soon." Taking her bags, she entered the front door. She called for Maurice several times as she walked through the house before acknowledging he was not there. Walking into the studio, she studied the goat sketch he'd left on the drawing table. *He hasn't been home. This picture looks about the same as it did when I left. Where could he be?* Going upstairs to the bedroom, she emptied her bags and put her new clothes away. Then she removed her sandals and lay on the bed. Opening the music box lid, the soft bell tones were soothing. *Sophie is just trying to cause more trouble between me and Maurice. I believe Tara. She and Maurice are friends, period.* Rolling from her side, she lay flat on her back, staring at the ceiling. *I don't get it. Everything here is always going sideways. Why Maurice would want to stay here is beyond me. Our life in New York was so much more peaceful. I cannot wait to leave New Orleans. Sophie said I should be packing. I knew she didn't want peace. Once we prove he's not Lindsay's baby daddy, we are out of here.*

I bet Maurice is right. Sophie's behind the Lindsay drama, too. The doorbell rang. Snapping the lid of the music box closed, she scampered to answer it.

Philippe grabbed Grace's hand as she opened the door. "Maurice is in the hospital. He had a car accident."

Dread gripped her heart. "Oh, my God. Is he all right?"

"He is. He's got some bruises and a broken leg. It's a bad break, and he needs surgery. I will take you to him. The doctor needs your consent for the surgery."

Running upstairs, Grace slipped into her sandals and bolted back down to the foyer. Following Philippe to the car, her heart was racing. *Please let him be all right. Please, God.*

"This is my fault," Philippe said, staring at the road ahead as he drove. "I should have never given a new driver such a powerful car. He lost control of the Porsche and crashed into a tree."

Her hand went to her throat. "What? Where?"

"I don't know for certain. An ambulance brought Maurice in. The police called me since I registered the Porsche in my name. He was unconscious when I arrived at the emergency room. The nurse told me he was in a lot of pain, and they had to sedate him."

"Why didn't you give consent to the doctor for the surgery?"

Philippe glanced at her. "I cannot. I am not legally his father."

Nervously twisting her hands in her lap, Grace tried to remain positive. *At least he is alive. He will recover from a broken leg. I was hurt much more badly, and I made a full recovery. Please, God, let him be fine.*

Tears blurred her vision as she entered the Emergency Room, eyes locking on Maurice lying on the gurney. A pronounced purple lump graced his forehead, and his left arm was bandaged. A sheet covered him from the waist down, preventing her from seeing his legs. The doctor explained Maurice had a compound fracture, and the shinbone had broken through the skin of his left leg. Surgery was necessary to reset the bone. After signing the forms the doctor put in front of her, they wheeled Maurice to the operating room.

Philippe held her as she cried into his shoulder. "He's going to be okay." Rubbing her back, he led her to the waiting room and sat with her.

Slowly, Grace pulled herself together and sat up straight. "Will you take me back to the house? I want to get a few things while they operate on him. I can drive myself back. I'm probably going to be here all night."

"Of course, Buttercup." Philippe took her hand and led her back to his black Mercedes.

Exiting the car in the driveway, she thanked Philippe before entering the studio door. *Seeing him like that, I didn't understand everything the doctor said.* Entering the master bedroom, she stopped in the center. *What should I bring? What do I need*? She stared at the closet before going to it and opening the doors. Removing her cardigan sweater from the rack, she froze. *What happened between him and Sophie today? She didn't seem to know about Maurice's accident. But I have a feeling she has something to do with it.* Going to her nightstand, she picked up her newest romance novel and, in the bathroom, her travel toothbrush and a trial-size toothpaste. Throwing it all into her black hobo bag, she hurried back to the hospital.

Philippe was still in the waiting room, leaning back in his chair with his eyes closed. Grace sat beside him. "I'm back."

"Hello, buttercup. I'm taking a little nap. It's been quite a day." Opening his eyes as he sat up and winked at her, a small smile formed on his lips. "You don't mind, do you?"

"No, no." Grace held up her book. "I can read."

He leaned back again, and she opened her book. They sat there for a few hours until, finally, the doctor came out. "The surgery went well, and he's in recovery. We will move him to a private room from there. I'll have the nurse let you know where once he's settled. He should be awake within the hour, and you can see him." Grace asked about the next steps. "He'll be on antibiotics and pain medication for a few days. Once the incisions on his leg heal and we know there is no infection, we will put a cast on his leg, and your husband can go home. At first, he'll need crutches, but he should be walking on his own in a few weeks. The cast will probably need to stay on for at least eight weeks. We'll monitor his progress. He was lucky he wasn't sitting on the side of the car which collided with the tree, or things could have been much worse. The bump on his head and the bruises on his arm will heal in time." The doctor touched Grace's arm. "Don't worry. Your husband will make a full recovery." After shaking Philippe's hand, the doctor proceeded down the hall.

"Thank God, good news," Philippe said, yawning. "I'm going to go home, and I'll come back in the morning." He kissed her cheek. "Goodnight, buttercup."

"Thank you, Philippe. Goodnight." Relieved, Grace sat back down and read her book until the nurse came and told her Maurice's room number. He was awake when she entered the room.

Forcing a smile, Grace approached his bedside. "How are you feeling?"

Maurice's voice was a faint whisper. "Like I've been in a car wreck. I can barely move. Breathe."

His droopy eyes made her want to cry, but she kept smiling. "It will take some time for the full effect of the anesthesia to wear off. The good news is you're going to be fine. The doctor said you can come home in a couple of days." She reached for his hand to rub it between her own. "I'm going to stay here all night and watch over you. I want you to rest and not worry about anything." Taking his hand to her lips, she whispered, "I love you." His attempted smile or wince of pain was hard to discern, but Grace gently laid his hand back on the bed as he closed his eyes. Pulling the armchair from the corner closer to his bed, she curled up with her book until she fell asleep.

A nurse entered the room early the next day with a cheerful wake-up call. "Monsieur Maurice, time to get up." Startled, Grace sat up in the chair. "Oh," the nurse, a squat, middle-aged black woman, eyed her. "I didn't know anyone else was here. Is this your husband?" Grace nodded. "You should get yourself some coffee and breakfast while I care for him. Give me a half hour, will you?"

Taking her bag, Grace left to find a ladies' room. Rounding a corner, following the posted signs, she ran right into a casually dressed Agent Wolf. "Good morning, Mrs. Chenault. How's your husband doing?"

Grace stepped back. "What are you doing here?"

"I'm here to speak to your husband about the accident. I saw it happen and called an ambulance. Is he awake? Talking?"

Her eyes widened. "You were following him?"

"Yes, lucky for him. Without immediate attention, he might be in worse condition than he is now. Did he tell you what happened?"

"No. The nurse is with him now, and I'm going to the cafeteria for breakfast."

"May I join you?"

Grace shook her head. "No. You can speak to both of us in about half an hour." Stepping around him, she entered the ladies' room, relieved he could not follow her. Glancing at her panicked face in the mirror, her heart began to race. *I hope Philippe doesn't return while we are talking to Agent Wolf. What will he think if he sees us talking to the FBI?* Sitting in the bathroom stall, a brief wave of nausea swept over her. She washed her face and brushed her teeth before going to the cafeteria. The thought of Maurice condemning the hospital's cheese omelet on her plate made her smile. *At least the coffee isn't too bad.* Monitoring the clock as she ate ensured she was outside the closed door of Maurice's room in half an hour. The nurse emerged, leaving the door open. "He's all ready for you now."

"Bonjour, mon cheri." Maurice was sitting up and smiling as Grace entered.

"You look much better than yesterday. How do you feel?"

"High." He lifted the button device, activating the pain medicine dispensary intravenously connected to his arm. "All the morphine I can stand. No pain."

She kissed him softly on the lips. "Don't get too carried away with it."

"I cannot. The machine prevents overdose."

She sat in the chair about to tell him about the FBI when Agent Wolf walked into the room. "Good morning, Mr. Chenault. Are you well enough to talk? I have some questions regarding your accident."

"I don't remember much," Maurice said. "What do you want to know?"

"How did you lose control of the car?"

A thoughtful expression clouded Maurice's face. A moment later, his eyes widened, focusing on the agent. "Oh, my God. The woman in the street. Did I hit her? Is she all right?"

Agent Wolf pulled a small wooden chair closer to Maurice's bed before sitting. "You did not hit her. I believe your maneuver to avoid hitting her with your car caused you to collide with the tree. I had you under surveillance the entire time. Seems you lost control of the car much earlier than that. Can you tell me what happened?"

Gnawing on her thumbnail, Grace held her breath.

Maurice shook his head. "I don't remember. All the pain medication has made my memory murky."

The agent had a skeptical look on his face. "Let me try to help you remember. You left Sophie's looking a bit shaken, but you were steady on the road at first. The trouble started after you turned onto Tchoupitoulas Street, and you barely missed hitting a truck."

Maurice glanced at Grace. "Is that what happened?"

"Did you have trouble with the brakes?" Agent Wolf continued. "From my vantage point, you appeared to be shifting into a lower gear, attempting to slow the car, which caused it to fishtail out of control."

"Your vantage point?" Maurice asked. "Where exactly?"

"A few car lengths behind you." Agent Wolf leaned forward. "I called for an ambulance when you hit the tree. You could have been killed. Are you certain you don't remember anything?"

"Not right now," Maurice replied. "Maybe in a few days, after I'm off the morphine, my memory will return."

Upon standing, Agent Wolf's eyes went from Maurice to Grace and back again. "I'll come back in a few days. Glad you're all right. Next time, you may not be so lucky." He started toward the door. "We will be examining the wreckage to determine if someone performed any mechanical sabotage on your car. I'll let you know what we find." Then he left, closing the door behind him.

"Are you telling the truth?" Grace asked. "Do you remember what happened?"

"I don't remember everything, but he is correct. My car had no brakes."

Grace's mouth formed an O. "What happened between you and Sophie?"

"She tried to kill me. Apparently, more than once." Slowly, he recounted the horrific scene. "Sophie wins. As soon as I can walk, we are getting out of New Orleans."

Philippe walked in. "Why are you leaving?" He sat in the chair the agent had vacated. "You're going to be fine. Already, you look much better today."

Maurice glared at him. "Please, do not pretend you don't know why I am leaving. Your daughter is completely insane."

Philippe chuckled. "I'll admit, Sophie can be a handful, but she would never harm you. The gun she pointed at you wasn't even loaded." He shifted his gaze to Grace. "May I speak to him alone for a minute?"

"No," Maurice said. "She is not going anywhere. Whatever you have to say, she will hear."

"I take full responsibility for the accident," Philippe said. "As I told Grace, I should have never given you the Porsche. You're not an experienced driver. You weren't ready for it."

"Sophie tampered with the Porsche's brakes. She sent someone to do it while we talked in the office. Probably the bartender."

Philippe's eyes squinted. "Are you certain?"

"Of course, I am certain. The damn car would not stop," Maurice shouted. "She is trying to kill me. What part of this are you not getting?"

Grace went to his bedside, rubbing his arm. "Calm down, please. Philippe, maybe you should leave and come back later."

"No," Maurice said to Grace. "He needs to tell me about the will." Glaring at Philippe, he said, "Sophie is angry because you added me to your will. Have you changed it? Because until you do, Sophie will continue down this murderous path."

"Why are my children telling me what to do?" Philippe's face got red. "I am the one in charge, not you."

"You are not in charge of anything," Maurice said in a low voice. "Especially not Sophie. How could you not see how jealous and angry she is? If my mother had died of anything other than cancer, I would accuse Sophie of her murder. She thinks Nettie stole you away from her."

"You are overreacting. Yes, Sophie has a few issues with you and your mother. But she did not cause you to have an accident. She is not trying to kill you."

"The FBI was here this morning. They're going to go over the Porsche with a fine-tooth comb. And when they find my brakes were fucked with, I'm going to tell them Sophie did it. Unless you change your will and you and Sophie stay away from me and Grace, I will talk. And if Sophie goes down, most likely, you and your whole rotten business will, too."

Philippe stood. "I thought we had made more progress than this." He strode out of the room.

Grace nervously gazed at Maurice. "Are you going to talk to the FBI?"

"Hopefully, I won't have to. If Philippe removes me from his will, Sophie should be satisfied, and all this craziness will end."

Late that night, Grace left the hospital after Maurice drifted to sleep. The phone was ringing when she entered the studio. "About time one of you answered. I've been calling you all day." *Lindsay*. "I set the appointment for the paternity test. It's tomorrow at 10 am."

"Maurice had a car accident, and he's in the hospital. I'll meet you in the lobby for the paperwork, and they can get his blood anytime to do the test." Grace's body trembled as she hung up the phone. *What will Philippe do now? Will this nightmare ever end?*

Chapter 24

Getting around on crutches was not as simple as Maurice had imagined. When they pulled into the driveway, he opened the car door and struggled to reach the crutches stashed behind his seat. Grace circled to his side, swung open the back door, grabbed the crutches, and handed them to him. *Right leg out, no problem, left leg?* He had to use both hands to move his left leg with the heavy cast to the outside of the car. Grace kept saying, 'Take your time.' *What the hell else am I going to do? I am moving as fast as I can and barely moving.* Leaning on the crutches, he steadied himself to a standing position. Grace closed the car door and started toward the studio. There were two steps leading to the door he'd always taken for granted. Hobbling behind her, his eyes stayed locked on the stairs. *How am I going to get up there?*

Grace unlocked the door and disappeared inside. He stood there, staring at the open door. Coming back, she looked down at him. "Are you coming in? What's the matter?"

"I don't know how to go up the steps with these. What should I do?"

"Uh." Grace came down a step. "Give me one crutch, and you use just one. Put your right foot up first and use the crutch to hoist yourself up." She grabbed his arm as he came up the steps, and he hopped on one foot into the studio.

Taking a deep breath, he put the crutches back under each arm. Maneuvering around his easels, he made it to the hallway.

"We'll stay in the guest suite, so you don't have to worry about going up and down the stairs," Grace said as she walked down the two steps into the great room. Maurice sighed. *I never realized how many stupid steps there are in this house.* Fortunately, going down the two stairs proved less taxing than going up. Upon entering the guest suite, his left leg started throbbing with pain.

Grace scurried around, fluffing up the bed pillows and pulling back the comforter. "I already put fresh sheets on the bed and brought some of your clothes down here. Sorry I had to cut the pant leg of some of your jeans." She gently patted the mattress, making a place for him to lie down. "I don't know which side you'll be more comfortable on, so if this side doesn't work, we'll move you to the other side. But this side is closest to the bathroom door." She stopped talking to move closer to him. "Are you all right?"

"My leg is killing me. I need to lie down." He hopped to the bed and sat on the side. Slowly leaning to lie down, he tried to use his sore left arm to lift his heavy left leg onto the bed. Grace rushed over to help and adjust his pillows as he stared at the ceiling. *I feel like an infant. How long will I have to depend on her to do anything?*

"I left the bag with your painkillers in the car. I'll be right back."

After being in bed for days at the hospital, Maurice could not wait to leave. This morning he felt strong, and the practice walk using the crutches in his room had gone well. *Why am I struggling so much? I hate being a burden.*

Returning with a glass of apple juice and the painkillers, Grace offered a warm smile, handing over two pills. He took the pills and juice as she settled beside him. "At least we got the good news today that you are not the father of Lindsay's baby."

Maurice gazed at her eyes. "I am so sorry for talking you into moving here. Jacque was right. It was crazy and stupid. I have put both of us in danger by coming here."

"You don't have to apologize. I thought it was a good idea too. And I encouraged you to get to know Philippe. Neither one of us had any idea how crazy Sophie is."

"The craziest part is, I was starting to like Philippe. I was starting to feel like he's my father." Maurice sighed. "He is not at all the way I imagined."

"It's all right to like someone without liking what they do." Grace ran her fingers through his hair as she leaned over to kiss his cheek. "I'm glad you are getting to know your father and see the good in him, as your mother did."

"You are the best wife in the whole world." Tears welled in his eyes.

Kissing him softly on the lips, she whispered, "You are the best husband. Now, lay back and get some rest. I'll go make something for dinner."

Within minutes, wooziness from the pain medicine took over, and he fell asleep.

As the days passed, Maurice got more comfortable with the crutches and less reliant on pain pills. With his cast-covered leg propped up on a cardboard box, he sat at his drawing table and completed his sketch of Cancer and Capricorn. *My photos of the other paintings should be ready. I need to pick them up and meet with the printer to make the posters.*

The doorbell rang, and a moment later, Marie stood in the studio doorway. "I'm sorry I didn't come to see you in the hospital. How are you doing?"

"I'm coming along." Reaching out his arms to her, she stepped into his embrace. "How are you?" Releasing her, he pointed to an easel in the corner. "Your portrait is done. Go see."

Lifting the drape from the easel, Marie let out a gasp. "No way. This is awesome." She whirled around with a bright smile. "How did you do this? It is so cool. I am a beautiful warrior princess. I love it."

"Yes, you are. Do you think Darius will love it?"

"I know he will." She gave Maurice another hug. "Thank you. What a wonderful gift. Can I come back tomorrow with Darius to pick it up?"

"Of course." Maurice's expression shifted to somber. "Marie, I want you to know I have truly enjoyed spending time with you and getting to know you. But Grace and I are leaving here. We are moving back to New York."

"Oh." Marie walked toward the window, gazing out at the lawn. "This is because of Sophie, isn't it? You should never have gone over there with the car. I told you she wouldn't take it."

"I know, and you were right," Maurice replied. "But I learned quite a few things by talking to Sophie. Things I needed to know."

"What will you do with the house? Are you going to sell it?" She spun back to him. "I would like to live here if you're not going to stay. Darius and I are planning to live together after we graduate in June. This place would be perfect for us."

Maurice chuckled. "Does your mother know about your plans?"

"Not yet. I will tell her after receiving my acceptance letter from the nursing program at Tulane. I'm going to be a nurse."

"Good for you."

"This house is so close to the university. I can't see her saying no. I don't expect her to be too keen on the Darius part. I may wait to tell her that part."

Maurice laughed. "As far as I am concerned, you may live here, with one condition. You must hire a cook, housekeeper, and yardman."

"Uh, yeah." Marie laughed. "You don't think I planned to do all that myself, do you? I don't know why you and Grace never hired anyone."

"Grace is a do-it-yourself kind of girl. Believe me, she was already getting worn down, and if we stayed, we would have eventually hired someone. This house is too large for one person to manage."

Marie approached to clasp his hand. "Can I come to visit you in New York?"

"I would love it if you would come to visit. Any time, okay?"

She kissed him on the cheek, and he did the same. "I'll see you tomorrow."

Marie and I are fine. We don't have the criminal gene, only Sophie. Good to know it doesn't have to affect all the offspring. Grace and I could have normal children. Please, God, let us have normal children.

Taking up his crutches, Maurice made his way to the kitchen, finding Grace deep in her textbook, scribbling notes. "Tomorrow, will you please take me to the photo shop to collect my pictures? And to the print shop. I want to order posters to sell in the park this weekend."

"You're feeling well enough to sell posters in Jackson Square? What happens if you need to use the bathroom? Is there even one there? Will anyone work with you and watch your table while you're gone?" Grace showed concern. "I think you should wait a bit longer. Soon you'll be able to put pressure on your leg and be more mobile. And you need a partner. I'm not sitting in the park while you sell posters all day."

Maurice snorted. "I need to have everything prepared, regardless. Will you take me?"

"Of course," Grace smiled. "Come sit down. I'll make you something to eat. Did Marie like her portrait?"

"She loved it." Taking a seat at the table, he glanced at her pile of books. "One day back at school, and already you have so much homework? Your teacher is a real taskmaster."

"Yes, he is, but it's good for me. It's what I need to pass the CPA exam."

"Was Xavier in class today?"

"He was, but we didn't talk much. I was in a rush to get back here to check on you." Rising from the table, she got bread and cold cuts from the fridge. "I'll make us some sandwiches."

The photos Maurice picked up from the camera shop the next day came out perfect. After reviewing them all, he chose pictures of Lily Dumont and Marie's portraits to be enlarged for his portfolio. Then he selected the best shots of the horoscope series to take to the printer for posters.

The man at the print shop said the posters would be ready in a couple of days. *I will ask Claude to hang out with me in the park on Saturday. We can talk about the business plan for the arts center, and I can give him the paperwork from Blaze. Maybe Raymond will come too. I hate I will not be here to see the cultural arts center come to fruition, but at least I will have had a hand in the nonprofit's creation.*

When they got home, Maurice went to the studio to begin painting his final horoscope picture. *Oh my god, Blaze. He knew about the will. That's how he knew I would have a lot of money. I hope Philippe has changed it. He's been avoiding me since I threatened to talk to the FBI.*

The doorbell rang, and a minute later, Grace appeared in the studio doorway. "Agent Wolf is here." Maurice followed her to the formal living room, where Agent Wolf sat on the sofa, dressed in a black suit. Maurice sat in the light teal chair across from him as Grace stood behind him.

"I wanted to update you on the car accident investigation. Someone punctured the line from the brake fluid tank, which would have caused a slow leak, eventually rendering the brakes useless." Agent Wolf leaned toward Maurice. "Hitting a tree could not have caused the puncture. Have you remembered any more details from the accident?"

"Yes, I remember the car lost brake power, just as you said. I noticed it when I tried to slow down to avoid hitting the truck."

"Any idea who would want to cause you to have an accident? Possibly to harm you?"

Maurice shook his head. "No."

"I followed you to Sophie's, and the car was operating fine. Someone who works at that sports bar is responsible. I wish I had kept a closer eye on your car, but I went inside shortly after you did. I only came back out when I saw you leaving," Agent Wolf sighed loudly. "Clearly, someone at the sports bar doesn't like you. You don't have any idea at all who it could be?"

"No."

"I know it's difficult to implicate family, but are you having problems with your father? I know he was there that day."

Maurice chuckled. "Agent Wolf, do you think my own father would try to kill me? No, it's not him. I don't know who did it, but it was not Philippe."

"What about your half-sister, Sophie? We know she's deeply involved in your father's drug business. Does she have an axe to grind with you?"

Maurice plastered on a fake smile. "Sophie? No. We get along fine. She wouldn't do it."

Agent Wolf stood up. "Please call me if you change your mind about helping us." He glanced at Grace. "I'll see myself out. Have a good evening."

Maurice started back to the studio. "I'm going to call Philippe right now and find out what is happening. He has not contacted me to tell me if he changed his will. I won't keep lying to the FBI if he's not going to change the will."

Philippe didn't answer when he called.

***************** *************

Grace wore her purple boho overalls with a white t-shirt for class on Wednesday. *I love this outfit. It's perfect for this warm spring weather.* After pinning her hair in a French roll, she admired herself in the master bath mirror. *Cute, very cute.* Going to the guest suite, she peeked in on Maurice, still sleeping. She made coffee, scrambled eggs, and toast and ate before making a tray of food to bring to Maurice. *I'll save him the trouble of hobbling to the kitchen today. He's doing much better getting around, though, thank goodness.*

Despite her concerns, she had left him to attend school on Monday at his insistence. Finishing the class before they left for New

York meant her work at Tulane would not be in vain and go toward her accreditation.

In class, Xavier was already in his seat when she arrived. "Hey, Grace. Look at us. We're twins." He pointed at the bib of his denim overalls. "I like your overalls better than mine. You hustled out of here so fast on Monday that I didn't get to ask you. How did you do on the exam?" He smiled. "Thank God, I passed with 75."

"I got a 95. I told you I aced it." Grace took out her notebook as Professor Collins walked in, slamming the door behind him.

Following the lecture, Xavier escorted Grace to her car. "I need to ask you a favor," he said as they approached the Benz. "My car was acting up this morning, making weird noises. I dropped it off at my mechanic's shop for a check-up. He gave me a ride here. Do you think you could drop me off there on your way home? It's only a few miles down St. Charles Avenue." He opened the driver's side door for Grace.

"Sure," Grace said, sliding behind the wheel. "Hop in."

Xavier closed her door and jogged around the front of the car to the passenger side. "Thanks, I appreciate it."

As Grace drove to the parking lot exit, Xavier directed her to take a right turn onto Audubon Boulevard. "I'm sorry I have to do this to you because I like you. You're a nice lady." Xavier slid a handgun from under his overall bib, pointing it toward her side. "I need you to get onto the highway ramp up ahead."

Grace's mouth dropped open as her heart started racing. "Xavier, what are you doing? Why do you have a gun? What do you want?"

He stared at her. "My boss wants to see you."

"Who is your boss?" She stumbled over her words. "Are you FBI? Is it Philippe?"

"Sophie Le Coeur. She wants to meet you and your husband. She figured bringing you in first would guarantee he'll show up when she calls him with an invitation."

Grace fought to concentrate on driving, struggling to keep calm. "You don't have to do this, Xavier. If Sophie wants to see me and Maurice, we can pick him up at the house right now. He'll come with us to see Sophie."

"I am sorry, Grace. We have to do this her way. Keep going until I tell you to stop. We're going to cross the bridge."

Grace's hands were shaking on the steering wheel, and she gripped it tighter, trying to steady herself. She glanced over at Xavier. "How long have you been working for Sophie?"

"Not long. Sophie is a business client of my sister's. My sister really is a CPA, and I'm an accountant. I was taking classes at New Orleans University. Sophie offered me an opportunity to go to Tulane tuition-free. All I had to do was court a beautiful lady." He smiled at her. "It was an easy job. I wasn't too thrilled when she asked me to do this to you. You know, force you to drive here. But she said you won't be hurt. It'll be the last thing I ever have to do for her."

They crossed over the Huey P. Long Bridge and entered Bridge City. Xavier directed her to an abandoned warehouse close to the base of the bridge.

Chapter 25

Unable to pace, Maurice sat at his drawing table, incessantly tapping his right foot. *Where could she be? Did she get a flat tire? An accident?* He drew in a deep breath. *This isn't like her. Something is wrong. I don't even have a car to go look for her. Please, God, don't let it be Sophie.*

The doorbell rang. Philippe stood at the door, holding a large manila envelope. "May I come in?"

Leaving the door wide open, Maurice went to sit on the formal living room sofa, propping the crutches beside his good leg. Philippe handed him the envelope before sitting in the chair across from him. "Where's Grace?"

"I don't know, and I'm worried about her. She went to school this morning, and she's not come home or called. It's not like her." Maurice stared at the envelope in his hand., before glancing at Philippe. "Will you take me to Tulane to look for her?"

"How long has it been?"

"Two hours. Her class ends at noon, and she always comes right home afterward."

Philippe sighed. "You know, women. She probably stopped to buy something, but I'll take you anywhere you want."

"The FBI came by. They found evidence someone sabotaged my car's brakes." Maurice held up the envelope before opening it. "This is the new will?" His fingers quickly tore into the envelope, and he scanned the document. No trace of his name. He looked up at Philippe. "Have you shown it to Sophie?"

Philippe nodded.

"Thank you." Maurice headed toward the studio. "I will put on a shoe, and we can go to the school."

As he entered the studio, the phone rang. "Hello, big brother."

"Sophie."

"I've got your wife here with me."

Desperate, he shouted into the phone. "Sophie, please do not do anything to hurt Grace." Philippe came and stood in the doorway, putting his fingertips to his lips and shaking his head. "Where are you? Why would you take Grace?"

"I want to see you, and I won't take no for an answer." Sophie cackled. "You won't let a broken leg stop you from coming, will you?"

"I will meet you anywhere you want. Tell me where you are, and I will come. Please don't hurt Grace."

"Do you have a pencil to write with, or will you remember?"

"Sophie, please. Tell me where you are."

"Bridge City. Take the first exit ramp and make the first right once you cross the bridge. Go slow and pay attention, or you'll miss it. Follow the dirt road and come to the back of the warehouse. Don't be stupid and bring anyone with you. Grace and I will be waiting."

While Maurice laced up his shoe, Philippe said, "I know exactly where she is. I cannot believe she took Grace. What the hell is wrong with her?" Hastily, he dialed the phone. "Charlie, bring a cab to 2025 Napoleon Avenue. Quickly. You will pick up my son and bring him to the Bridge City warehouse." He put down the phone and gazed at Maurice. "You were right. She has become unhinged. I had no idea she was so far gone."

Maurice sat up. "Why are you calling a cab? We should be leaving now. Right now."

"You will take a cab, so she thinks you are alone. I will go there and make sure Grace is safe." Philippe took Maurice's hands into his own. "Do not tell her you saw me or talked to me. I will surprise Sophie and subdue her before she can do any harm."

Maurice shook his head. "No, you should take me there and talk to her. This is all your fault. Why couldn't you just leave me alone as I asked you to?"

"Now is not the time to argue. One day, when you are a father, maybe you'll understand. Right now, we need to handle Sophie. She's not rational. Please, let me do this my way. I promise I will be there when you arrive. Will you trust me?"

Gazing into his father's blue eyes, Maurice nodded.

"Good. Do whatever she says until I can get to her. Understand?"

"Yes."

Philippe grabbed his arm. "Come on. I'll help you to the street for the cab."

Standing on the curb, Maurice stared at the taillights of Philippe's Mercedes as he drove away. *Please, God, don't let anything happen to Grace. Please. I hope Philippe knows what he's doing.* His heart was pounding, and his hands were sweating, fidgeting around the crutch handles.

After what seemed an eternity, a small white minivan cab pulled up. As he got in, the elderly white man driving asked, "You Philippe's son?"

Maurice nodded. "Please hurry. My wife is in danger."

"Don't worry," the white-haired man replied, "I've got you." Revving the engine, they sped off.

The dirt road shrouded under the canopy of trees was dark and bumpy as the cab approached the warehouse. Maurice's stomach was in knots as the crackle of the rock and gravel pinged the undercarriage of the car. The driver turned to Maurice as he got out. "I'll go to the end of the road and wait for you. I won't leave you out here all alone."

Maurice took a deep breath before he thanked the driver and navigated his way down the rocky road toward the long, low warehouse building. A single spotlight above the door lit a circle on the ground in the building's shadow. Sophie stepped out in a black jumpsuit, waving a large handgun. "You do love your wife."

"Where is she?" Maurice pleaded. "Please let Grace go, and I will do whatever you ask."

Sophie pointed the gun at him. "You will do whatever I ask, no matter what. Come a little closer. I want to see the fear in your eyes."

Creeping closer, Maurice continued to beg. "Please, I am the one you want. Grace has nothing to do with this. She is innocent. Please let her go."

"I'm not going to hurt Grace. I like her. After I finish dealing with you, I will take her to the airport and put her on a plane to New York myself." Stepping nearer, Sophie kicked one crutch out from under his arm, and he stumbled. "Get on the ground."

Falling to the rocky ground, Maurice's cast made a cracking sound as he landed. He closed his eyes, wincing in pain, heart racing.

"Sophie, put the gun down." Philippe raised his hand toward her, slowly walking out the warehouse door, with Grace closely following behind him. "I am the one you are angry with, not Maurice. His mother didn't steal me away from you. It was my choice."

Maurice lifted his head as Philippe approached Sophie and pulled down her arm, holding the gun. Grace raced to Maurice and squatted down beside him. He quickly kissed her. "Are you all right? Did she hurt you?"

Grace held his arm, shaking. "I'm all right. Scared to death, but all right. Xavier works for her," she whispered. "He forced me to drive here at gunpoint and Sophie locked me in a broom closet."

Wide-eyed and trembling, they huddled together as Philippe spoke to Sophie in low tones for a moment. Suddenly Sophie jerked away. "No. I cannot believe you are willing to let him go. He will go to the FBI and turn us in. You told me he said it."

"Maurice," Philippe shouted, holding her arm, "Tell Sophie you're not going to the FBI."

Maurice yelled. "I won't talk to the FBI. I swear, I won't tell anyone," He whispered to Grace, "Stay down and slowly crawl back away from her. Then run. There is a cab down the road." Grace didn't move a muscle.

Sophie pulled away from Philippe and raised her arm, pointing the large handgun at Maurice. "He is a liar. You can't believe a single word that comes from his mouth."

"No, Sophie, he is telling the truth. He won't talk to the FBI. He and Grace are leaving, and you will never have to see him again. Everything I have is yours and Marie's. Why are you doing this? You saw the will. You said you were satisfied."

Still holding the gun on Maurice, Sophie turned to her father. "You love him more than me."

Philippe rushed to her side, pulling down her arms as he embraced her. "No, no, no. You are my little girl. My special girl. We do everything together. We work together, we live together." He took her face in his hands. "I love you more than anyone. You were always first place in my heart, even if I didn't always show it. There is no one I love more than you. No one."

"But if he goes to the FBI, we will both go to jail. That is what he wants. To be rid of us so he can take our money. I cannot let him do it. He doesn't deserve to live." Sophie quickly extended her arm, pointing the gun. Reaching out, Philippe pulled the gun into his stomach as it fired.

Maurice's eyes widened as his father collapsed on the ground right before him. "Philippe!"

"Papa!" Sophie looked down at his body, moaning. "What did you do, Papa?"

A loud voice called through the trees beyond the warehouse. "Sophie Le Coeur, this is the FBI. Drop your weapon and raise your arms slowly." Sophie spun in the direction the voice came from. "Fuck you, FBI," she yelled before firing her gun. Seconds later, return gunfire struck her, and she fell next to her father as a pool of blood formed around her.

Agent Wolf emerged from the wooded area beyond the warehouse and stood over the bloody bodies. He looked at Maurice and Grace. "You two all right?" His blond partner stood behind him, holding a sniper rifle.

Maurice crawled over to Philippe and put his hand on his face. Philippe's eyes fluttered. Looking up at Agent Wolf, he said. "Call an ambulance. He is still alive."

"One's already on the way." Bending down over Sophie's body, Agent Wolf felt for a pulse. "She's dead." He looked at Maurice. "Why didn't you call me? Why would you come here alone?"

In a strangled voice, Maurice replied, "I was hoping you would follow me." He continued to cradle Philippe's head in his hands. "Isn't there something you can do for him?"

Philippe opened his eyes, raising his hand to Maurice's cheek. "My son." His arm dropped as the sirens of the ambulance and police cars got louder. Grace held Maurice as he held his father, weeping.

The agents questioned Grace and Maurice as they loaded the bodies into the ambulance. Shortly after, Agent Wolf dropped them at their house. "We'll contact you if we need more information, but I think we wrapped our case up as far as you're concerned. Once we thoroughly go through your car, we'll return it to you in a day or two."

They silently went to the guest suite and stripped off their clothes before bed. They held one another and sobbed as Maurice whispered in her ear. "It is over. It is all over."

Chapter 26

The following day, they sat in their robes in the great room, watching the local news coverage of the death of the notorious Philippe Le Coeur on television. It included footage of the FBI rounding up several people connected to Philippe's criminal enterprise in the city. Maurice's mouth dropped open as a video clip of Yves in handcuffs being led from his house came on the screen. He turned to Grace. "I have to call Jacque."

Going to the studio, Maurice phoned his cousin with the latest news. As he set the phone down, it instantly rang. "Maurice, I need to see you." It was Blaze. "May I stop by your house?"

A half-hour later, Grace led Blaze to the great room, where Maurice was sitting, glued to the television screen. Dressed in somber black, Blaze settled on the sofa next to Maurice. "I'm so sorry for your loss. I loved your father very much. He was a great man and a good friend to me." Handing Maurice a large manila envelope, Blaze patted his back in sympathy. "I know money is not a substitute, but Philippe wanted you to have this. Look it over and call me when you are ready to discuss the details." Upon standing, he bowed before Grace. "Madame Chenault, my condolences." Grace led him from the room as Maurice opened the envelope. There were deeds to three houses in his name. The accompanying paperwork listed the previous owner as his mother, Antoinette Louise Chenault. In a separate smaller white envelope, a key with a business card for a banker at Louisiana National Bank. On the back, a number. 522.

Grace came back and rubbed Maurice's back. "What is it?"

Handing her the package, he started to cry.

A week later, dressed in black, Maurice and Grace quietly rode to St. Joseph's. The church was quickly filling for the funeral service for Philippe and Sophie as Maurice and Grace sat toward the back of the church. Marie sat in the front pew, and he assumed her mother was beside her. *I imagine Philippe's wife hates me as much as Sophie did. I don't want to upset or offend her, but I would like to offer my condolences. Maybe I'll try to speak with her after the service.*

Grace squeezed his hand, gazing at everyone attending the service. "This is quite a turnout. I guess Philippe was telling the truth when he said the people of this city love him."

Marie moved down the aisle toward them, wearing a long lacy black dress. He stood, holding the back of the pew for balance as she approached. Gazing into her wet brown eyes, he asked, "How are you holding up? Is there anything I can do for you?"

"My mother would like you and Grace to sit on the front pew with us. You are family."

Following her lead, they moved to the front pew. Maurice sat next to Marie as he handed Grace his crutches. "I'm so sorry about everything that happened."

Marie glanced at him as she took his hand. "It's not your fault. I'm glad you came today. I wasn't sure you would."

He nodded, glancing at the woman seated next to Marie, wearing a long black veil over her head. "Your mother, is she all right?"

"She is coping."

The priest praised the good Samaritan works Philippe and Sophie had performed over the years. He preached only God could judge or condemn any soul on earth and all should pray to receive His Mercy.

After the service, Maurice stood, and the woman with the veil lifted it, revealing an older version of Sophie's face with an ugly scar marring her left cheek. She gazed at him from her seat with dry, dull green eyes. "We haven't officially met. I am Mia, Philippe's wife." She held out her left hand with massive gold and diamond rings sparkling on her fingers.

Maurice took her hand, gently kissing it. "You have my deepest sympathy. I am profoundly sorry for your loss."

"We have all lost loved ones." Mia stood in her long black lace dress. "Please don't bear the burden of unnecessary guilt over what's happened. It was inevitable. I knew this day would come. A reckless life leads to a tragic death." Her gaze settled on the closed caskets. "Now, they are at peace." Taking Maurice's hand, Mia squeezed it tightly. "I knew your father loved you and your mother deeply. I never held it against either one of you. Please accept his provisions. It gave him great joy getting to know you. Will you come to the burial?"

Maurice gestured at his cast leg. "I'm sorry, but I'm having a bit of trouble getting around. I'll say my goodbyes to Philippe here. Merci beaucoup." Maurice and Grace moved out of the pew, allowing Mia and Marie to pass toward the church exit amongst the mourners.

Placing his hand on Philippe's casket, Maurice whispered, "I am sorry I didn't ever tell you I love you. I know it was what you wanted to hear. Rest in peace, Philippe. Father."

Their journey home was silent. Sitting at the kitchen table, Grace poured two glasses of Chardonnay. "Are you hungry?" she asked.

"No, are you?"

"Not really." They silently sipped their wine, occasionally glancing at one another. Abruptly, Grace bolted from her seat, rushing to the sink, retching. When done, she rinsed her mouth and wiped her face with a paper towel. "Ugh, that was awful. Sorry."

"Don't apologize. Are you all right?"

"Yes. I probably shouldn't be drinking on an empty stomach." Taking out a loaf of bread and some butter, she gave him a weak smile. "I'll have a piece of toast. Would you like one? You should eat something, too."

"Okay." Maurice twirled his wine glass, watching its contents swirl. "I guess I will call Jacque today and ask him to start looking for a place for us."

Grace stood near the toaster. "Oh no. We are going to find an extended-stay hotel and call a realtor. We will find our own place."

Nodding, Maurice replied, "You're right. We will find our own place. Are we looking in Greenburgh only?"

"It doesn't have to be in Greenburgh. There are several towns in the vicinity we can check out." The toast popped up, and she quickly buttered it and sat. After biting and chewing a piece of toast, she said, "Now that we're rich, we can buy any house we want."

"I still feel bad about taking the money." Maurice took a small bite of the toast.

"I don't. After all the crap we have been through with your family, it's only right we get something good out of it."

Maurice glanced at her. "You're still angry?"

"Very." Grace took his hand. "Sophie kidnapped me and tried to kill you. I don't think I'll ever be able to forgive her."

"I know this will sound crazy, but after thinking about it these past few days, I understand Sophie's anger and jealousy. When I was younger, I was mostly away in France. I didn't have to hear it often, but when I was here, I heard nasty gossip about my mother and Philippe, which hurt me. It hurt a lot, even though I never believed it was true." Maurice snorted and looked down at his hands. "I thought my mother sent me away to boarding school to have the best education. Now, I know that wasn't her only motivation. She didn't want me to see how she was truly living her life. My mother lied to me my entire life, telling me Michel was my father and that he died serving our country. I never, ever saw Philippe and my mother together, not once. It shocked me when she told me Philippe was my father right before she died." Glancing up at Grace, he continued. "But Sophie was here. Philippe told me he didn't give a damn who knew about him and my mother. I imagine Sophie probably saw them together quite often. She knew all the terrible things people said about Philippe and Nettie were true. I still don't understand how Mia could permit Philippe to carry on an affair with my mother. It's a miracle Marie is not crazy. A child cannot process the complicated situations their parents get into." Grace finished eating her toast. He touched her hand. "Are you feeling better?"

"Yes, the toast helped." She looked around the kitchen. "Tomorrow, we'll start packing."

For a moment, they sat in silence before Maurice cleared his throat. "Is there any way I can convince you to stay here? Now nothing is standing in the way of us raising a family here. We can open our art gallery as we planned and fund the cultural arts center, too."

Grace raised her eyebrows. "You want to stay here after all that's happened?"

"It can't get any worse. What else could happen? Bad things happened to us when we lived in New York, and we stayed there anyway. We came here to start over, and now, we really can. You told me you liked New Orleans, and if not for Sophie and Philippe, we could be happy here. Well, they're gone now." Bringing her hand to his lips, he kissed it. "I want to live here. It's important to me we make this work."

Grace eyed him warily. "I don't know. If it's really important to you, I will need to think about it. Can I think about it?"

"Of course. I'm grateful you're willing to consider it. There's no rush to make a decision now, is there? I know the wounds are still fresh, but I hope you will change your mind." Maurice gazed at her. "I couldn't believe that safe deposit box was filled with cash. Thanks to Yves's book cooking, the feds couldn't tie a lot of Philipe's money and property to his drug business. And somehow, Blaze fixed it so Yves could avoid doing time." He sighed. "I'm going to give a big donation to St. Leo's. And whether we stay or not, I'm going to fund the nonprofit for the cultural arts center.

They sat silently for several minutes before Maurice said, "I need to pick up my posters from the printer."

"To do what with them?"

"I'm still going to sell them. I am still an artist, regardless of how rich we are."

Grace got up for a glass of water. "We will also need to hire an attorney and a financial advisor to help us invest the money. We are not entrusting millions of dollars to Jacque."

Maurice raised his eyebrows. "You're not going to handle our money?"

"I'm not trusting myself. No, we'll leave it to the professionals. I will handle the day-to-day expenses, and I'll keep tabs on them to keep them honest." After finishing her water, she took his hand. "Come on, let's go lie down. You look tired."

The next day, Grace drove Maurice to Central City. After helping him out of the car, she said, "I'm going into the drugstore to pick up a few things while you're in the print shop."

Examining the posters in the shop, he was extremely pleased with how they turned out and requested they deliver them to his house. Arriving home, Maurice looked around his studio and picked up an empty cardboard box. He started packing sketchpads into it and then stopped. Sitting at the drawing table, he gazed out the window. *I hope Grace changes her mind. I want this to be our home.*

"Finally, some good news." Grace entered the studio, a big grin on her face. "The stick turned blue."

Maurice was confused. "What stick?"

"This one." She held up an unfamiliar white plastic tube. "I'm pregnant."

Maurice's eyes widened. "Really? You are certain?"

She approached to show him the indicator box on the home pregnancy test. "See right here. You pee on it. If it stays white, not pregnant. If it turns blue, pregnant. It's blue."

Pulling her into his arms, passionately kissing her slowly and deeply, he whispered, "I told you it would happen."

Epilogue December 1988

Maurice turned the door sign to CLOSED before stepping into the back office. The gallery was quite busy in the days leading up to Christmas Eve, with exceptionally brisk sales of the posters printed from his horoscope series. His original oil paintings of the astrological pairings became highly coveted as well and led to many custom orders from clients who wanted their personal astrology pairing, whether they were compatible or not.

Unable to contain the huge grin across his face, he collected the final invoices to take home from the desk. *The gallery is doing so well. With Grace managing the books, I can focus on my artwork and my customers. Next year, we will finally break ground on the New Orleans Cultural Arts Center. We make a great team. I don't know why I ever thought I had to do this all on my own.*

The bell above the entrance jingled. *I must have forgotten to lock it.* Stepping back into the gallery, Maurice called out, "Sorry, we are closed."

"Your door was open." Dressed in a sleek black suit, Jacque stood in the entry, smiling. "Bonjour cousin." Nodding his head, he gazed at the paintings covering the gallery walls. "This is quite a place you've got here."

"I am so happy to see you. I didn't know you were coming for the holidays," Maurice said as they embraced one another, kissing checks.

Jacque chuckled. "Between my mother and Anne's begging, I couldn't say no. Besides, I want to meet my godson and nephew. And it's about time you officially meet Jackson."

"How are Anne and your son? Where are they?"

"Dropped them at my mother's. They're great. Now, give me a tour of this eclectic wonderland. You've got some unique items for sale. I like the horoscope calendar."

They strolled together around the large store with Maurice narrating as he pointed out certain sculptures on podiums and the posters and paintings gracing the walls.

Puffing his chest out, Maurice gestured toward his artwork on one wall. "Yes, Grace and I decided we want to have something for everyone and not cater to only wealthy clientele. I partnered with some local artists willing to have inexpensive replicas of their work for sale, along with posters of my oils. After launching the gallery with a showing of my horoscope series, we're getting a great response. The business is doing well."

After a brisk tour of the gallery, Jacque pulled Maurice into a bear hug. "I'm damn proud of you, cousin."

Maurice lowered his head. "Merci beaucoup. Will you and Anne stop by my house tonight for a drink?"

"Of course." Jacque headed for the door. "Catch you later."

Hurrying back to the office, Maurice picked up the invoices and his keys. *This is going to be an amazing Christmas. I can't wait to get home and see Louis.*

Outside, as he locked the door, he admired the golden scripted letters that spelled out "The Chenault Gallery" on the glass pane. Pride swelled within each time he saw it, and a broad grin broke out on his face as he hustled down the alley to his silver Mercedes. Driving through the French Quarter, he reveled in the dazzling Christmas decorations lighting the streets as he headed home.

Entering through the studio door, Grace's laughter greeted him. "Yes, Maurice is obsessed with his son. He wants to hold him all the time. Yesterday, I practically had to force him to put Louis in his crib so he could take a nap." Placing the phone receiver on her shoulder briefly to kiss Maurice on the cheek, Grace whispered, "It's mom." Returning the receiver to her ear, she continued. "Yes, we're all ready for your arrival tomorrow. Maurice will pick you up at the airport. I can't wait to see you and Dad."

Climbing the stairs to the nursery, Maurice's heart raced with anticipation. Upon entering, he found Isabelle, the nanny, rocking near the crib. She put a finger to her lips to signal that Louis was asleep. Gripping the crib rail, he leaned over to kiss his son's cheek and then stood there staring, smiling. *He is so perfect. I didn't think I could love anyone this much.* Reaching down to caress Louis' crown of soft black hair and tiny belly through the soft, green onesie, he listened to Louis breathe, savoring his baby powder scent.

After a few precious moments, Maurice reluctantly tore himself away to shower and change clothes. When he joined Grace in the kitchen, she offered him a sample of freshly made madeleines prepared by their cook. "Babe, you must try these," she said. "They taste like heaven."

Taking a bite, he nodded in agreement. "Delicious. Are your mother and father excited about coming for Christmas?"

"Absolutely. They can't wait to meet their grandson. And to see us, of course."

Maurice wiggled his eyebrows. "Guess who else is here? Jacque, Anne, and Jackson. This is going to be the best anniversary and the best Christmas ever. All for Louis' first Christmas."

"Wow, I can't wait to see them." Grace handed him a glass of Chardonnay as they sat at the kitchen table and they toasted.

Leaning back in his chair, Maurice sighed. "I'm sorry my parents didn't have a chance to meet our son. But I'm certain they're here in spirit. At least now I understand why Philippe was so determined to have a relationship with me. I cannot imagine what I would do if someone tried to keep Louis from me."

Grace smiled. "Well, no need to worry about that. You're stuck with me and now Louis, too."

Maurice laughed. "I wouldn't have it any other way."

Did you enjoy reading this book?

Dear Readers,

I hope you enjoyed Grace and Maurice's story. If you did, I would appreciate it very much if you wrote an honest review. It does not need to be long or complicated. Just a simple statement that you liked the book and what you found interesting about it – or for that matter, why you did not like the book.

Anywhere you post the review will help spread the word about this book and I thank you for it.

I would truly appreciate an Amazon review.

Please help me fulfill my dream. A review goes a long way to help sell books.

Thanks! I truly appreciate your support.

And please go to my website, https://lorilynwhite.com, to sign up for my newsletter and stay up to date on the news related to book signing, new book releases, and additional content.

Lorilyn White

In case you missed it…………..

She Wouldn't Wait is the prequel to *No Big Easy Love*

Learn how Grace and Maurice met and became a couple through a variety of trials and tragedies.

She Wouldn't Wait is available now on Amazon.com.

ABOUT THE AUTHOR

Lorilyn White is a retired corporate finance manager and teacher who lives in Virginia Beach, VA. Originally from New York, Lorilyn relocated after retiring. She began writing poetry and short stories at an early age for school publications and pleasure and now fully indulges in her passion. Lorilyn is also an avid reader and loves to travel.

You can connect with her by visiting her website, www.lorilynwhite.com,

or via email at lorilynwhite@gmail.com.

Made in the USA
Middletown, DE
12 June 2024